For Uwe
Heidulf Krawolitzki
And to my father

Evelyn Guevara Lohmann

# Spies-C.I.A-Lies-Terrorist-Che Guevara

*Bibliografische Information der Deutschen Nationalbibliothek:*
*Die Deutsche Nationalbibliothek verzeichnet diese Publikation in der Deutschen Nationalbibliografie; detaillierte bibliografische Daten sind im Internet über http://dnb.dnb.de abrufbar.*

*copyright© 2017 Evelyn G Lohmann*

*Illustration:* Evelyn Lohmann

*Herstellung und Verlag: BOD – Books on Demand, Norderstedt*

*ISBN:* 978-3-7347-148666

Che, Ernesto Guevara was my father.

Ciro bustos        Che Guevara

The reality of the propaganda Hero Che Guevara only came to light when I started to look for my birth parents. My first statement was, he was still alive! I met him, he was my father but everyone has to die sometime; he died on 1.1.2017.

After sixteen years of research and many questions Che Guevara/Ciro Bustos could have answered, I found out how he was created into a propaganda hero. The family connections are not as I first thought they were.

'Gabriel Garcia Marquez the creator of Che Guevara' explains how he came from a Mexican political family, 'Jurado' and the dark side of why! The visual evidence underlines how the fake was created.

This book takes you through the jungle of how I found out and why I was looking. I did not expect to find a world of drugs and weapons, political intrigue running through events like J F Kennedy's assassination, the Contras, Watergate.

One thing is clear whatever Che Guevara's real name was he was a master spy!

I want to point out that this is not a literary work of art but an account of how history has been misled.

# Spies-C.I.A-Lies-Terrorists-Che Guevara.

## Part One-
## Why was I looking?
## Che, Ernesto Guevara was my father.

### Chapter one.
### Why was I looking?

The biography, 'Che Guevara, a revolutionary life.
By Jon Lee Anderson
What now?
Curtained information!
The album.
The three travelling companions.
Omar Perez Lopez.
Che Guevara de la Serna's children.
Ninth of October.
The Life and Death of Che Guevara-
   -Companero. By Jorge G Castaneda.
Open eyes reflecting Light.
Full head of hair.

### Chapter two.
### Cuba

Omar in Cuba.
Centro de Estudios Che Guevara.
Gilberto and half brother Camilo.
Goodbye to my brother.
Waiting for the DNA results.
Che's brother had identified Che's body?

## Chapter three.
## Ebay's Che Guevara CD.

Che Guevara CIA- State Dept-
Dept of Defence Files.
Twisting snake of the DNA.
'The Way To Revolution.'
A list of names Che is known to have used.
Monika Ertl.

## Chapter four.
## To Sweden Malmo

Mundane Place.
Eyes.
The blue cards.

## Chapter five.
## The three wise men.

The DNA again.
 Wikileaks.
The Bond girl again.
Internet notes.
Che in disguise.
Association plots!
Ultimate Sacrifice
Letters Sent.
Chile wanted a revolution.

## Chapter six.
## Elizabath Burgos-Debray
## and Regis Debray.

Who knows Che became Ciro?
Archive Chile.
Christoph Röckerath.

## Chapter seven.

The movie busyness.
Che's double, Cantinflas a Mexican movie star.
Ana Maria, Che's sister.
Elizabeth Burgos-Debray's news paper cuttings.
The biography is by Josef Lawrezki.KGB
World News- Garderen Weekly-
Ciro's pension and prison Camiri.

### Chapter eight
### Their Lawyers!

The script writer!
Why are there so many of Che's family involved?
Elizabeth Burgos-Debray's files.
Archive Chile Pagina 12.
Trying to find advice.

### Chapter nine.
### Errol Flynn.

Jorge Ricardo Masetti.
To see Ciro again.
Army Advisers surprise uncles!
Jon Lee Anderson lived in the flat above Ciro Bustos.
Why does Ciro have my photo in his glass case?
More films to look at.

### Chapter ten.
### Pierre Kalfon

Pierre Kalfon.
A list of who knows?

### Chapter eleven.
### A Brazilian guerrilla in Bolivia.

Inty. One and two.
Luiz Renato Almeida Pires.

## Chapter twelve.
### Looking for evidence

The DNA is not of any use at this time!
Monika Ertl and Ann Wright.

## Part Two-
### There is more to this than I thought.

## Chapter thirteen.
### Susan-Monica-Ann.

Gary Hart American politician, author, lawyer, professor.

Democratic presidential nomination.

Democratic Daniel Ellsberg.

Christoph Röckerath.

The Congo Diaries.

Giangiacomo Feltinelli.

## Chapter fourteen.
### Guests at the death party.

Supporting role guerrilla warier.

Fifty million dollars.

Feltrinelli- Sine Weg in den Terrorismus.

-By Jobst C. Knigge.

Pier Paolo Pasolini.

Now what! Feltrinelli and Pier Paolo Pasolini.

Feltrinelli and Pier Paolo Pasolini.

Haydee Tamara Bunke/Susan Sontag.

Ulises Estrada Lescaille.

## Chapter fifteen.
### The truth about the Revolution
### Cuba exported.

Juan F Benemelis.

Fidel Castro.

Rafael Munoz Rivero.
Cuban guerrilla group Guerrilleros 17group.
Ricardo Alarcon De Quesada,
   -Cuban minister.

## Chapter sixteen.
## What now?

My photo.
Carlos Nestor Kirchner.
Hector Perez Marcano and Raul Menendez Tomassevich
Alberto Bayo y Giroud. From the Spanish Civil war.

## Chapter seventeen.
## -WATERGATE 1972-

The Democratic National Party.
Castro was putting money into their political party.
Slate Magazine.
Felix Rodriguez.
Eduardo- Howard Hunt.
Cuban Museum, Inc.
Otto Reich.
A normal person can only die once.

## Chapter eighteen.
## There can only be one account.

There should only be one account.
It is known C.I.A men shared the same code names.

## Chapter nineteen.
## The map.

## Chapter twenty.
## Letters found.

Norberto Forgione.
Jorge Denti.

Raul Lynch was Argentina's ambassador to Cuba.
Collective Third World Cinema.
Rodolfo Walsh's name on this list of those that had gone missing-
Film Industry in Latin America
Alfredo Guevara controlled Cuba's film industry; controlled all of Latin America's as will.
Members of the Guevara family.

## Chapter twenty one.
### My father's book.

Che Wants to see you.-
    The untold story of Che Guevara.
My notes.
Manuel Pineiro Losada
Tania Bunka.
Che had thirty different names to travel around the world with.
Alfredo Hellman.
Lenardo Werthein.
Pampero Cordubensis. By Masetti.
Alvaro Vargas Llosa.
Mario Vargas Llosa.
Gabriel Garcia Marquez- *was also a CIA agent.*
Is it my imagination?
Ricardo Rojo's daughter Marta.

Pierre Kalfon used Jorge Alvarez an editor!

## Chapter twenty two.
### Continuing surprises from my father's book.
Celia de la Serna Llosa.
Hilda Gadea.
Julia Urqnidi.

Celia de la Serna Llosa, my grandmother.
Froilan Gonzalez- Adys M Cupull.
Political publisher- 'Unfinished Song.'
General Jose de la Serna was the last Viceroy of Peru.
Cayetono Cordova Iturbara.
Jorge Edward Valde- Chili's ambassador.
Julio Cortazar-

> Chapter twenty three.
> Other writers/poets/journalists!
> With family members!

Lucho Loayza.
Raul Porras Barrenehea.
Jorge Luis Borges.
Guillermo Cabrera Infante.
Jose/Pepe Rodriguez Feo.
Nicolas Guillen.
Jorge Edward Volde.
Pablo Neruda.
Romules Gallegos.
Carlos Barral.
Vidadyo Telleboim.
Emir Rodriguez Monegal.
Alberto Szpunberg=Albertito.
A founder member of 'Brigada Masetti.'
Ciro Algaranaz- The Mayor of Camiri.
Ricardo Gadea Acosta.
Ricardo Gadea Acosta is Hilda Gadea Acosta's brother.
Hilda Gadea Acosta was Che's first wife.
Aurora Camacho Schmidt.

Cata Podesta

## Chapter twenty four.
### Fidel Castro's Big Guns and their Supporters.

Fidel Castro.
Manuel Pineiro.
Luis Hernandez Ojeda.
Colonel Roberto Quintanilla
Giangiaccomo Feltrninelli
The Bolivian Minister Antonio Arguedas Mendieta.
Gabriel Garcia Marquez.
Tania Bunke.
Ulises Estrada.
Elizabeth Burgos-Debray.
Daniel Alarcon Ramirez 'Benigno.
A short list of members.
Carlos Barral the leader of the publishing house Seix Barral.
Alfrado Guevara.
Giangiaccomo Feltrninelli.

## Chapter twenty five.
### My conclusions at this point.

The proceeds went to revolutionists to fund their battles in South America.
Foot notes.
How to organize a death party in Bolivia.

### Part three
## Chapter twenty six.

There is something I did not expect to find out!

## Chapter twenty seven.
### Hand written note books and diaries and other things.

## Chapter twenty eight.
## Korda's photo!

Before Che's death.
50,000,000 $
Che Guevara was a mass media produced hero.
Manuel Pineiro well known as Castro's Spy Master.
Luis Hernandez Ojeda.
Jan Stage was an accomplice at the shooting of
Roberto Quintanilla in Hamburg?

## Chapter twenty nine.
## My Grand Mother.

Cilia de la Serna Llosa.
Clair Sterling.
Anna Magnani.
Pier Pablo Pasolini.
Carlos Barral.
Saverio Tutino.

## Chapter thirty.
## Katy Jurado

Maria Cristina Estela Marcela Jurado.
Luis Jurado Ochoa and Luis Raul Ochoa.
Emilo Portes Gil. Mexican President.

## Chapter thirty one
## My Grand father.

Family members and friends.
Ricardo Gadea Acosta
Pablo Escobar Guviria
Mario Fortino Alfonso Mareno Reyes.
Ciro R Bustos.

Chapter thirty two.
Family members and connections.

Conclusion
Listed where information came from.

Part one
Chapter one.
Why was I looking?

Do they say when you want to tell a story you should begin at the beginning? Do I start in London where I was born? Or where I was conceived or do I start at the point where I discovered the strangest things that lead me to find I had four half-sisters in New Zealand and six more half-siblings in Cuba? (There are others I could call relations)

I was born in London just before Christmas in nineteen fifty-five. Where I was adopted; to an English family that thought themselves noble.

I am olive skinned and had dark hair and funny brown coloured eyes. Giggled to music and had to live with the words 'Ladies don't do that!' said about most things I my problem I don't know where the beginning was.

'Ladies don't do that', seemed to cover everything! Especially when asking why I did not look the same as anyone around me.

The husband I married did not seem to think trying to find out about my roots were something ladies asked about either.

When he left after twenty-five of years of marriage, I went with my new partner to Cuba.

We had a holiday of a life time! Made all the more special by discovering my adopted father had been to Trinidad, in Cuba. I remember the photos of him standing in front of the church. Trinidad was not where the strange things started to happen.

The moment I set foot on Cuban soil I felt at home, really at home for the first time in my life! 'Going through a bad divorce' so I thought!

Seeing a place where my adopted father had been; was strange enough! But when we got to Santa Clara things became even stranger!

There were people with similar eyes, like mine and skin like mine.

People are trying to talk to me! And trying to talk to me even though I am surrounded by the folk we are enjoying our jeep trip with. I don't have enough Spanish to say good day!

When the older man came to ask if I would like to give him money as his wife was in hospital, I had another shock.

The name of the hospital was Evelyn something!

Strange that is my forename. I thought I had had to have this name as it was a family name on my adopted mother's side.

I did not know it was a name to be seen in Cuba!
  'Having a difficult divorce.'

We are moved on to the next place of interest the mausoleum of their hero. His triumph in the revolution is also remembered in Santa Clara railway station!

'Having a difficult divorce.' must be going to my head!
We are now walking around the mausoleum of one of the best remembered heroes of any revulsion. When someone said:
'You look so like his sister.'
This is the point where I give up to- 'Having a difficult divorce.'
I decide that a little Cuba labara might be the best way to cope with the fore mentioned.

The trip to Havana was one of the next strange events to happen to me! The Hemmingway walk through the old part of the city was planed. But, then I saw the family name of my adopted father on a restaurant door… Farnes.

Others are saying she is 'Having a difficult divorce.'
All the way back in the bus tears are flowing down my face!

*I am back in the world again, I have roots!*

All folk that have parts or their lives puzzle missing will understand this last remark.

'Having a difficult divorce' gets off that bus with a clear mind, even with a glass of Cuba Libra that never seemed to empty no matter how much was drank from it.

This is the time where I have decided to look for my birth mother again, other attempts were stopped by my adoptive mother's and my first husband's disapproval.

There are not many facts to suggest my thoughts could be true, but there are a lot of circumstances that could.

My adopted father lived in the city of London; His busyness was to investigate companies to safeguard other companies that wanted to invest their money.

His offices were two hundred meters away from the offices in charge of importing sugar into England, from Cuba!

His father was a merchant sales man. At that time 'merchant sales' meant handling goods brought to London by ship.

My adopted father had been in Cuba, I don't have the pictures any more.

I was to find a photo that could be of my adopted father in an autobiography listening to Che Guevara speak; in Peru.

My adopted mother and father had also been to New Zealand. I do not know if they went together. My adoptive mother spent a year in New Zealand with her brother, on a sheep farm. New Zealand was where I learnt my birthmother came from.

New Zealand is where I find four sisters. I sadly misted my birthmother by seven months. She died without being able to tell me the strange things I needed to know. The English courts did not help me in time to talk to her.

For me to talk about my birthmother was not something I could do with my adoptive mother. I knew her name but trying to look for someone with only a name, without knowing the year of their birth, nor where they came from, did make that search difficult, bordering on imposable. I found her but it was a long hard job.

After that first trip to Cuba in 2000, nearly two years went by. Letters and telephone calls crossed the English Channel. I had my birth mother's name, Beverly Norelle Frost.

A letter had arrived telling me the judge was authorised to tell me my birthmother was 23 in 1955 and she came from New Zealand.

There was an email waiting for me when we returned from that trip. Mandy, Joe, Susan, and Maree appeared in emails to follow.

I have four sisters in New Zealand!

If you have been alone in this world, and find you are very much part of life, part of a chain, there are others like you!

There are not enough words in the English language to cover how you feel!!

My birth mother was a nurse. I learnt that from my youngest sister. That our birthmother decided to travel the world, she started the trip at the end of nineteen fifty-four.

I believed my birthmother was in Mexico City for the P.A.M games, at the time I was conceived. Where it was said Che is training to be a doctor at that time, and he was involved in Fidel Castro's military training camps.

Letters in Spanish and English are being sent to every hospital I can find were Ernesto Guevara could have worked.

Che, Ernesto Guevara had been a reporter at the 1955 P.A.M games. Despite writing to every hospital I could think of and trying to find out if hotels would still have records of their visitors from that time, I could not find the one bit of information I needed. I found nothing about either person, looking back it was strange as there must be other sores of information other than the official versions. But I did ask if as a nurse with my birth mother's name had work there with Che, as I lived in Germany it did seem an imposable task.

I sent letters to the Che Guevara centre in Havana that have not been answered. Not surprising as it is run by Che's second wife! But it was said that Che Guevara kept dairies about everything he did and of his conquests. They have been stored in the Havana centre. Along with photos taken by Che at the P.A.M American games nineteen fifty five, where 'they' could have met!

I knew the photos existed from the time we had been in Santiago De Cuba, were we had seen an exhibition of cameras Che and Fidel Castro were interested in, our guide told us about the photos and that they were in Habana.

The photos I felt then were an important link, maybe my birthmother could be found on some of them. At this time I cannot say why I feel this way, it is just a strong feeling.

I and Uwe spent hours running round Habana looking for them on our next trip. I had to leave without knowing where they were.

I had to wait till we were sitting in a waiting room months later for Uwe to say the photos ware in Hamburg. Just down the road from us, compared to Habana! I did not think to try and meet the young man in charge of the photos, Camilo, Maybe seeing someone that could be a half brother would have helped me, but I had missed meeting him and if I had what was I going to say? 'Hi, I think I am your half sister.'

The photos brought me a feeling of being a step closer but not the evidence I wanted. What did I expect photos of girlfriends and associates?

Had my original birth certificate said the name of my birth father, I would not have needed to run around the world with emails, looking for the missing links.

There are not many that can wonder at seeing the face of a man, that you think is your father, tattooed on muscular chests or staring down on you from bright posters, oh the t-shirt!

The biography, 'Che Guevara, a revolutionary life. By Jon Lee Anderson.' I have the paperback version, did help me to make a farther connection, it dos confirm my birthfather and my adoptive father met!

My adoptive father's profession took him around the world; his job would not have prevented him from making such connections.

It is photo during a lull in the August 1961 economic summit in Punta del Este, Uruguay.

Nether knowing how they were connected, connected by a little girl.

It is not conclusive evidence I know, but I want to explain why I was looking.

I am not able to find any more connections, other than my adoptive father's profession, and where he was born, where he lived and worked in the City of London. Two hundred and fifty meters from where sugar imports were controlled in the city. His father was a merchant salesman, it a time when that meant he handled with goods from incoming ships.

What now?

I did not have anything other than a good after diner story!

Mandy had said there was a photo album my birthmother had made of her trip to London. A photo of her preparing to leave with a ship, on it's the back a date confirming when the trip started, it was nineteen fifty four.

A ship! A Photo, an album! They have got to help!

I sent a photo of my birth father to my sisters in hope they would look in the album for me.

The four years that have passed since my younger sister and I sat together and she told me of the album. It had got lost, they did not think about it anymore.

It is not that I cannot understand I have come into their lives, at a time when their mother had died. What a time to discover there is another child coming out of the past. Two of the five girls born to my birthmother were given up for adoption; myself in London and two years later Maree in New Zealand.

The next surprise was to change the negative winds of Christmas 2006! A wicked twist of fate saw the satellite receiver decide it did not want to work anymore. The day that happened, the local supermarket had a special offer with satellite receivers. It did not look any different than the last one. But it had Cuban television! Wonderful I could now watch English, American and German television and now have an eye on Cuba! Not as easy as one would think as most of their programs are in Spanish. But their charm, the music and art, the travel programs showing place I know were enough to keep me happy.

I am watching a program celebrating Fidel Castro's eighth birthday, I am interested in all things Cuban. I had at one time thought Fidel Castro could be a father candidate, in the daydream years.

I had to stop what I was doing a woman was speaking, I look into a face that was familiar, she spoke like I do when I am talking about the things in life I love. Was I looking into my face? I was so shocked I only just caught her name- Guevara! When the spell was broken I ran to the internet for every photo, article I could find about Aleida Guevara March.

I have felt the same feeling with all four sisters in New Zealand; the x factor, the factor you cannot explain with your practical side, but it is so strong you cannot ignore it.

The early months of 2007 were the hardest for me. I am frustrated I know the information connecting my feeling and reality are out there! Where is the album my sisters have been talking about? Which ship did my birthmother take?

A young woman of twenty two/three would be so excited about a trip of this kind she would have kept a record of it. Kept the ticket maybe, a diary, had a photo album. The information I was asking for from New Zealand was not forthcoming.

More letters go out to Mexico hospitals this time in Spanish!

If I had the name of the ship, I could find out about its route. I am online nosing in passengers list, shipping companies.

I did not know from which port she left New Zealand. There were two ports in question, Auckland and Wellington.
The ships passing through the Panama Canal were the most interesting to me.

It all happened over fifty years ago, time losses interest in the facts. I did not have a date of my birthmother's departure to work with or a confirmed date of arrival in London, other than my birth date, if that can be trusted.

I now have to question everything I have been told. Somewhere in the different piles of emails from my sisters living in New Zealand and the books and strangely translated diaries. With the old letter from my adoptive mother, memories of photos from my adoptive father, and facts floating on the internet, there had to be away forwards!

    The ship is the subject to stick to for the moment. Three ships names start to come forward.
>Rangitoto.
>Ruahine.
>Rangitane.

They were ships on the route from New Zealand to England at that time.

    The internet's line to my computer is trying to help me, it is happy to tell me of immigrants wishing to travel from Europe to the new worlds. The ships were popular till the middle of the sixty's. From then on airplanes took over as passenger transporters.

    The New Zealand Maritime Museum.
        www.nzmaritime.org

The Maritime Museum came up with useful information about the route taken to London and back again. The time the trips took and the interesting price charged for the voyage.

    For Ten Pounds you could travel half the world, for not more than twenty the world!

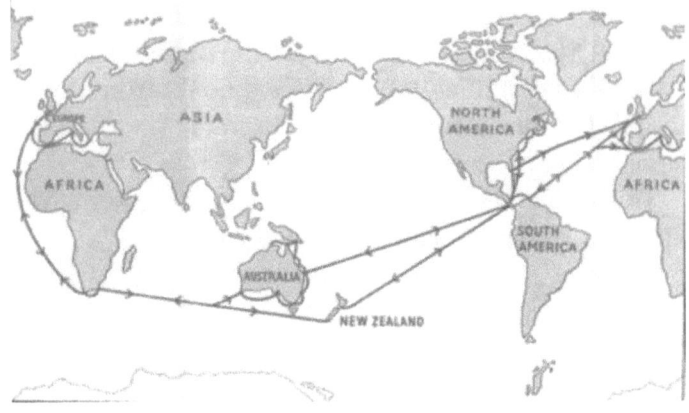

The rout taken by the ship, from an old catalogue.

# PASSENGER AND CARGO SERVICES AND PRINCIPAL CARGOES CARRIED

**PASSENGER SERVICE BY "RANGITOTO"** until mid 1969

London to Auckland or Wellington via Curacao, Panama and Tahiti returning via Tahiti, Panama, Kingston, Port Everglades (for Miami) and Bermuda.

## CARGO SERVICES FROM UNITED KINGDOM

London to New Zealand via Curacao and Panama Canal.

London to Fiji and New Zealand via Curacao and Panama Canal.

Continent and Genoa to New Zealand via Curacao and Panama Canal.

Newport, Swansea, Glasgow and Liverpool to New Zealand via Curacao and Panama Canal.

Newport, Swansea and Liverpool to Australia via Cape of Good Hope.

**Cargoes.** Chemicals, fertilisers, iron and steel, machinery, manufactured goods, motor cars, textiles and whisky.

## HOMEWARD SERVICES

New Zealand to United Kingdom via Continental, Mediterranean, South and West African ports.

Discharging in United Kingdom—Hull, London, Southampton, Avonmouth, Cardiff, Liverpool and Glasgow via Panama Canal and Curacao (if direct).

South and West African Ports—Durban, Cape Town, Lagos and Tema thence Continental, United Kingdom ports via Cape of Good Hope and Las Palmas.

Mediterranean—Piraeus, Famagusta, Genoa, Marseilles, Barcelona and Lisbon thence Continental and United Kingdom ports via Panama Canal and Curacao or Cape Horn and Las Palmas.

**Cargoes.** Butter, casein, cheese, fruit (apples and pears), meat, milk powder, tallow and wool.

Australia to United Kingdom, Continental and Mediterranean Ports via Cape of Good Hope and Las Palmas. Discharging at Piraeus, Malta, Genoa, Continental Ports, London, Avonmouth, Liverpool, and other occasional ports.

**Cargoes.** Butter, cheese, eggs, fruit including canned and dried, hides, lead, meat, mineral sands, sugar, tallow, wheat and zinc.

## THE NORTH AMERICAN TRADE

Canada and East Coast U.S.A. to Australia and New Zealand Ports via Panama Canal.

Loading at Montreal, Three Rivers, Quebec, Cornerbrook, Philadelphia, New York, Newport News, Savannah and other occasional ports.

**Cargoes.** Agricultural machinery, chemicals, manufactured goods, motor cars and tobacco.

Australia and New Zealand to East Coast U.S.A. and Canada via Panama Canal.

Discharging at Charleston, Norfolk, Newport News, Philadelphia, New York and Boston in U.S.A. and

Questions like did my birthmother stay on the ship she departed on? Did she stop over to sightsee or earn some money for living expenses? Nurse could always get work even if they were qualified or not.

The piles of copies of every email are spread over my table. Every remark anyone made is being scrutinized.

I don't have every email ever sent to me as the computer of the time died of old age, it could have put into writing, my birthmother had attended the P.A.M games as stated by Mandy. It was from Mandy I heard that my birthmother was interested in sport and would have attended the PM games in 1955. It was her remarks that woke the interest in Che's photos.

I am not sure the photo album still exists! It is being said there is only a photo marking my birthmother's start of her trip, with the date 26 November on the back of it.

Without a confirmed point to work from I am stuck, the album must hold at least a key so I can move on. But it is stuck behind that wall!

The name Helen O'Conner appears in an email. Sister Joe remembers her; she was a friend my birthmother made on that trip to London. Was she from or going to Ireland, no known date of birth, I had that problem before!

Joe remembers that Helen's husband had worked as the harbour master in Cork, Ireland. With just that information to go on, I was back up on the internet. Funny how fate works!

The Harbour Master working for County Cork knew Jack before he died; and as far as Pat knew Helen was alive and will, living in Waterford. He gave me her address!

The excitement! After fifty-one years and twelve days I felt I was getting closer.

There was someone who knew your birthmother at the time you were born. A letter was put in the post! That morning my companion and I had shared a Champaign breakfast.

Helen has not replied, I cannot get her telephone number from the directory inquires. Check with Pat the address sent another letter to Helen. Was she is over one hundred, buried and forgotten and no one knows. Handy caped or her hearing aid is broken along with her glasses!

Mandy offers to write to Helen on my behalf, maybe Helen is upset by the letters I have sent!

I showed the address Pat had given to me for Helen to my companion. He asks, 'is it a small village?'

I am ready to jump into a plain and bang on her door!

'If it is a small town the post mistress would know.'
My dear man suggested.

I turned to the internet again for the telephone number of the post office in Waterford.

Yes she knew Helen, she was not there. I was sure she meant dead, not there!

No not there, gone away! I had to explain what was troubling me. The Post Mistress was so sympathetic I was to ring back. I cannot tell you how long it was till I was to call back but every second hang heavily.

The Post Mistress had gone down the road to knock on the door of Helen's son. He said I was to put a note on the door… How was I to do that from Germany?

After explaining to him why the mad lady from over the water wanted to talk to his mother, I was able to write down a number of telephone numbers.

Helen was in Dublin. Much easier to get to! She was staying with her daughter. I rang left messages on the answer phone.

While I was waiting I returned to investigate the ship, it is interesting to see the route returning goes through the Mediterranean, and some ships used the Sues Channel.

If you have a description of a ship you can identify it even without knowing its name, I didn't have even that!

Were they (The ugly sisters) telling me there wasn't a photo album?

Then there was a photo album but Fred had it. Fred was my birthmother's husband and father to three of my sisters.

Fred had remarried and moved away with his new lady. I did not see why the album was not available!

A letter has arrived from Helen. She is more than surprised to hear from me and puzzled how I know Pat the harbour master.

Helen did know my birthmother had a baby when she was in London. But she did not know about Beverly's second daughter Maree. I had omitted to enclose what had happened to me! A thick litter was stuffed in the post, and best wishes to the Post Mistress!

I am hopeful Helen can fill in more of the blanks; there are photos and a letter written by my birthmother, in the letter she sent me.

Mandy had given me a ring my birthmother had, somehow to have a letter written by my birthmother and the accompanying Christmas photo of her and three sisters and Fred was comforting. It is dated November 1979. It is still a funny feeling seeing words from my birthmother, Beverly.

She is to be seen in France, Monaco and Lugarno Italy, it was shown in the photos, Helen had sent. There is also one of Beverly standing in a doorway of a workingman's house.
(Helen told me later it was the door of the house Perry and Beverly lived in, in London)

(Copies of the same photos turned up in the copy of the photo album and more. When it did allow its self to be copied and sent to me.)

This is supposedly the photo taken the day mum left!

26 November 1954

We have a ship name now — M.V. Rangitoto — these were postcards in the album.

The name of the ship is now on the computer's screen, in an email, and confirming the date my birthmother left New Zealand! 'The twenty-six of December 1954' that is what it says on the photo copy of the photo, supposedly taken on the day she left. And on the same copy are of post cards of the lounge and bar, of the ship. I have seen the Lounge and bar before when wondering if this was the ship! Rangitoto.

(It Departed from Wellington; its exact route was not recorded that year.)

There is a photo of Perry Shanks, a policeman. Is he a candidate as my father? He cannot be, the timing, dose no allow Perry Shanks to be. Nor does his blue eyes, my eyes are brown.

My birthmother met him in London in 1956, my birth year is 1955, end of! When I saw his photo I said to my companion I wish he was my father, he looked so nice. From the photos I have seen since he looked so in love with Beverly.

There is also a photo, Mandy thinks is of Helen, on the back of the photo, Mandy, says is written, 'Beverly and self, Feb 1956.'

Helen did not meet Beverly till the February after my birth in December. Helen does not know of Beverly's adventures before meeting her. My birthmother's movements were not traceable from the time she left New Zealand till my birth.

Helen was hard to reach; her daughter has given birth to a new grandchild! I do understand, least she is all there and not gone, as the Post Mistress said.

        Curtained information!

Why can I only have curtain information from the album? Why do I have to say, I only want to find my father? I don't want to pry into others lives. There must be more troubled lies hidden!

Beverly has a brother and sisters. Brother and sisters she had to come back to New Zealand to look after, during and after her mother was dying from cancer. That was how the story was told. Beverly had to give Maree up to look after them all.

I would not have thought to question this. But all I have had were a few bones thrown to me to chew on. They said album did not have any photos of Mexico, there is nothing in it that could help me.

Joy was a friend that Beverly had from childhood. Mandy says she is the only person that knew in New Zealand Beverly had two children before she married Fred. And that they were conceived on that European trip.

Joy was so sweet to talk to; she was excited that someone was talking to her form so far away.

Beverly had not told her much about her time away. According to Joy, Beverly had made a fool of herself with a charming, dashing young man, she described the type of lover the accounts I have read about Che Guevara describe.

The name Allen White was the name of the man, Joy used. He was supposed to be the one night stand.

Allen White was the name of the man that Maree had been told was her father, the best friend of Perry Shanks and a college in the Metropolitan police in London.

I reported back to Helen what Joy has to say. It strikes me as strange when Helen did not know the name, nor does she recognize him among the photos I sent her, from part of the copy of the album I was able to have.

Beverly and Helen were among a group of girls from around the world. There is Pearl and Audrey Baird. Margaret Hawker. And a German lady; Beverly stay at her house in London. They all odd jobbed in and around London, some were looking after children in Norway and other places or jobbed in restaurants, shops. Anything they could get so they could enjoy living it up, in and around the Mediterranean.

I happen to say to Helen I did not understand how Beverly could have flown back to New Zealand, as compared to the ship which cost ten pounds in 1957. A flight was one thousand pounds! The flight took up to six days, by sea six to eight weeks.

Beverly and Audrey took a ship; Audrey wanted to go home to Australia! Beverly did not want to stay with Perry Shanks so was happy to go with her!

Audrey's name is in the letter Helen sent to me, with Christmas photo, dated 1979.

I do not feel comfortable; this is really Maree's sphere, not really to do with me. But there are questions running around my mind. I asked Maree if she wanted to know what was being said. Maree confirms her interest in an email.

How could I keep what I have been told to myself? I know what hell it is, trying to knock down walls. Not when I am still asking to see the whole album. I hear is stuck with Fred, Mandy is hoping to pick it up the next time she visits her father: the visit is planned for the coming months.

The album.

The album or its photo copies are spread on my table! The original doesn't want to leave New Zealand. Frustrating I want to feel the paper of the photos, look at them in the light for water marks.

Why am I worrying? There are some that match the photos that Helen sent me, from when they were in Europe together.

The album is mostly life with Perry. Polices men's outings; with coach trips to the sea. I have seen that type of photo before! Down at the pub, mugs of beer in their hands with their arms round their wives.

I was a 'wife of' with the British Army long enough to know when Helen said she visited Beverly and Perry in their house in London! That would have meant they were married!

It was the rule then as it is now, with the British! Unmarried couples did not get accommodation from the army or police or any of the services for that matter, and 'living in sin' was frowned on.

I had to live with the grumbling from sergeants and other irate ranks, as youngsters of nineteen or so were given flats as they had wives extra, whereas they were only offered a single man's room in barracks.

One day I may investigate my conclusions from the talks from Helen and Joy, and the photo album. But for now the copy of the album is in front of me!

What did I expect, to see a man with wild hair and a berry with a silver star?!

(My mother's travelling companion and, seen again with my mother.)

I see a lady with a polo neck sweater and glasses, on the first page of the album; she is also in the pool with my birthmother. I think they are on board a ship. Now, she, the lady with the polo neck sweater, can clearly be seen in a photo in the biography written by Jon Lee Anderson. (This photo had been sent in a litter to a friend Calcia Ferrer, it is simply dated Guatemala, 1954) I cannot use the photo to show you, as it does not belong to me. I can show you in the next photo of my mother and her companions; she is the lady on the left.

(The same photo was shown in a program about Che Guevara's life, on Cuban television on the Saturday fifth of May 2007, where my birthmother can more clearly be seen.)

At first I take the order of the photos from the album as a guide. But as the album is somehow strangely incomplete for a record of such a long trip away from home! I started to look at it without the restraint of saying, the journey out, Panama channel.

Time spent in Mediterranean. Life with Perry. And, back home with a ship.

In Jon Lee Anderson's biography, Che Guevara A Revolutionary Life, there is a photo of my birth mother and two of her travelling companions can, standing in a group, with Che and his first wife Hilda Gadea Acosta, she can be seen in the photo.

## Hilda Gadea

Guatemala, 1954. Ernesto standing next to his future first wife, Hilda Gadea, a Peruvian political exile. Before long, they would become lovers. From right: Ricardo Rojo, Hilda, Ernesto (wearing white suit). Gualo García is squatting in the foreground. *Courtesy of Carlos "Calica" Ferrer*

My mother is standing under Ricardo Roio, the man with the hat.

She is with her traveling companions.

In Jon Lee Anderson's biography, Che Guevara A Revolutionary Life, there is a photo of my birth mother and two of her travelling companions can, standing in a group, with Che and his first wife Hilda Gadea Acosta, she can be seen in the next photo.

*Ricardo Rojio was present at Ciro Bustos and Regis Debray's court case at the time of Che Guevara's death party.

There in another photo on the same page of the album showing my birthmother standing in the same group.

As I look at the photograph I begin to see Hilda Gadea Acosta! With her is the Cuban flag! I am trying to find out if I can identify any of the men in the photos. The internet is not being too helpful, but I think one could be Frank Pais.

I had accepted I was the result of a one night stand, but those photos mean there was something more. It means my birthmother knew much more about those times than she wanted to tell.

My birth mother was at the military training camp before the revolution planed for Cuba.

Hector Perez Marcano and Raul Menendez Tomassevich (((I have seen since the men in those photos playing foot ball with Che in other photos. On the internet.)))

Raul Menendez Tomassevich was a general in Castro brother's army. A close friend of Alfrado Guevara the head if films. A close friend of Fidel and was at school in Santiago de Cuba. Fidel Castro was also schooled in Santiago de Cuba.

Hector Perez Marcano was also a high ranking commander. He was known to have been with the Castros from the nineteen fifties onwards!

       What a secret to have!

This is the page as I received it.

There was one more surprise from me! The same lady with the polo neck sweater and glasses is sitting in a car with my birthmother. My birthmother is sitting at the steering weal and Che Guevara is on the front seat beside them.

Here I would like to put in a copy of the two photographs from 'A revolutionary life' Jon Lee Anderson and 'Back on the road' (Otra Vez) Ernesto Che Guevara. But I do not wish to get impeach any copyright.

Page five of the photo album is a strange mixture of pictures. Beverly with a nun, Helen and I suppose the lady in the polo neck sweater, but Helen did not recognize her, it is difficult to see as she is so raped up in winter cloths.

A man dressed to look like a mod from the mod and rocker time. A photo of Beverly in a long skirt in front of a tent and a copy of the same photo Helen had previously sent me of my birthmother on the beach in France. With, 'Bevy in France.' written in the back.

Che with my mother, pip and all.

It is the top right has a picture that catches my eye. Is it of my birthparents, Beverly Norelle Frost and Ernesto Guevara.

The three travelling companions.

The photo, were my birthmother and three of her travelling companions is also to be found in Ernesto Che Guevara. (inedito) Otra Vez, confirming it was taken in Guatemala, but does not put a date to the photo. The same can be said about the photo in Che's diary, it does not have a date. But my birthmother is there. I would like to have included them in my account but as I can't find them in the open domain.

Omar Perez Lopez

I thought this was the end but I now know I am at the beginning, at the beginning, of trying to find away to contact my half brothers and sisters in Cuba. Omar Perez Lopez is said to be a son Ernesto Guevara.

I want to say I had fun looking for way to find Omar Perez Lopez, I did, but it stressed me as well.

I found poems and essays that led me to a poet society in Holland, but I was two years too late. Would they have an address for him? There were many calls made to their head quarters, till I got an address in Italy! As I was waiting for an address in Holland, just down the road from where live. I saw a blog where it said he was working as a translator in Holland;

Kirstein Dykstra had translated some of Omar's work.

As a poem presented on the Holland poetry society's web site had been translated by her I thought it would be a good idea to see if her name as in the Dutch telephone book. The idea being if Omar was working as a guest he would not have a registered telephone number, but she might! The might was just a thought I had no idea from where she came.

I was soon lost in the Dutch internet the telephone book!
I have my problems in German and with my dyslectic English I thought I was not moving forward, till I found there was only one Kirstein Dykstra. Her internet page did not tell me anything, only it was pink! Nice colour if you like pink. I had to wait till she answered the telephone in person. I did not understand her recorded massage.

She was very nice to me even as we were talking at cross-purposes. When she asked me if I needed a midwife, I understood why her internet side was pink! I said I was looking for a brother. She wished me luck as I thanked her; she was not the translator I was looking for.

The poet society came up with a few addresses in Italy and something in Spain; the letter I sent there came back, without my visiting card, don't know what that meant.

Letters went to every address I got hold of, I do not know what I said. It depended on my mood and how frustrated I was as to what I wrote in those letters. The poet society in Italy did not offer me any help, I did not try to ring them just in case midwives could get muddled with the mafia.

I spent days exploring the internet, collecting email addresses and anything to do with Omar Perez Lopez.

I had a reply from a man in Florida he did not know why I should want to talk with him as he was in prison. I would have liked to talk to him; maybe he thought to talk to a lady in Germany to much as he did not answer me again.

If the Che Guevara Centre was not talking to me, even after all my enquires Omar may also not want to. I have only hope.

There was a short email saying. 'I am Omar Perez.'
No one can speak to me, as I was walking on a cloud!
What do I do now? All I want is to make contact, and tell my truth; hear the truth! I have been here before; if I want the truth I must tell the truth, even if he does not want another half sister.

As I write this he is not answering my emails. As I had heard Omar is a Zen Monk: he must understand what I am looking for?

Back on the internet again looking to understand as quickly as possible Buddhism; Hamburg is helpful, and the Buddhist lady in Holland say's she knows him! Now I know I could sit on a beach with a Cuba Libra in my hand and talk... But he is not talking to me. I spent nine intensive months on my search for him.

I did find the real Kirstein Dykstra she is in a university in America; I did have an email ready to send to her before Omar sent one to me. This might have been the moment to try to contact her, ask her for her help.

I have not come, this fare to stop now!
If I had not stood alone without another human to connect me to the human world and if I had not gone on holiday to Cuba to set me on this rollercoaster, I would never have found out who my birthmother and birthfather were.

When I saw the royal family in Cuban television, I had the chance to watch them as a family, I had the feeling I could understand why they would find another half sister difficult. But understanding does not make anything easier for me.

To know you have two more half sister and two more half brothers living, I want to find away to reach them.

### Che Guevara de la Serna's Children.

With Hilda Gadea.
(Married 18 August 1955; divorced 22 may 1959)
 * Hilda Beatriz Guevara Gadea.
 Born 15 February 1956 in Mexico City; died 21 August 1995 in Havana, Cuba.

Hilda Beatriz Guevara cl
oture institute in Havana and she worked on Che Guevara's biography.
(CeiberWeiber- Frauen Onlinemagazine- Artkel 'Herstory' jhd `Freauen um Che'. And Biograph Castaneada.

With Aleida March Torres. (married 2 June 1959)
   *Aleida Guevara March.
Born 24 November 1960 in Havana, Cuba.
Alaida Guevara March is a doctor of medicine, specialising in allergic and asthma medicine, based at the William Soler Children's Hospital.
(Image:Aleida Guevara March.jpg- Wikipedia)

   *Camilo Guevara March.
Born 20 May 1962 in Havana, Cuba.
Camilo Guevara Marsh works for the Ministry of Fishery.
He accompanied the collection of his father's photographs in 2002.

   *Celia Guevara March.
Born 14 June 1963 in Havana, Cuba.
Celia Guevara March is the chief veterinarian at the Havana National Aquarium.

   *Ernesto Guevara March.
Born 24 February 1965 in Havana, Cuba

(No information known about his currant life at this time)

Extramarital.

With Beverly Norelle Frost.
   *Evelyn Guevara-Frost.
Borne in London 17 December 1955 in London, England.
Evelyn Guevara-Frost is an artist and author living in Europe.

With Lilia Rosa Lopez,
   *Omar Perez Lopez.
Born 19 February 1964 in Havana, Cuba.
Omar Perez Lopez is a poet and translator.
(www Poetry international web.)
(Omar's birth date was confirmed by him when I visited him in Habana. 2008)

(A search for another half brother. Did not bring me much)
   *Mirko.
(CeiberWeiber- Frauen Onlinemagazine- Artkel 'Herstory' jhd `Freauen um Che')
(from the first call with Omar, I hear I am the only one making enquiries)
Much information is confirmed in Jon Lee Anderson's
'A Revolutionary Life.'

There is scene on the Cuban television where I saw Aiada, Cilia, Camilo, and Ernesto. Aida March is talking to Hugo Chavez; they are celebrating the fortieth anniversary of Che Guevara's death. 2008

I was over the moon when Omar sent me an email, but when he did not reply to my emails my thoughts started to wander as I waited for him to contact me.

I know how it feels to have sisters from New Zealand use emails to announce their presence. For Omar to find out I was claiming to be a half sister may not have been as delightful as it was for me. Trying to communicate with Cuba is not easy at the best of times.

Ninth of October.

The ninth of October was the date Che was said to have been shot; his death is portrayed in many films. The German television channels are showing so many; I have to try to remember which film say's what! I decide to acquire some of them after I saw 'Die Letzten Tage einer Legende. 500851065.

Two people catch my interest, Regis Debray an alleged journalist and an Argentinean artist Ciro Bustos.

Interesting Jon Lea Anderson's biography mentions Ciro Bustos on page 506 of the copy I have. Bustos was reported walking down the street in Havana. He was walking into the Cuban revolution, on that very page! He became a lieutenant to Che, but any other references are difficult to find in 2007.

 The only explanation I could find for his low profile was Bustos was involved in preparing the way for Che's future plans.

The Life and Death of Che Guevara Companero.
     By Jorge G Castaneda.

 In this book Bustos is only mentioned in passing. In the notes to chapter eight from Castaneda, the reference makes a remark about… 'Bustos telephone conversation with the Castaneda. September $7^{th}$ 1996- but there is no reference in chapter 8. Castaneda- page 433. In fact the chapter is about something else!

 I made a remark about this to my partner, he finds Bustos's photo on the internet. As it happens it is the same photo used when advertising the film 'Sacrifico who betrayed Che Guevara?'

 I had a hard time getting this film, it was restricted and not for sale in America! The television station was not a loud to sale it! Then my partner traced it to its makers in Sweden, only find the film had disappear somewhere! After a month of sending them many emails and bothering them on the phone, a copy did get to me.

 I had studded Wilfried Huismann's film, 'Schnappschuss mit Che.' The more I studied the films the more questions I had. None of the people in the films can agree on anything! The only fact they can agree on is the date Regis Debary and Ciro Bustos were said to have been captured. There are many dates given as to when Che was shot!

    Open eyes reflecting Light.

One thing that dose worry me is the fact Che's eyes are open and reflecting light. The nun that cleaned Che's body was supposed to have remarked about his Christ like appearance. Did she mean something else?

If my partner had not made a remark about the photos I was looking at, I would have not looked further. I had been looking for a scar on Che's face, ear. It had been reported he had accidentally shot himself. The reference is a few paragraphs after the first mention of Ciro Bustos in Jon Lee Anderson's book.

I was beginning to question everything, I did not find a scar in any of the photos in those presented on the internet but a book by Christopher Loving, 'Che die fotobiografie.' had one with a plaster over his left eyebrow. And, the book shows different 'looks' Che uses to more about without attracting attention; with hair without, with glasses…

It was looking at the self-portrait Che had taken as a young man where he looks like a man reading a book in the copy of my birthmother's album.

I had sent Ciro Bustos a letter to ask him if he had meet my mother, at first in English and after ring him, in Spanish.

The idea behind this was; I so wanted to contact someone that could have met my birth mother and father.

My partner pointed out for someone that cannot speak Spanish and the other said he was without the English language twenty minutes on the phone was a long time!

I would like to put the fore mentioned photos.

I try to find more photos of Ciro Bustos, not easy! There is one with a woman and child in a program Pageina/12.com. (he is said to be 30 at the time of the photo.) Then there is one in the opening of the film 'Sacrifico' the man there has a broken nose. Then there is the one taken some forty years later, no sign of such a broken nose. Used on the back of the cover for the film 'Sacrificio.'

Many features change over the years ears grow as do noses. Fat can come and go, with age, stress or with the help of a skilled scalpel! But hands don't change, nor does the shape of ears. There is one thing you cannot change is the shape of your head, unless you run into a bus!

Is it possible two men can have the same shape of head?

There is a photo of Che as a baby, where the shape of his head can be seen. I place the photo of Che bald head as he poses for a passport and one I took from the film 'Sacrifico' of Bustos (in his late thirties) at his trial with Regis Debary, I placed them over each other to find they match!

I spend some time on ears till I diced to look at hands.

It could be my imagination taking me down this road, but without it I could not find my way forward, that and the sharp mind of my partner put balance to my ideas. I find Che has long large hands with a thumb that turn upwards as dose Ciro Bustos! I took a photo of Ciro's hands from the film 'Sacrifico.'

Full head of hair.

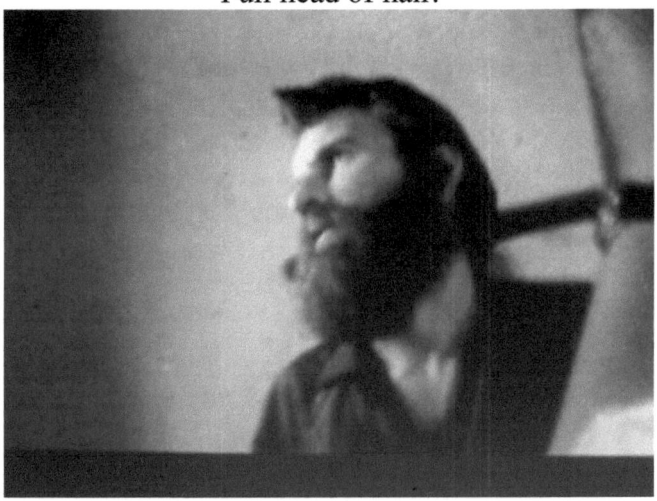

In the part of the film, 'Schnappschuss mit Che' showing Regis Debary and Ciro Bustos at the time they were to be released from prison after serving three of their thirty year sentence. The film shows Ciro Bustos with a full head of hair, a hair line coming to a point over his brow, a shape often seen in photos of Che.

The question crossed my mind as to how a bladed man can grow such thick hair?

I thought for a long time how all this could this be possible? I stopped trying to puzzle my way through (how) … Che was a doctor! He would know what to take and how much. And! He has used disguises before.

*My muddled mind cannot get round the idea if Che Guevara is my father then so is Ciro Bustos.*

I wanted to try to write this without emotion but I have the feeling I am on a rollercoaster that is mixing my feelings as fast as it can into a blur.

Chapter two
Cuba

It is Christmas, I have to find away to contact Omar and I have not decided just what I am going to do with what I think I know. But I have to get the best proof anyone can have, a DNA test. If I could just run my hand through his hair; difficult, pointed out my partner, difficult as the photos of Omar at the Buddhist DoJo in Havana show him as a monk, without hair!

The internet had to send emails again for me, to anyone that might get a word to Omar. I rang the Dojo in Havana; the man said Omar did not work there! He did not have any ideas as to how I could contact Omar, but he did promise to say, I called if he saw him. Another man did not speak English but asked if I was family and which hotel I was staying at. That rollercoaster car was starting to send everything into a blur again!

I was running out of ideas; but Uwe has found another telephone number. This time the lady says she knows Omar! No wait he has just moved! Are the brakes on my coaster car? I am to ring back at nine o'clock, it is seven there in Cuba. She will give me his number.

It is Christmas day and Uwe and I are going to Christmas lunch with his mother will she mind if I ring Cuba?

Omar's number stared up at me from the piece of paper, my want feet want to dance a gig but my mind wonders just how mad I am!

There can only be a first time, only once! What will he be like to talk to on the telephone; does he want to talk to me? His last email had been over a month before, it did ask, when would I be coming; then there was again nothing.

That there was nothing was because his computer is down, he is so easy to talk to! His voice is clear just a trace of American in his easy English. I come away with the impression he is just as curious as I am. All I have to do now is book my ticket/hotel and say when I am coming.

The rollercoaster is playing with my emotions, again! To meet a brother! He can fill in some of the missing gaps in my life. I have no idea how to tell him I am your half sister and by the way throw away all history books, I think Che lives.

Omar in Cuba.

As I had sat on the step outside the hotel waiting for the first time I would meet Omar, I was feeling like a fridge trying to cope with a heat wave!

Meeting Omar was so easy! He could not be anybody else other than my brother! Half a brother but a full friend, is what he said, I do hope so.

I am in Cuba it is not my home base, just the fact I don't speak Spanish puts me at a disadvantage. I have to find answers to questions I am too nervous to ask!

Omar asked me why I wanted to have a DNA test; I could not tell him my thoughts about the man in the back of my mind. That we were related did not need to be confirmed between us; just like the sisters in New Zealand there was something there. Not just we cannot tolerate cow's milk nor the fact we are both can use left and right hands, something more in the way we use humour, you are not always sure if we are joking or are serous.

Omar did not meet the father, 'The Father,' is how we decided to refer to our father, somehow there seemed to be a need for an understanding, maybe because he was told when he was twenty five who his father really was.

Omar's forty fourth, birthday was on the nineteenth of February not March; we met the week before this date.

As we were painting the living room of the sweet villa Omar has just moved into with Sandra and a wonderfully lively four year old boy! Omar tells me the 'Royal Family.' 'That is my name for the Guevara Marsh family.' Have not acknowledged him, he has only met one on passing, one of the sisters, but I have forgotten which one it was!

I have the feeling he is not happy about this situation. I would not be, well I am not, they, the Royal family have not replied to any of my communications over the years; no matter how I have sent them. I have even sent them a copy of some of my findings through the Cuban embassy in London.

I had thought there could be others, lost children, trying to make contact like me. But Omar said I was the only one. There is another's name on the internet, Mirco. I found this name on a blog but have not been able to find out anymore. Omar said the biographer Pierre Kalfon had written something about someone called Mirco. I wonder if I can find out more, Pierre Kalfon name is mentioned on the credits on the film 'Scrificio'.

The paint does not cover the walls as well as it does in Germany, but it does give you time to think. Omar does not think the Royal Family will welcome me with open arms, he could be right; they have not even tried to contact me.

The copyright for that photo by Alberto Korda has been given to the Royal Family. So Omar tells me. They are frightened of claims being made against their estate. Just how it comes together I don't know nor do I want to.

I just wanted to be acknowledged. That thought brought me back as to why I was here, to get some proof. I was too frightened to just take his, Omar's tooth brush, pull out his hair. Stick one of those swabs into his mouth; wait for him to cut his toe nails.

I am not in my base country. 'Note I do not say my home country, I feel so at home in Cuba, there is no place like it on earth and she has given me more than I could ever have wished for.'

Omar's parent-father was in the government, his mother is still alive and he knows his way around.

The James Bond girl trying to cope with the hot spell found the address of the package service and other ways into the hotel using the back entrance. I have been told I look Cuban many times, just don't open my mouth!

It has taken my thirty years to speak German with a Dutch accent. I did not have that much time. I had the British embassy's address and a map of the surrounding city.

I also had a dog support team; the one dog brought a friend. 'I did not offer any dog any food, nor promised any.' He brought two more chums, now whenever I when for a walk the four chums came too. If I was trying not to be noticed, the pack of four made me look just as eccentric as I do at home. I live with four little dogs and they accompany me and my partner on walks around the country side.

The Cuban four only left me when I was at my brother's house, Packo must have told them I did not need their services. Packo is a large German sheep dog already a friend of mine. What did strike me was Bustos also has a dog like Packo. I had asked the makers of 'Sacrifico.' what Bustos's dogs name is. That and other questions, but they did not take me seriously enough to answer me.

I am here to get nearer to the truth. Up until now I have been indulging in my feelings, I must to learn to except my feelings trust my instincts, but they are not enough for the rest of the world.

Omar does not have time to be a brother every day, so I got into a taxi. I wanted to go to the Centro de Estudios Che Guevara. I had said I wanted to see the original photo, where my birth mother's face can be seen in full. It was not a lie, but, I did have another reason.

If Jorge G Castaneda had written in the notes for chapter eight about Ciro Bustos and Jan Lee Anderson had said Ciro Bustos had walked down the main street in Habana in nineteen fifty seven and as Che's lieutenant there must be some pictorial record of him, if there was, my theory would have to be ready to be thrown away.

Centro de Estudios Che Guevara.

The last time I stood in front of the house my father shared with his second wife, the centre was under construction, a building site! Now the building was standing impressively as I got out of the taxi.

There was a, but, it was closed. (Did they know I was here?) My taxi driver told me they were renovating the centre, just my luck! He was kind enough to take my photo in front of the building. But it did leave me with a problem.

As it turned out it was not a problem, there are books everywhere! Books with photos! And most of the books have come from the presses getting their information from Centro de Estudios Che Guevara.

Books in Cuba are everywhere to find and the hotel had many, I was a loud to run through them, collect ISBN numbers. The excuse was not being able to read Spanish! I did not say buying so many books was not in my budget.

The photo book depicting life and times did not have anyone looking like Ciro Bustos, the only photo where a man had a hat on so I could not see his hair line turned out to be someone by the name of Sanchez. The girl behind the counter must know, such subjects are taught in school.

Another book with the title of 'Evocacion' by Aleida March had photos I had not seen before, a bawled headed Che in Africa, but no lieutenant Bustos.

'Ei Diaro del Che en Bolivia.' The diary about the time in Bolivia was very interesting! It was interesting, because the only photo of Bustos was from back view with Debray, you cannot tell who was supposed to be who!

The only other photo I have seen of a supposed meeting where Bustos and Debray and Che is in the film 'Snapshot Che' by Wilfried Huismann, that photo is so out of focus it also not clear who is who.

(Interestingly when I looked at the film 'Sacrificio.' again.

I noticed Bustos pointing at a man with a full head of hair and say it is himself. But Bustos is bald, and always was partly baled; the hair he had did not grow on top of his head stroked the sides. But there again both photos of that moment are so out of focus. The photo I mean is often on show. (In the base of Che's guerrilla base, Nancahuazü. In the spring of 1967)

(((The issue of hair bothers me, if bald men can grow hair its news to me. Someone would have become very rich, the TV ads would leave gingilis ringing in my ears and every man would have a head of hair that would look good on any rock singer!)))

There is another pair of points; Ciro Bustos indicates he is the man on the far right of the photo I have been writing about. He say's that in the interview in 'Sacrificio.'
Point 1. Bustos in the beginning of the film show a Bustos as a dark Latino type.
Point 2. In the photo from the guerrilla base the man indicated by Bustos is NOT of that type. The man hair is too light!

I am so glad they are tolerant of tourists; no one in the antique book market in the old city minded my nose in their books. They even spent time writing down IBNS numbers for me, I spent such a happy afternoon sitting chatting and just drinking in the atmosphere.

That I went back to my hotel in the oldest taxi waiting in the rank it was a wonder, it did not have seat belts I did wonder why the driver rolled the wonderful car up to the traffic lights as it did not have brakes either!

I should have guessed, they did have to push the car out into the road and bump start it, but the love hart's light flashed on the dashboard. I loved very minuet of the drive, even if I did think I would have to walk back to the hotel.

### The Book Fair first trip.

After the disappointment of the Centro de Estudios Che Guevara, being closed I got the taxi drive to take me to the book fair in the old castle on the hill by the light house El Morrow. This is Cuba, everything is an adventure. I ran up the light house after waiting for Raul Castro to do his walk about as he was opening the fair.

I forgot I was not use to running up spiral stairs, paid for that the next day. There were stalls selling fresh food and drinks along the way I walked to the fort. I still had to wait for Raul to see the all the book stalls.

As I stood in the sun in a line of folk waiting to buy their entry tickets, I met Gilberto, he had been in the old Germany the DDR and spoke a bit of German and bit more English. I spent a happy two hours in that queue without sun cream or a hat!

When the lady turned up to open the ticket hut I decided the lack of tickets was going to be a problem.

No one had any idea where the tickets were, no one mined it was all enjoyed as a fair should be, the smell of food mingled with the heat.

I made the decision to return to the hotel, promising to ring Gilberto and make a date with him for another day. I was worried there would not be any taxies left when I wanted to go back. Gilberto later pointed out on our date, 'no Cuban ever uses a taxi.' I blamed the sun!

That trip back to the hotel was an enjoyable trip as the sea was splashing water over the wall flooding the road.

With the window open and my driver trying to keep the car dry I took photos of the playful sea. He even stopped to show me it was not all fun; the sea was undermining the old sea wall pushing into the old drains sending water fountains into the road. I was glad the drain covers had gone missing long ago the sea water was came up with such force!

I had to admit there was a lot of restoration work needed to bring Habana back to its original glory. Buildings that are held up with wooden supports do give the city a charm; though there was clearly work, underway. I had to wonder if they will manage to repair everything before it all falls down.

I have another day to look around before I am invited to breakfast with my brother. This time I am going to strip the old vanish of his table. Painting his walls while he and his neighbour play music; was one of my highlights. Omar was beating rhythm on a wooden box drum as the neighbour played the saxophone. The paint brush liked the rhythm.

I went to the Aquarium the reason I wanted to go there was half-sister Celia works there as a vet, I did not expect to see her, but if I could get a contact email address with… say, one of the other vets I would have a way to contact her.

I was going with Gilberto to the book fair on Sunday, but the blisters on my feet needed a rest, if a walked around anymore I would be lame for weeks. Sunday was spent running round Habana's old city, seeing places that had been so important at the start of my strange adventure.

The Farnes restaurant that had been so important to me on that first trip. Werner a fellow traveller and I past on one of those tricycle bikes and the places where Uwe and I had parked the hire car on other trips to Habana.

Werner and I were trying to get to Hemingway's roof top café the driver of the tricycle took us over high pavements tipping us sideways it made me laugh but Werner was not as happy as I was. Werner is eighty one with a new knee! He's grumbling it did not match my laughter.

The drink waiting for us after we had asked for new directions returned harmony, we were so disorientated it helped settled both of us. The roof tops of Havana are special to me; the mojito cocktail in my hand remained me of the tears that started to fall the first time I was here. Werner did not understand me at all, nor did I. I was here to get the DNA of my brother, I was having fun!

The night was long, and getting longer; the problem how to get the DNA was keeping me awake, that and the chap next room being very sick in his bathroom… bathroom, toothbrush. I had it! If I took the brushes from the do it yourself kit and rolled them in his toothbrush. Maybe take a few bristles from the brush and flick some of the gung from the bristles base into the little plastic bag would solve my problem. And save me any trouble stealing his toothbrush could bring.

That would mean he would not know what I was up to; till I knew how was I going to tell him, his new half sister thinks there is a man in Sweden that might be our father!?

There was the special moment were we sat on the kitchen floor a normal thing to do when you are renovating your house. I gave him a copy of my catalogue of my paintings and he gave me a copy of his book of poems he even did a thing in the front of it for me. Who needs words when we have so many! Between us we did not need DNA I knew but my feelings were not going to be enough.

I did fall asleep even with the next door's roommate groaning in his bathroom.

The breakfast next morning with Omar was followed by coffee and tea and another piece of luck, a toothpick straight from the horse's mouth was added to the bristles from the toothbrush!

Second trip to the book fair.

I rang Gilberto to confirm our date; he rang me back to ask how my feet were as I had put off our date because of the troublesome blusters. The telephone had made me jump, could it be because I had been playing with Omar's toothbrush? I don't like being a Bond girl.

We were going to meet outside the Capital. He would be wearing a yellow shirt; did he know how many people would be wearing a yellow shirt that morning?

My offer of a taxi was brushed aside, we were going by bus! For me the idea was wonderful, many were waiting for the bus to the Book Fair, so to smuggle me into the bus was easy.

I bent down to pick up a coin gave it a kiss and put it in my bag for luck. The little girl watched me do such a strange thing excepted Gilberto explanation with a razed eye borough.

The buses were newer that I remember seeing before. The bus was not a loud to leave till the bus could not fit in anymore people; every space had to be occupied and the standing room filled. The man on the pavement kept pushing more folk in till he was satisfied it was full. I did not feel squashed even though the bus was so full.

The bus dropped us all on the road in front of El Morrow the festival feeling is still here even though it was not the opening day. The little girl stooped down a picked up another coin, she handed to me! Was I showing myself up as a tourist? I kissed the coin and handed it back to her with its luck refilled. Gilberto told her, the good luck in it was for her.

As we were walking towards the entrance with tickets in our hands a man strode past us. Gilberto saw his date running back the way we had come, shouting Camilo!

Gilberto and half brother Camilo.

Camilo stopped what now? He does not speak English my Spanish did not cover you are my half-brother! As Omar had suggested this might not be a good time to say such a thing. I took his photo and one of him and Gilberto. It has got to be useful sometime.

Camilo had been in Hamburg accompanying the photos I had run around Habana looking for. I did try to say so with the help of confused Gilberto; he did not understand why I was so excited, nor why I was trying not to hug Camilo.

I had to tell Gilberto what had just happened to me. He is the only person in Cuba that knows why I was there. I did not mention the man in Sweden though.

Gilberto understood why I wanted to see the office my father had worked in, overlooking the city of Habana.

I found a comic about Che Guevara my father at one of the stalls and Gilberto found a map of Germany where all the places Gilberto had been to so many years before were marked.

I told him the whole of my story as we eat a large tourist lunch I wanted to treat him to as thank you for the lovely lucky day we were spending together. He was shocked when I said I could not eat anymore, could they pack the rest of my meal so I could take it with me. He said it was not Cuban to do something like that! I said we were tourists and could and we did.

Goodbye to my brother.

I went to say goodbye to my brother and tell him just how lucky that coin was. Omar want to know, what did I feel on seeing Camilo? Good question, not the same feeling as with Omar, but just as strong or I would not have run down the road before I could think better of it.

On Wednesday morning thinking I was flying home that day, I rang up to check with the lady from the travel company, she said there was a holed up on all flights, as they, the Americans were going to shoot down a satellite.

I was not to fly out till Thursday night. The wait upset me, I was homesick, and a storm did not help, not even the rainbow could cheer me up. Was that

because Omar had said things like rainbows were only there to impress tourists?
I was not going to cheered up I wanted my four doggies and Uwe, James Boned could keep his job!

Least this way I had a half brother and a full friend, met Camilo, even if he did not know I was a half sister waving my arms in front of him and an email address that could lead away to Cilla. The rest will find away somehow!

Waiting for the DNA results.

Waiting for the results for the DNA was the most difficult thing I ever had to do; and there seemed to be no end to the waiting.

I sent the toothpick and the bits from the toothbrush along with two of the little brushes in their packet to the firm promising me ninety to ninety-five present, not knowing they were talking a load of bubble. But, how was I to know that then?

Firstly the ten days they promised ran into two months, I must have made a thousand phone calls, they added to the plies of emails I sent asking how things were going. On television it only takes two minuets! I even paid another ninety Euros for the toothpick to be tested somehow the toothpick was a difficult thing to test unlike their brushes.

When two months had past I was at the end of my tether, how long was this going to go on for? I knew it is not easy to do a half sibling test across the sexes.

I was not expecting to get an email at midnight saying they could not make the test due to a lack of material. Strange to say I did not sleep that night. I did not have enough money to fly back to Cuba nor could I find another excuse to descend on Omar again so soon! I was lost in despair till my partner said ring this number.

The number was for a DNA tester with a forensic background. I must have been on the phone for hours, the man how's name I did not catch was so interesting!

I did have enough DNA to test, the toothpick would have been loaded not to mention the bits from his toothbrush they would be more than enough. But, but, I did not have them, 'they' the others did.

The man whose name I did not get was saying something about letters from men that had died in the Second World War had been used to identify bodies found in unmarked graves.

I had Omar's book of poems, I had not read it as I was saving it to read in the next winter.

Omar had made a ballpoint pen impression in the inside cover of his gift! The first page after the cover is not a place where fingers usually linger. I did still have the first set of little brushes I had rolled in Omar's toothbrush; 'they' had said they would be useless!

The man how's name I did not get said, sent everything I had to him and he would see if there was enough DNA to make a test possible on the things I had. And he would not charge me anything to check, if there was enough I could send down my DNA and his payment later.

I had told him everything! Later when I though over the long telephone conversation I realised it was April the first! If I was to plan an April fool on a forensic expert could I have thought of a better story?

So now I was worrying again as I waited to hear if there was going to be enough DNA to use.

He did say, he had stranger April fools played on him and stranger 'stories' than mine had been investigated, he had not taken my call as an April fool.

I am waiting again! It is not any easier than the first time, the ten days are moving slowly, not helped by bank holidays and post strikes. I even rang to check again that he did not think it had been an April fool stunt.

I was not able to ring up on the day appointed as I was too stressed to ask, waiting had got to me; my partner had to take over for me. The two months had now stretched into three months and twenty eight days; Uwe had to pick up the phone as I was not able of doing anything.

It was not a result I was expecting, it is not the percentage in front of the point that is important, it is the match behind it that is. To get that information I need my birthmother's DNA and Omar's mothers. My half sisters could help but there again they are only half sisters.

It took me sometime to understand my cup is half full not half empty! I felt I was sitting in a cul-de-sac with no way to go because no one will talk to me, but that does not mean my cup is empty.

As it is we could be cousins as well as half siblings. It could be our mothers that are the connecting link, (though I don't think so somehow.) how could they be connected?

Half brother's and full friends are not continually falling out of trees, I have decided to put that search behind me, to enjoy the sense of peace I have from meeting Omar and seeing another half brother at the book fair. Just knowing I do not stand in the world alone and I have roots twisting in mankind make me feel more human than I ever have before; even if the DNA cannot be conclusive.

Trying to unravel my roots would cost me more time and time is not in my control. With Omar's DNA I can try to find out if the man in Sweden is Che Guevara, May the fourteenth could be his eighth birthday.

Che's brother had identified Che's body?

I did not make the trip to Sweden. I have become unsure. The outside world does not seem to want to know.

The maker of the film 'Snap shot with Che.' Wilfried Huismann did come and see me but ran away as soon as I told him I thought Che still lives!

I have to say I cannot understand why, do I look like a crazy middle age woman? As he left he told me he had talked to Alfrido/Ruberto Che's younger brother. As Che's brother, he had identified Che's body.

But, but when I saw the film from Raffaele Bruntti, 'Che Guevara- Der Tod und Der Mythos.' The film confronted me with a young man with down cast eyes stating he had not seen the body of his brother.

The film also reports reporters of the time had been waiting to see the body in a hotel next to the hospital's morgue; they were unable to see the body. Raffaele Bruntti's film says the body went missing two hours after life was said to have been taken from it.

This film also stated there were discrepancies as to where the body was supposed to have been buried. The remark that sticks in my mind is that the remains that were said to be Che's remains were not subject to DNA testing!

Of course I tried to tell him, Raffaele Bruntti, about Ciro Bustos and he is the reason maters don't match! I don't want to understand I am a crazy middle age woman.

I have not gone to Sweden to meet Ciro Bustos, I don't know how. I don't know how to meet a man that could be my father.

## Chapter three
Ebay's Che Guevara CD.

I saw on the internet, Ebay's had a Che Guevara CD on offer.

Che Guevara CIA- State Dept- Dept of Defence Files. When I first saw it I was not going to buy it, something to do with the crazy middle age women, thing.

I was sceptical, my partner was sceptical. The thought crossed my mind that I would give out more for a book and eight Euros was not a loss I could take if it was the rubbish I was expecting.

Two things happened, the first being Helen the girl friend my mother made in when she first came to Europe, sent me an email. She and her daughter were curious to know if I had found out more about Beverly. I wrote her a long updating email about my trip to Cuba and how I felt I had gone as far as I could, considering the muddling result of the DAN.

Beverly and Omar's mother does not feel to me the right way forward, how could they be connected? Che had two brothers and a half brother. I only know the half brother is connected on his father's side.

Uncle Roberto, Omar told me he is connected to the Cuban film industry. Juan Martin as Che's other brother, I know nothing about. I only found his name when I felt I had to check up in 'Che Fotobiografie.' If it was I, that had made a rueful mistake about Che's eye colour.
It is a shame that Omar is not able to enjoy knowing them and his other four siblings.

I do not know even the name of Che's younger half brother! Half an uncle! I seem to be collecting a lot of half people.

* Uncle Reberto was not the head of the Cuban film industry as Omar said; Alfredo Guevara was; he delighted being a member of the Che Guevara family.*

Reference in the book- Gabriel Garcia Marquez the creator of Che Guevara.

The other thing that happened was I had finished the dictionary I was compiling. The idea of idle hands guided me to my desk and take out the CD I had got from the United States. The thought of over thirty thousand pages would replace the space the dictionary had left.

I enclose the number of the files, it is in the public domain.

Che Guevara CIA -State Dept- Dept of Defence Files.

The CIA files are from Informer Enterprises.

A list of the pages that caught my eye.
DOS
Pages 15 to 18 DOS.
White House
Pages 8 to 10.
DOD
Pages 4 to 8.
Page 8 to 10 White House.

Says that the guerrillas were captured, seriously engaged and one of them was thought to be Che Guevara. (seriously injured! This is only the start of many discrepancies.)

Pages 4 to 8 of DOD, add the question as to where and how Che was supposed to have died.

Pages 15 to 18. DOS -They made me sit up, since when did Che Guevara have light blue eyes?

The man who did the autopsy states- the man in front of him had-

LIGHT BLUE EYES.

In the same report it says that the man was shot through the thorax. (In the film 'Sacrifico.' in spite of the direct camera shots this is not to be seen.)

That the body had been covered in preservative, I had not at first though the fact was interesting, but now I think it is important. (The smell was reported to have been very strong! This would keep people moving not wanting to ask question as to whether the body was still alive!) If you want to keep a body like that would it stop you from being able to say when it became lifeless? I will not speculate anymore this is not my field.

The **light blue eyes!?**

If the autopsy had not mentioned the eyes being light blue, had it only said blue you could say it was a slip of the tong but to say light blue!?

Ciro Bustos is not mentioned in any of these files. (In the whole of these documents the name is only once to be seen, an Index. Where 174 is said to be the number of his file, where ever it is…. All references are document numbers.)

There is more said about Regis Debray. I get the impression that he is thought of, on the same leave as Fidel Castro and Che by the CIA.

Now there are so many discrepancies!
I feel I am in over my head, the little crazy middle aged lady is not an expert but what I do have is my feelings and-

a) A man leaving prison with a full head of hair, 'Sacrifico'
   Ciro Bustos is shown as being partly bald.'
b) The film 'Schappschuss mit Che.' Shows that CIA agent
   Felix Rodriguez's account is not accurate.
c) The fact that Che/Ciro have matching head shapes and their hands match also.
   Baby Che head shape matches, older Che and Ciro Bustos.
d) The 'light blue eyes.' In the CIA autopsy report.
e) Bald headed Bustos points to a man he says is himself as a younger man with hair a lot of hair, when all photos state he was as a young man bald.

One thing the experts don't have as a guide is---
*I am looking for my father*.
I do not know how 'they' managed to twist events nor why, I only know it happened. I can only say 'they' had the tools and used them. If I was to try to decide how it was done I might as well write a thriller, but I would still get lost in the maze of none matching facts.

Twisting snake of the DNA.

I am free to take up my thoughts again! I met Rena, I met him at a compotation for firemen, he was the reporter for the local news paper; he agreed to look into 'my story.' With his questions grow more questions.

How do I prove that Omar is a son of Che? He says he is, but how can that be proved? Omar says he was told when he was twenty five. His birth certificate will have the man's name that brought him up, not Che's.

Omar told me, they, the Marsh family do not recognise him, as Che's child. How can it be proved Che is his father? There are other children in Omar's family that don't share the same father. Could his half sister living in Italy be connected to Che? How to prove every child in the Marsh family have the same father?

Is this why Omar did not want to give me his DNA?

I would have to ask each and everyone, sisters, brothers, any living uncles and aunts to provide their DNA in hope of identifying Che Guevara's DNA. And now we are talking about resources I do not have! Would the family willing undergo such a search just to provide a DNA to match with Che's or find which DNA matches so I could prove my theory!

That Omar and my DNA need our mothers' DNA to make sense of the connections no longer upsets me. I learnt from Rene that folk from that part of the world have a closer DNA that in Europe. All of this means the only way to prove my point is with a forensic photo program.

Such a program can measure points on a face and can say even with stretching years, if there is a match. You can change the look of your face but to change the basic measurements.

Just how I am going to get someone to do such a thing for me, I just do not know. The cost of this program is too expensive for me. (Face book is using this technology now so it is a matter of time; before a match can be made without the need for an expert!)

This is not the main reason why I find myself sitting in front of my laptop. I have found another film that asked more questions. The films name is 'Che Guevara, The way to revolution.'

I found this copy in my local supermarket. You could say it found me, as most things have up until now.

It is a film made in Cuba dated 1968. It includes testimonies from intersecting members of the group around Che at the supposed time of his capture. It is directed by Manuel Perez.
Manuel Perez was born in Havana, he directed documenters made in Cuba. His film leaves me asking, how one man can appear in so many films/books under so many different names? Pictured as busyness man, revolutionist, prisoner, expert in guerrillas maters working for the Americans.

'The Way To Revolution.'
The first point is;
The intervened were young men that were said to have been with Che, they made their testimonies were made sometime after their return to Cuba.

Their testimonies do not match with what they say in 'Snap shot with Che.'

I could match, point for point their interviews in both films, I will leave that to those better than me at such things.

I know time can change the way you look at things, though the facts should stay the same, cross reference somehow, like teeth in a comb!

It is the moment in the documentary where it shows a man looking like Ciro Bustos getting into an American jeep, made me look twice. They name this man as Ramon Benitez. He looks like Ciro Bustos! And I think Ciro Bustos is Che! And I thing Che was my father.

In the film 'Wege Der Revolution' www.icestorm.de Regie: Manuel Perez, you can see Felix Ramos an adviser to the CIA getting into a jeep- Looking like Ciro Bustos with one of the Che Guevara code names. Ciro Bustos with one of Che Guevara's code names-

I am told by the film 'Weg Der Revolution.' 'He' is an expert in guerrilla war fair, working for the Americans.

The film cover tells me other copies can be obtained by looking on their website www.icestorm.de. It is a film with in the film produced by Paco Prats that I find most interesting.

A list of names Che is known to have used.

Ramon Benitez= a business man
              From a Revolutionary Life, Jon Lee Anderson.

Adolfo Mena Gonzalez= to be seen in a self portrait, taken in hotel room Bolivia.
              From a Revolutionary Life, Jon Lee Anderson.

Filex Ramos= the expert on guerrilla maters. A C.I.A agent
              working for the Americans.
              From Wege Der Revolution,
              Ice Storm.

  Had Rene not questioned the point about eyes reflecting light, or not after death, I would not have been interested in talking to Gunter.(remember this name) He has retired but once an expert in pathology always an expert in pathology, so I asked his opinion. Gunter confirmed eyes do not reflect light the instance life leaves a body.
  When he was asking why I wanted to know such a thing,
I noticed there were car number plates nailed on the doors of his garage. Venezuela, Bolivia! If I had not seen the car number plate for Bolivia I would not have told him my reasons for asking. Gunter had been to Bolivia, he had met film maker Hans Ertl.

Hans Ertl's daughter was Monika Ertl, she was supposed to have come to Hamburg to the Bolivian embassy and shot Andres Selick. He was the man that was supposed to have given the order to execute Che.

 * I did not know at the time he was Klaus Barbi's son.*

Monika Ertl.

I got the film 'Gesucht Monika Ertl. The woman who revenged Che Guevara's death.

 The film did not confirm what Gunter heard from Hans Ertl that Che was such a good son in-law. The film did not make a clear the contact, relationship between Monika Ertl and Che; but it did say their farm was in the same district as Che was running his campaign.

It is an interesting film, to learn Klaus Barbie was considered as an uncle to Monika, and she knew Regis Debray. Seeing that made me think! What did I think? I had found loose ends, but I do not know from where they come from!

Monika was a woman how looked like my mother, the same type as his second wife. Monika liked to be on horseback, could use a gun. She often went with her father on filming trips and enjoyed camping with him.

Regis Debray and Ciro Bustos were arrested on the same day. Regis Debray was a close college to Che-Bustos and now I know he was connected with Monika Ertl. The film shows them planning to plot against Klaus Barbie. When they were in Cuba!

Klaus Barbie had to leave Europe at the end of the Second World War, as did many others. Bolivia found their expertise valuable, and used their skills to train their own men. Their skills were a needed in tracking down those coursing problems for the Bolivian government.

If Bolivia found emigrants from Germany helpful in Bolivian organisation, so could Cuba! The DDR and Cuba sheared the same political principals; both lands ran under the same rules.

This thought became real after seeing a news paper article pointing out how East Germany's fishing fleet was connected to Havana and its fishing industry and sent boats to Namibia.

I just have to point the east cost of Germany supports the Baltic Sea. And I have heard that those from the broken Nazi party had found homes in Sweden.

I don't know what this all thesis facts means, they are like a photo which is out of focus and you do not even know if they are photos that should be there.

Gunter cost me a year, he was sure that the CIA would bother me. So sure they would, he told someone who I thought was a friend; they did not speak to me again. I thought they had been members of the DDR's no longer wanted political party. (I think now there may be other reasons behind his remarks.)

Chapter four
To Sweden Malmo

It is not the first time I have thought I have come to an end only to find I am at a new beginning. When I first came to the island about a year ago I knew Malmo was not far away. The thought that Klaus Barbie and other members of the broken Nazi party were involved in Bolivia, slowed my need to go met the man in Sweden. Being told that if I was anywhere near the truth I would have been shot a long time ago did not help me either!

I used a lot of other excuses not to get on the ferry. When it came to the day before Uwe was going to take me to the ferry I came up with the excuse I had broken a finger nail! Perhaps that is why he put me in the car next day telling me to go, to get the whole thing out of my system.

Uwe was right it was time to get the whole thing out of the way so I could look into the future. I had put my trip of the week before due to someone's remark. 'Emotion had taken over from common sense.' At times I have used the same remark to hide behind.

I am on the ferry, what is the worst that can happen to me?
I know he is there, I rang last week. I decide not to think about it, just enjoy getting there.

I met two lovely ladies enjoying a five day trip around Sweden. After getting lost on the boat as we tried to find their bus, they persuaded the trip organiser to give me a lift to Malmo. Without the stress of trying to find a bus to take me from Trelleburg to the centre of Malmo I could enjoy the

unfolding landscape and admire the Bridge connecting
Denmark to Sweden. On that day the wind was blowing so strongly that traffic had to move over it slowly.

I did not want to get my map out and make my way to the address marked on it, I wanted to stay on the bus and enjoy the interesting facts the organiser had to tell about the city of Malmo.

Mac Donald's provide me with lunch and a place to brush my hair and a man who said he was a reporter reminded me yet again that the story I had to tell was just my emotion playing tricks. What did I have to lose? No one believed what I have to say nor what I thought I have found out. Nasty men would not be coming to take me away! I was here to try to meet a man that I thought was possibly my father or find the thoughts that had been with me for so long a resting place.

I would need a resting place for the night, there happened to be a stopover on the same street where I his flat was. Sacrificio had scenes of the street before the block his flat was in. Strange to think the film had shown me glimpses of how his flat looked inside.

I was let inside the building by the nice Turk; he was from the shop next door; as there were only numbers on the door bells I could not guess which was his!

Standing outside the door with Ciro Bustos on its nameplate my heart was thumping, when my hand reached up to press the bell it thumped without mercy! There was no reply, will that it then! Use plan B come back in the morning, ask the Turk when he is likely to be back. I took a photo of the door just to prove to Uwe and myself I had been there. As I was putting away my camera when the door opened! What was I going to say?

I managed to say, 'Halo I am Evelyn.' There was a moment I cannot describe and then he asked me in.

His brown eyes are rimed with blue/green; I want to look into them as if they would tell all I wanted to know. His eyes have thrown me my mind is in neutral, I am trying to tell him why I am here. Trying to tell someone who does not speak English that your mother met Che in Mexico in nineteen fifty five, and you wanted to meet him because. A) You want to meet someone who met Che. B) You are Che, you are my father.

Thank goodness my mind is in neutral! The flat is as the film shows it, only it is more so. His work hangs from the walls, his pictures have feelings I understand. I call myself an artist.

There is a wall with books about everything on one side of the room the opposite wall has a work bench and another bookcase between the computer by the window. This bookcase is full with books about you know who, Che! Books I know and books I don't, most were in Spanish. There were two a copies of Jon Lee Anderson one in English, good to see an old friend. I remarked it was not a hundred percent correct, he remarked he thought it was, with it I tried to explain my birthmother probably met Che at the Pam Am games.

I did see the photo of the girl that I think could be a portrait of the young Che first love. I did not ask who she was.

I like his paintings, they are studies of the human form with feeling and emotion worked in to inherence their closeness. They do not have faces, they don't need expressions their bodies tell you what you need to know. I had read somewhere he painted portraits of people without faces; which was one of the things that woke my interest in him in first place.

Now I come to writ this down I remember, I could not find any records of him in the university he was supposed to have studded at, in Argentina. But then they might not have put that kind of information for me to read on the internet.

((((Ciro Bustos name came to my notice in Jan Lee Anderson's book a page before Che shot himself and the doctors sent him into shock when they gave him a jab.

I don't have a copy of the film I saw on the television, it said He and Debray travelled with Tamara Bunka. The two men were journalist, they wanted to move around Bolivia discreetly but Tamara Bunka made sure they were noticed wherever they went. Trying to find a copy of that film I had found 'Sacrificio.')))

'Sacrifico' had given me a glimpse into flat I was sitting sipping juice in.

We were together two hours, my mind was still in neutral and I was so tired could not wait for a bed with a television to go to sleep with. I was too tired to realise I should put the code for Germany before my number, I did want to tell Uwe I was ok, that there were no bad guys under the bed. That the man I had come to visit had strange coloured eyes had put my mind into neutral. I want to tell Uwe that I was going to have breakfast with Mr Bustos the next day.

I was late as I wanted to know if I could open a post box. I could not decide the night before if my letters had reached him, if not, the men under the bed might have them! Once a Bond girl always a Bond girl!

I had been a Bond girl when I had visited Omar, so when Mr Bustos said he did not have any milk for our coffee I did not react there are many folk that cannot digest milk. Omar had told me that he could not drink milk, I cannot. The thought Omar was both left and right handed as I am, crossed my neutral mind it was then I looked at Mr Bustos's hands. (I had looked at many photos of Che's and Bustos's hands when I was looking for connections) the hands I was looking at were familiar. Black and white photos are not the best way of trying to make comparisons with someone some forty years older. But they were familiar, long practical, the top of little finger of the right hand tip bends inwards, like mine. They are like mine. Omar's hands were small, child like, they had bothered me, they did not seem right.

I am here to end that kind of thinking; I have been going round in circles for ten years trying to find connections, jumping at shadows of emotions. No, this must be the end.

Mr Bustos and I talk about art, we feel comfortable, and he shows me all of his pictures: I like them so much they are about contact and love. I tell him I want to keep in contact, He is an artist I am artist, and we have pictures stacked in corners as the walls cannot carry any more, but the ideas keep coming.
The market for art is so slow we would starve if we lived from
our work. He gave me copies of the brochures he had printed for expeditions of his work; I hope there is enough DNA on them. I must fire that Bond girl.

I have Jan Lee Anderson's book in my hand, I did not bring anything with me but, this book does have a picture of my birthmother and her two friends with Che and Hilda, I still not know where it was taken. And the copy has the photo of my adopted father listening to Che speak in Uruguay.

Mr Bustos asks me what my mother's name was, he remarked that he told Ricardo Rojo, also in the picture with my birth mother; not to write a book about his friendship with Che, that book is not now taken seriously. How could have Bustos told him not to write that book, he, Bustos was not in Mexico (so he said,) I did not know Bustos knew Ricardo Roco!

Wasn't Bustos supposed to be in Argentina studding art at that time?

I did not take up the remark at the time only when I was telling Uwe later did the remark seemed strange.

I wish I had not taken croissants as they shared their crumbs everywhere, the flat was tidy and clean, I wish my house looked like that, when people drop in they have to put up with whatever project I am working on!

As we go back to the Che Guevara book case he points to a photo of Hilda the first wife of Che, she had been pregnant at the same time as my mother was. From the description in Mr Anderson's book she was supposed to be a dragon, but the little woman looked sweet and totally charming. Older than the photos I had seen before but defiantly Hilda.

Camilo's name came easily to his lips I was stumbling over it, I was trying to explain about wanting to see Che's photos, about running about the world trying to see them, being dyslectic can really be a pain at times, people think you are a fool when names won't come into your mouth at the right moment!

I want people to believe me, I want to believe me, I wanted from the photos, from the Pam Am games proof my birthmother and Che met. That need to believe to be believed had built a wall of frustration, it was no longer there!

There was a man sitting opposite me and I felt at peace! He is asking about my birthmother and what my adoptive father profession had been. My adoptive father was an adviser in the investment world it explained why he had travelled the world, but children of three years old are not told much about their parent's previous lives, then I was old enough to ask he was dying; he died the same year as Che. Strange to have a parent and a father die in the same year! Strange to think they met, not knowing they were connected by a little girl!

We left the flat with its bookshelves and paintings and large leaved plants in the window. It was then I got out my camera and asked to take his photo. He waved his hand as the building next to his flat was being renovated, it was hung with nets.

I was not going to be stopped by safety nets! When a young man pushing himself up the hill on a skateboard was close enough I asked him if he would take our photo. One was not enough so he took a second; this gave his skateboard the chance to start down the hill without him.

We walked towards the city the way I had come, the sun was shining, as the travail agent had said Sweden's southern lands liked to hide in mists the sun must be shining for me.

We crossed the main road then through the small market place I had seen the day before, before entering the older part of town, we entered a long green park that ran the whole length of the old town.

He stopped, I knew we were going to say goodbye. I said I was going to leave Che Guevara behind and look into the future, I hope the future was with him. I do not know if he understood my words, I don't know if he, we understood anything I just felt we did.

We leant towards each other, the hug was natural and easy, he kissed me on my cheek. As he drew away I saw tears rundown his face before his sun glasses hid his eyes from me.

He walked away as I did; my way was under the trees his way was back the way we had come. I only looked around once; he did not turn when I did.

After finding again the Mac Donald's that had been my starting point, I went to find the bus that would take me to Trelleburg and the ferry. If I had known the bus would pass the small market and stop a little way from the crossroads we had walked over!

Will I know now, you just get off the bus and walk down the pedestrian street with a telephone shop, with a nice girl to remind you to use the country code when you want to ring home! Walk straight into the buildings of the ferry company. If the ferry had been there I could have just walked onto it as well.

As it was I had a couple of hours to walk around the shops. Even though my mind is still in neutral I found myself standing in front of Che-posters and mugs and a clock. I don't have a Che t-shirt! (I have other things!) Thank goodness my mind is in neutral.

It was when I was telling Uwe about my time with Mr Bustos that my mind came out or neutral. How did he know Ricardo Rojo? (A close friend of Che's in Mexico.)
Why was Hilda's photo a treasure? Why did he ask so many questions about my birthmother, why ask, what her name was?

Uwe reminds me I was so sure Omar was my half brother. Because- when I went to see Omar I wanted a half brother. When I went to see Mr Bustos I wanted and end.

Making a decision to except what you have seen and felt is a long process. I was not sure Ciro was Che. With Omar I had to wait for the DNA test, when it came it only gave me a half result. The tester wanted more information the DNA had missing links, he wanted to have my birth mother and

Omar's mother's DNA. The tests could not get a closer match.

I now think I know why! Ciro did not react when I mentioned Omar was Che's son. What if Omar was a fake not me!? Omar did not want to give me a DNA sample; he did not want me to see the March family. Omar did say he thought they would throw me out of Cuba- I did not want to risk being thrown out of anywhere, but I did find out where my two half sisters worked. And I did stand outside their house opposite the Che Guevara centre. And I did see Camilo at the book fair, even if he did not know what I wanted.

When a friend asked me how my trip went I did not know how to answer her, all I could say was why did he cry when we parted? It was good to have a friend put an arm around you in that moment.

      Mundane Place.

Why do great moments have to be in mundane places?
I had to go the WC while Uwe was putting gas into the car, the WC filed with light, without its help I would not have looked into my eyes. It felt as if I was looking into them for the first time in my life. They are brown with a blue/green edging. Funny I though, I have always thought of them as mud coloured. The colouring is not as striking as Ciro's but it is still there! What now? I don't need a DNA test and even if I had one, no one would believe it. No one wants to believe it.

How can the world believe that the whole Che Guevara story should be rewritten!?

At this moment I do not know what I want- I do want to remain in contact with Ciro, I will even learn Spanish if he will communicate with me, just another mountain for a dyslectic! He did say he would come and stay with me but he has not yet taken up my offer to write to me by email, the telephone is so difficult I can understand much more when hands and expression are there to help me.

## Eyes

I have spent many hours on the internet, looking at videos, frame by frame, to find evidence to present not only to myself to confirm the eyes. I found pictures of a young Che with those eyes, I found a picture of him with his mother; she also has the same eyes as he does, (as I do) I did not mark this reference to clearly. There is evidence to show the same eyes are to be seen on the death bed at the death party!

Funny Man. TV=   Eyes of grandmother and a young Che.

Cheguevaravideos.blogspot.com
    Guevara, Part 3
        Part 4
            Part 5- As Castro reads Che's
                farewell letter.
        Part 6- At the very beginning of the film.

=At the moment where locks of hair are being cut from his head the eyes can be seen.
(Concluding it is Che's own body they used in the allusion. I have to remark the body was not thin enough for someone that had been starving for so long!)

The films are repeated in many languages and have been put on the blog early in the year. (2010) I studded them around the 28/6/2010.

The Eyes can be seen that photo by Alberto Korda. A clear light copy shows them.

While I have been waiting to see if Ciro will talk to me by email, I have taken three Spanish lesions, managed to get someone to write a letter in Argentina Spanish! Then worried he would be alarmed by me simple gesture! I did try to write my own messages in Spanish, after my first lesson in Spanish I realised it is not so easy, goodness knows what I said!

The weeks of this hot summer are made more difficult because there have not been any emails; to have wait is not easy for me! I am getting more restless, the weeks go by.

Ok, I will go again to Sweden.

I know we cannot speak with each other easy, my solution to that was to sit down and ask myself what do I want to ask Ciro? Not easy! Firstly as I am not getting any feedback from him, secondly where do I begin?

My first questions were about depression, did he suffer from depression? I do not know why it was the first question I wrote down. It was one of the questions I presented him on blue cards he answered openly.

Other question was about seeing people again from the past, people like my half brothers and sisters. Could he go to Cuba as Bustos? Can he travel anywhere he wishes, worldwide or Europe?

There is something else on my mind. Who knows he is still a live? The Marsh Family in Cuba? Obviously Regis Debray dose, he was imprisoned in Bolivia with Ciro Bustos.
(Ciro did say he could not go to Cuba or Argentina.)
*That is strange he sent me an email around Christmas saying it was 32 hot in Binaries 12.2010*

The blue cards

Armed with thirty-six blue cards with questions in English on one side and the same question repeated in Spanish on the other, and a small traveller's guide to Spanish, I board the ferry for Sweden again.

I get to Malmo to find most people have given into the heat and gone to the beach. It is a hot summer; the trains in Germany have over heated compartments where as in Sweden the railway lines have buckled!

Could the heat explain why I cannot find Ciro? Or does he not wish to see me? I had sent him an email- would he like to have coffee with me between two and three tomorrow?

I have to admit I could have been sent such an email earlier, and I have to admit I don't want to be rejected. Fear did play a part as well as not having Spanish to use as I wish.

The Bond girl is back, the nice man working in the pizza café says he knows the man in the photo I show him, Ciro's name did not produce any reaction with the folk I asked if they knew him.

The Pizza man told me Ciro had only five friends, when he told me he had a car I was interested. I did find it in the car park opposite the traffic lights; I knew it was the car even if the colour was not quite was the Pizza man said. On the back seat were Ciro's sun glasses, the same ones he had on when he walked me to the buss the first time I was here.

It was a frustrating afternoon, the first time I got into the building Ciro's door did not open. The Bond girl is trying to decide wither there is anyone in the flat or not. The nice lady in the Thailand massage shop next door tried to ring Ciro's number for me, but there was no replay. If I had not gone to the WC I might not have missed him! His car has gone from the car park!

I take myself off to sulk around town, but I am two bad tempered to enjoy the Swedish stores. But I do have time to think; I should book a room for the night. Bond girls don't give up even if they are hot or tired. And it was nice to dump my bag on the bed. I do want to go home, it is hot, my foal has hurt herself, I miss my dogs and if Uwe was with me I would feel a lot better.

I am getting to know the surrounding roads; I am surprised how easy it is to get into any building I want to. I want to see if I can see into Ciro's building. Have the blinds been reset? From the front of the building I can see the balcony door is open!

The Turkish man from the shop next door lets me in to the building. I ring the doorbell outside his flat for the umpteenth time, but this time I can hear voices behind the door. A hand came out! Not Ciro's! Do I have to have my heart in my mouth?

Ciro is surprised to see me! I am glad to see him! I am told to go in; he is a little flustered, so am I. He went down stairs with three men he had been talking to.

Bond girl went straight into the bathroom; the small brush used to clean between Ciro's teeth was in a prepared plastic freezer bag, was safely in my pocket! I was too frightened to take make a copy of the photo of Hila Gadea, Che's first wife or the photo that looks like his first love. Maria del Carmen.
My excuse was if I am right then the DNA I had in my pocket was all the proof I need.

Will my tripe was not wasted even if he did not want to talk to me! I cannot say what language they had been speaking when they had opened the door, the young man did speak English! (I know this is not the time to have an intermit decision, can we trust the young translator with the subjects covering my blue cards back in the room I have taken?

Ciro said he had sent me an email to say he did not have time to meet me today. As I had left at six am I did not see his email that showed up on my email account at eleven.

It did not hit me then; Ciro was watching my emails, my letters were on his table. So good to know!

I when back to my hotel room much happier than before, we have agreed to meet the next day at twelve, please ring to confirm if he is at home.

Malmo was presently quite the next day as everyone that could, had deserted its hot streets for the beach. I had time to check up when my bus would leave to take me to the ferry.

It is twelve, I am in the Turkish pizza Bar; the nice man has rung to ask Ciro if he would like to have lunch with me. As I am waiting for him the irony of two photos of Che struck me. One is a copy of 'The Photo' where as the other is of Che clowning about, laughing. May be it was too hot in the bar, or Ciro did not want to sit down under a photo of John Lennon, that was also hanging there!

All Ciro's favoured places have their shutters up, gone to the beach! We had to trudge back into town to find something to eat. We sat at a little table outside on the pavement to take advantage of the cooler shadows.

My blue cards are not producing the success I wished for, they did not have the question or fazes I needed now! My questions ranged from what do you like to eat to, are among the people you would like to meet again are they my half brothers and sister, in

Cuba? The answer to my first question, he did answer. Depression was something he had to deal with. I don't know why it was my first question.

When I asked him if he remembered my mother, he said he, Bustos was not there at the time so how could he, but he did let slip he was eighty two. Che was born in nineteen twenty eight; Ciro Bustos is supposed to be four years younger. (It is July two thousand and ten, now.) He did say he could not go back to Cuba.

On card five I told him I had been studding him for about ten years. The amount of time I have spent on this idea even surprised me!

I did not get a clear answer to the question as to why, had he as Bustos made two films? The first film where I saw him showed him as an artist, the mere mention of an artist had attracted my attention. It was why I decided to contact him and not someone else, he was the one I wanted to speak to, an artist and he had known my father. Will, if he had not made them I would not be sitting here now!

It is getting difficult as the food needs the space on the small table. The Italian Pizza man is bubbling in Italian, Ciro is bubbling in Spanish; my brain is between English and German! So when Ciro asked for my blue cards I just hand them to him with an apology they might not be diplomatic. He was not impressed with my numbering system, nor was I, I had lost it! I had even forgotten to write the equivalent in English on the back of some of them, so I did not know what I was asking!

Didn't Ciro say he did not speak French on my last trip? He has just said he has a little French!

Ciro laughed at my 'who, what, why etc cards' naturally they did not have any of the words I needed now!

Ciro just said yes to question thirty four, that good he wants to be friends.

Questions as to, who knows who you are now; did not get a response. Any question that could lead in that direction did not get a response.

When was it in the blue cards questions or my dish of pasta did Ciro ask me just what I wanted?

I don't know what those that passed our table on the pavement thought when I asked Ciro to look into my eyes.
I am bending over my pasta staring closely into his eyes, as he looked into my eyes; must have looked funny! I remember thinking we have similar eyes.

Then I put my hand next to his, to show how our little fingers of our right hand match. I don't know why I did this I just did. I had a mouth full of hot pasta when he said 'No!'

Ciro did not through my cards at me. Now he knows what I am thinking. He bubbled something at me but there must have been pasta in my ears, I felt so calm.

When, the DNA has been tested all questions will be answered. I would have said if I had the Spanish to say it.

Card thirty six says. 'To be able to talk openly to you, for you to be able to talk openly to me is very important. I needed to use the word important again only to get impotent out of the dictionary. Good thing Ciro found my misshape funny.

I did say if I emailed him with the number thirty six in it, it meant I was upset at not hearing from him, I was only here because he had not contacted me. I had not known if he had got my post.

Ciro had said he is eighty two, Ciro is supposed to be four years younger than Che, he was born 1928, the year is now 2010. I have his DNA, why am I nervous when I hear things like that?

I think Ciro tries to cover himself at times, as statements he makes do not always match. Could be our communication problem, he named that as to why he had not replied.

What a thing to say! If you will talk to me I will learn Spanish, but I am dyslectic it will take some time. Sounded good when I said it.

Lee Anderson spent three years with the Marsh family as he wrote the biography. His children had the same nanny as Che's children had.

While I was visiting Ciro in Sweden for the second time Fidel Castro is to be seen on the news, most think he is dead!
(My half sister Cella is to be seen showing the old man the dolphins; she works as a marine vet in Havana, few days later on Sky TV.) Ciro's reaction to this was not even marked by a shrug.

Ciro worked in a hospital, as cleaner; one of the two men that made 'Sacrifico' told me that. Ciro should know the difference between a gallbladder scar and an appendix. 'I think most people do'.

There it was on the back of card thirty five, Ciro wrote nineteen sixty one, that was the date he was for the first time in Cuba. But the Jan Lee Anderson's book states nineteen fifty seven. Why has Ciro written in Spanish, 'The bay of pigs invasion under this date? The other side of the blue card asks who knows his true identity.

Card nineteen told him, as I had been looking for him I had met with a wall of disbelief. No one has believed what I have said about Ciro Bustos or any of my story!

I hope with the DNA to end all speculation.

## Chapter five
### The three wise men.

I never thought the three men I saw in Ciro's flat would be important to me.

Humberto Vazquez Viana, I was pleased to recognize him, a Wikipedia article informed me he had married a lady from East Germany, good I thought! I was hoping to find someone Ciro trusted to be our translator; hand and foot was not enough for the maters I wanted to discuss.

When I suggested the idea, Ciro emailed back suggesting I was mad! Humberto Vazquez Viana killed in Bolivia- but I had found him selling a book about Che!

Humberto Vazquez Viana was promoting his book in Italy; there are photos of him of him at the books opening. I did find his death certificate in another Wikipedia article that would have confirmed what Ciro had said if I had not seen the book promotion.

I sent copies of the photo and Humberto Vazquez Viana's address that I had got out of the Swedish telephone book.

Rondon Aristides Velasquez, he was the man that had stood with is hand behind his back; he had held himself upright as if he was looking over his glasses. His job is the running of the Che Guevara institute in Santa Clara, Cuba. There are photos of him and Ciro there, when Ciro celebrated his eighth birthday. An interesting remark is, he was one of Castro's teachers in nineteen sixty-one! I found that on his blog.

Christoph Röckerath was the young man that spoke English without any trace of an accent! He is an USA correspondent! I first saw him 'Insel au seiner anderen Zeit' a film about Cuba tradition. If they had not used the same music for 'Sacrificio' and an internet interview by Jean-Luc Godard/Monteagudo, I would not have made the full circle.

They all said they had worked with Ciro in the local hospital as Orderlies. Funny looking Orderlies now I come and think of it!

(((If the pizza man said Ciro had five friends then the other one could be Jon Lee Anderson. I was to learn later that he live in the flat above Ciro for a year.)))

(((The other could be Aleida March! I saw she had been in Gutenberg, two hours down the road.)))

The DNA again.

Months have gone by since the DNA test results lay before me. I have gone through a muddled kind of grieving, sorrow and sadness.

My first problem was to do a father shaft test in Germany I needed 'His' written permission: knowing the way some think, a lawyer would have to stick his stamp on it to state he is, who he says he is! As I have stolen his DNA asking for permission was not going to be easy!

The nice man, who had helped me when I had trouble with getting a test for me and Omar, offered a solution. The solution was to have the result sent from Austria! Which he did, but I had to tease him to give it to me in writing.

The nice man had said it was negative with connections that stated we came from the same fifty present, could mean something or nothing! I needed my birthmother and his mother's DNA. He had said something similar about Omar.

I wanted a yes or no! A yes or no without any possibilities of maybes. So ok the test was negative!

I have told those interested around me I am stuck at the point where I need permission for a DNA test. I need time, time to grieve.

That was where it would have stayed had Uwe not bought the book to the TV sires written by Stieg Lasson.

Uwe had his head in the first book said it was more complicated than those filming the program showed, the S:S had members living in Sweden since the war.
S.S members had moved to Bolivia. In fact they had been useful in building the country's industries.

Klaus Barbie had been Monica Ertl's godfather- she was supposed to have shot the man that ordered Che to shot, when she was in Hamburg.

Wikileaks.

The film that showed a man looking so like Ciro stepping into a jeep, told me he was Felix Ramos working for the Americans as a guerrilla expert, replayed in my mind.
Wikileaks only frustrated me more; I could only find files that I could not open with my computer. Or I had to go through Russian to look at lists of files- it is like looking for a needle in a hay stack.

I have found since the Wikileaks scandal there is more and more information appearing on the internet I will add some of the interesting comments. The Blues eyes of the body on the mortuary table, pop up in other document said to have come from the White House, can now be found openly in many reports.

Some say Felix Rodriguez was there where as others say he was not about when Che was shot. I know I have been at this point of thinking before, where statements don't match.

But how can they?

The people playing this game are members of S.S or the CIA. Leaders of governments, Bolivian, American, Cuban, and who knows who else!

And I expect to find answers among opponents like that!

Now more question start to run through my mind about the DNA test.

Why did it take so long for the first company to tell me they could not do a test they advertise they can do?

Can I trust the answer I was given from the nice man on the telephone?

Am I going to let my innocents and inexperience about what I am being told stop me form have the chance to have a relationship with a man that could be my father? When time is not on my side?

My conclusion is, I cannot trust what I am being told.

To trust my gut feelings maybe a better way forward.

All of this has been going on in my life for ten years now.

I have had gut feelings about Aleida my half sister when I first saw her on television years ago. And I must have had a gut feeling or I would not have leant over the small pavement table to let Ciro look into my eyes on a hot summer's day!

So there is a thing, I wanted Omer to be my half brother, and now feel he may not be, as Ciro did not know his name.

Were as I wanted there to be and end with Ciro, only to find a new beginning.

Ciro is answering my short emails
        The Bond girl again.

'The thought to return to Cuba with a new mission for the Bond girl has crossed my mind. The mission would be to get my Uncle's DNA, as well as all half brother and sisters!

*(I throw away Omar's DNA. That was before I understood I can no longer trust the written word.)*

Sounds like mission imposable!!! Will, I have done some funny things in the name of 'a gut feeling.'

But, the but for this idea is, where can I go to interpret the DNA? I don't know enough to stand behind anyone and see that they make an accurate test!

I have joked about being a James Bond Girl! That was long before I ever came to the idea there were others playing this game. I am just a little ant in this game, hope they don't tread on me.

        Internet notes

Here I will add my new internet notes. From the moment Wikileaks aroused my curiosity, I have wondered if the files he opened had anything I would find interesting; but I was not able to open them. So why was I surprised there was much more information available on the internet? I will put down anything I find interesting.

        Fund in 15,2,2011

Recruiting Nazis=www.angelfire.com.

"Torres turned out to be a populist- he exiled refugee Che Guevara and busyness like Gulf Oil."
*The thing that got me the remark was dated 1969.*

Jim Garrison's 1967 Play Boy interview   (part 1) www.maebrussell.com/.../Garrison. Oct 1967
This page states Che Guevara was in Dallas at the time J F Kennedy was shot. That Che was interested in arranging talks with the president. He was in contact with Miss Howard.

*Not imposable he had interesting talks with the CIA.*

Chehasta.navod.ru/bol_4.hfm.
The other side of the Barricades.
States(a)
   At the base near Santa Cruz, these skills were taught by CIA agents Captain Felix Ramos and Edurdo Gonzolez. (Cubans) with a Captain Margraito. (Puerto Rican)

States(b)
   Felix Ramos and Edurado Gonzoler worked for the  Americans!

States©
   Felix Ramos and Edurado Gonzoler were both present at the time of Che's capture and death in 1967.
Moment !!!!!
Felix Ramos was the name of the man I feel is Bustos !!!!!

Felix Ramos is the name given to a man getting into an American jeep. The voice over say Felix Ramos is a Guerrillas expert working for the Americans….

This short seen came after those that survived their adventures in Bolivia have given interviews in the film…

'Wege Der Revolution.'

Regie: Manuel Perez. Born in Havana in 1939. He began in 1959 to work on Documentaries and spiel films.

Just a gut feeling!?

Che Guevara became Ciro Bustos and Ciro Bustos took the name of Felix Ramos.

(((Remember: Che from a young man liked to disguise himself.)))

*My sense of humor finds the thought wonderful!*

*You get to plan your own demise, your last words, for the history books. Maybe it is horrifying as will.*

Found on, 16,2,2011.

In the internet side **Death of Che.**

Wwwgwu.edu/~nsarchiv/nsaebb/nsaebb5/-

National Security Ardine briefing, book no5.

States that Felix Rodriguez used the code name of Felix Ramos.

Felix Rodriguez was debriefed on 3.6.1975.

*Two men using the same code name?*

Another remark from Death of Che, dated September 26<sup>th</sup> 1967. Felix Rodriguez is convinced he knows Che's next move.

Another remark! *Ramon* was given as Che's nick name, Ramon and Willy.

(dept of defense Intelligence Information Report.) (RoJo 218)

Many names: one person.

www.amigospais-guaracbuga,org.oagmf026.pfp.

This program tells of the many names used by Felix Rodriguez.

There are six names, and one of them is Felix Ramon Medina.

*There is not a lot of difference between Ramos, Ramon.*

*But when I was trying to understand the difference: The Other side of the Barricade connects the names Felix Ramos and Eduardo Gonzoler, both Cubans and Captain Margarito from Puerto Rio.*

   *But when I try to connect Felix Rodriguez's name with the other two for mentioned, wwwwikipeda.org: says Hasenfus worked for (Max Gomez) this happens to be one of the alias's Felix Rodriguez uses and Ramon Media was on alias for Luis Pasada Carriles. He worked for the CIA.*

  *Secrets of the CIA: In bed with the Nazis states the same on its cover. Though this program- Murder of Che Guevara from Locoedro59. Said it was not available in this land (Germany)*

*With-* Felix Ramos+Edurado Gonzoler+1967+CIA.

I landed in wwwleandokatz.com/...
ChronoEnglishChefourhtml.

I was informed Edurado Gonzoler was a doctor and a harsh interrogator. As will as a CIA agent.
   *But it did not connect his name with Felix Rodriguez.*

The mysterious third person Roth that was picked up at the same time as Ciro Bustos and Regis Debray turned into George Andrew Roth who only has to say he collaborated with the CIA.
   *But I cannot connect him to Felix Rodriguez.*

Note…in the film from legion the last day in the life of Che Guevara. Bustos states there was never a man called Andrew Roth.

The program connected to wwwleandokatz.com/...
ChronoEnglishChefourhtml. Informed me in… Chronology: Che Guevara in Bolivia. *That Ciro Bustos had an Asthmatic condition.*

*Now that is strange!*
*Che Guevara was known to have asthma! And now Bustos as will!*
This statement was confirmed in-
Don't Shoot I am Che. By Grul Arnallo Sauoedo Palozor.
He was very keen on capturing any guerrillas.

*I am muddled over code names and now they both have asthma!.*

Code names… in the travelling adventures with Alberto Grando, Che's nick name is *El Pelao* -baldy.
Ciro Bustos's alias was *El Pelao* -baldy
        Ciro Bustos –Carlos O Pelao.

I found this out looking on the internet, looking for code name and aliases for Che and Bustos as well as looking for Felix Rodriguez aliases. -Captain Ramos. -El Gato.

*Alberto Grando.. States, that the adventure in Argentina failed, only he and Ciro Bustos survived.*
  I have added this note as it is the only one I have found. Alberto Grando was as a young man, Che's companion on his motorbike trip.

                Che in disguise.
  I have found a photo of Che in disguise in an internet program, looking like a member of the Mafia, where I also saw Marita Lorenz. I had seen the film where the story is told of how she met Fidel Castro when she was nineteen; she fell head over heels in love with him. Marita was unwittingly caught up in the intrigue and politics of that time.
  What was really going on then?

Castro is being backed by the previous president of Cuba, the previous president to the one he, Castro throw out.

The Mafia has three godfathers that were running guns, girls and drugs through Cuba, their gambolling casinos in Cuba bring in over on hundred million dollies a year.

Castro is happy to have USSA support his by now week economy. The Americans are not happy, having adversaries at their back door. I can understand.

The Bay of Pigs invasion could not bring Cuba back under America arm, Kennedy KFK could not send in an air force to back the men that had been sent: because the USSR was watching them.

Kennedy had been told by USSR they would not tolerate the USA attacking Cuba.

World War had been averted over the missiles everyone thought had been placed in Cuba. Castro was not happy when the USSR invited the USA to drop in, to see for themselves that Cuba did not have their missiles anymore.

Castro was not happy at the invitation the USSR had given.

Kennedy was stuck between the Mafia godfathers warring in his back garden and the USSR smoke Che was in Dallas at the same time as Kennedy e signals were not for pace.

Association plots!!!!!

Everyone seems to have been involved in planning to assonate someone!

The people I am looking at seem to be actors in a thriller.

Marita Lorenz was caught in this spider's web, I mention her as she was involved in attempts aimed at Castro and Kennedy. She is not the only one! One of her associates was Frank Fiorini Sturgis, he was over herd to say he was one of the gun men involved in Kennedy's death.

This is why I am looking this way, I have found two connections. The first the photo of one of Che's disguises in an internet program telling me about Marita Lorenz and the fact that Che was in Dallas at the same time as Kennedy…. The same time as Kennedy was shot.

I had the idea Che was a CIA agent as he had the same alias as Felix Rodriguez. (It was common practice to have agents use the same names, alias, code names etc)

I thought Che was involved!

He was, but not in the way I first thought.

Kennedy's way of coping with this smouldering cooking pot was to plan a coup, a coup to take over Cuba; point a finger at anyone standing in the kitchen should the pot boil over. He could then smile at the USSR and say it was not him.

I was hoping I would learn more when a got Mark Lorenz's email address. His mother knows Fidel Castro; she was caught in Frank Sturgis's net. She had met Lee Harvey Oswald; he had been in the same cell/network as Marita. She must have met Che!

I found a charming young man opening my emails; I felt he was a brother from the first word. To know you are not the only one with dyslexia, love of animals because they keep your feet on the ground. Try to get your father's attention while trying to cope with everyday, that kind of a brother!

There is a beach we are going to walk along when we have all the answers we need. I hope it will be the same beach.

What did I want Marita to tell me? I read everything I could about her, watched her film again. Interestingly by the same director as the film 'Schnappschuss mit Che.'

I made a wallpaper maps, I sent Mark one. Kennedy is on it and Castro, Marita and Frank Sturgis. Che it has been said under house arrest, Ciro Bustos of course (I mention the lack of family photos in his flat.)

The strange guest's at Che's death party, Felix Rodriguez being just one of them. (Felix Rodriguez and Che have the same alias.)

There is the name of the ex-dictator of Venezuela; he is Monica Lorenz's farther, Marita's daughter. The Chilean president Salvida Allende's and his ambassador to the USA, Orlando Lettelier, he worked to get Ciro Bustos and Regis Debray out of their Bolivian prison. And he was married to Monica Lorenz. Marita Lorenz's daughter.

When you look at the other side of my map Monica Ertl come together with Regis Debray, Klaus Barbie is also there.

(A neighbour of mine stated Monica Ertl's Father said to him, Che was a good son-in-law.) This idea could be possible as the letter Castro read while Che was supposed lost in the Congo say's; Che gave away all his writs legal etc and rank and properties in Cuba. In my mind Che is from that point a free man! Without home land or a legal passport in that name!

There are other CIA names on my map, Luis Posade Carriles he went to school with Felix Rodriguez, others that are present at Che's death party also are found involved with the Contras.

The same names can be found connected to Watergate!
(It has been said that the intruders wanted Castro's writings. Castro had written about assassination attempts on his own life.) What they really wanted were the records of payments made to the Democrat Party.
(I thought they were joking when they said Fidel Castro holds the world record for survived assassination attempts.)

The man I saw in Ciro's flat, Humbo Jorge Vazqez Viana, I put on the map. He was picked up around the same time as Ciro and Regis Debray were said to have been arrested.
(Humbo had a brother Jorge, I apologise if I have been muddled by the brothers involvement)
I added Ramón Velzquer who I also saw in Ciro's flat that day. (I do not remember where it was that

said he was the Cuban minister of industry. But he does run the museum in Santa Clara, Che's of course!

Talking about Cuba again I have added Rolando Cubela a man who was in the government and was in the Cuban army. And I have Almeida he is the next most powerful man in Cuba after Fidel and Roul Castro, and I suppose Che.
Almeida was the commander of the Cuban army, one of the strongest men in Cuba, next to Castro, and Che.

(I did not put in Commander Camello Cienfuegos as Frank Sturgis claimed he recruited/converted him to the CIA: which could explain why the commander aeroplane got lost.)

But I hope to show there are strange connections. I am trying to understand what is in front of me. I had gone through this poses so I could find the question I wanted to ask Marita.

What was the relationship between Castro and Che? Brother Roul was friends with Che, Roul was invited to Che and Aleida's wedding, were as Castro was not.

Castro exiled Che, Che was *Exiled from Cuba*. Why?
Because Kennedy was planning a Coup, assonate Castor, place Almeida Juan as leader, he needed Che as he was a white man in a white world, Almieda had black skin, he was the commander of the Cuban army and his men would back him.

For Castro it must have been imposable, not knowing who was with you and who was not. If you felt Che was plotting against you, place him under house arrest. How Che could get away from a man that must have been badly hurt by recovering you were involved in plotting against him I do not know.

## Ultimate Sacrifice

If I had not chewed my way through- http:ajweberman.com/nodulex25pdf and nodulx10. I would have been very confused when reading Larmar Warldron and Thom Hartmann's book (Ultimate Sacrifice)

In the nodulxs I had been looking for a name to match the photo of Che in disguise, any name I did not know I looked up on the internet. The result of doing this meant when I picked up the book Ultimate Sacrifice I already had an in idea who was who.

The Ultimate Sacrifice explained to me Kennedy's planed coup 'Amworld'. Why Castro expelled Che for his involvement in a plot or plots, assassinations/coup, not that this book is about Castro, it is out to explain Kennedy's assassination. They infer the CIA use of code names and alias to confuse anyone trying to put two and two together. In the case of Rolando Cubela his code name was Amlash, there were others using the code name, Amlash1 and Amlash2 and so on. (Making sense of Che having the same code names as Felix Rodriguez.)

People had the same code names when working on the same assignments. It is not surprising to note folk that worked on more than one assignment had more than one code name! Now you can see who was working with who and who on what.

I thought Che could have become a CIA member working against Castro. Or he had infiltrated the ring around Kennedy on behalf of Castro. On Cuba's behalf!?

I can understand Che not agreeing with the way Castor got things done, there is civil war in Cuba. Castro's revolution is covering conflicting interests within its self. The Mafia were using Cuba to traffic drugs, wash money, and run guns, upset Kennedy! The USSA are breathing down your neck!

I cannot answer all questions that were behind what Che was trying to do. Che was in Dallas at the same time as Kennedy in November, the same time as Kennedy was assassinated! Che was waiting to take his place in the Cuban Coup. The Amworld Coup was planned to take place at the beginning of December!

Che was placed in house arrest three times, the last time coincides with Rolando Cubela's planned assassination attempt. Rolando Cubela lived in Varadero in a house near Castro's house. Rolando Cubela and a Che were reported as best of friends. Interestingly Rolando Cubela was in Paris at the same time Kennedy was assassinated, he was discussing his plan to assonate Castro.

Everyone that wants to go to Varadero has to pass through a bottle neck, a good place for an ambush.

Expel Che from Cuba for his part in assassination plans; take way his writs for at least knowing about a planned Coup. Strip away his rank and privileges and throw him away, makes a man free to start something new! Buy a farm in Bolivia to grow whine as his second wife's family had done in Cuba, look for a new wife/life!? All this is now possible! (I have to say this idea was wrong.)

        Where do I go from here?
Bach up on the internet! What do I want to ask it? Who knows the real truth?

    A letter to my father.

It has taken me many years to come to the conclusion you are my father.

It is as strange for my as it must be for you. The only explanation I can give you is I need to understand from where I come.

The members on the stage are forceful group. The CIA, the Bush family, Skull and Bones, the German SS, Klaus Barbie, Monica Ertl. The U.S.A Mafia, There are many other names around you.

The players on the stage have made it hard to decide what is true and what is not, they have stirred the facts so much.

It was the little things that lead me to you. There are things that a child takes for granted; it is how they know how and where they belong- to a family. From the moment someone said I looked like your family I studded you, things like the shape of your head as a baby and now.

I thought I was stupid to do such things but when I saw Ciro Bustos, Che Guevara, Felix Ramon, Adolfo Mena Gonzalez, I knew I was looking at the same person.

/Your eyes reflected light. When the body has no life in it the eyes do not reflect light any more./

/Your body disappeared after two hours!/ as reported in
The Body and the Legend, a B&B film.

/ In The State Dept-Dept of Defence Files = The post-mortem report states you had blue eyes! (The report puzzled me at first.)

/In one film shows you as an expert working for the U,S,A an expert on guerrilla war fair. The name they use is Felix Ramon. The producer is Cuban. (The way to Revolution) bestell-nr 69095/

/You come out of prison with a full head of hair! Ciro Bustos is always shown as being bald./

/ The photo of a young Ciro Bustos shows a young man with a broken nose. Once broken the nose dose not grow any more.
Yours has not been broken./

/ I have matched your faces with my trusted ruler, the example I have sent is of poor quality. I send you another pair of photos taken from Facebook. Much changes in a man's face but known points don't./

(Ears and noses grow throughout life.)

/the film 'Snap shot with Che.' proves that the photo supposed to be taken by Felix Rodriguez. Is a fake!

The first time I came to your door was to be proven wrong.

I could be wrong. I wanted to be wrong.

I looked into your eyes, spent the whole weekend looking at photos. In a good copy of 'that' photo you can see your eye paten; your mother has the same eyes.

>You have the same eyes.
>I have the same eyes.

My skin is like yours, my eyes, and the shape of our little fingers. To find you have these things is strange. Many people have the same likenesses; they are not likenesses you can see on TV, old photos.

To be sure I took your D:N:A. but then realised it was worthless! I can never trust the results. Not with such players on the stage.

You have put you self into the public eye.
All this information I have found in open internets programs, films, TV, etc.

I don't know anyone that has had the same experience as you and I.

I am fifty five now and don't want any more time taken from us.

>LOVE EVELYN

The letter I sent to Ciro Bustos in both English and Spanish. I sent copies to 'Benigo' - Dariel Alaron Ramirez, (His letters came back as address was incorrect. Felix Rodreguez and Regis Debray. The note I added suggested we should get together to discuss how we should present the facts. More and more information is being released. And, that the authors' of the book Ultimate Sacrifice are asking the same questions as I am.

To the authors' from the Ultimate Sacrifice Lomam Waldren and Thom Hartmann. I also sent letters too.

I wander if anyone will answer.

I had decided to see what had happened to 'Benigo'- Dariel Alaron Ramirez. Should I have been surprised to see he became a member of Salvador Allande's private secret army, as did Harry Vallegas another member of Che's death party? He's nickname is 'Pombo.'

Benigno is to be seen standing among men grouped near Salvador Allende after Che's supposed death. See Che Guevara Legion and Myths.

One of the facts that had puzzled me was Bolivia did not want a revolution, many had reported that including Felix Rodriguez makes the statement in the opening of Wilfried Huismann's film. To read Chile had spoken of a need of a revolution made me sit up!

(Chile wanted a revolution.)

Salvador Allande and his diplomat Orlando Lettelier got Ciro Bustos and Regis Debray freed from the Chilean prison.

Orlando Lettelier was married to Marita Lorenz daughter Monica and publisher her book. Love Fidel.

The name Elizabeth Burgos-Debray caught my attention in Cristian Perez's study. Salvador Allende- Notes on his security Team. An account of the assignation of Salvador Allende! Elizabeth Burgos-Debray- She too was involved in Ciro Bustos and Regis Debray's release! It should not be a surprise, she was married to Regis, visited him in prison; in Bolivia. I found a picture of her as a very young woman sitting at a table with Fidel Castro.

Elizabeth was born in Venezuela; she must have met Regis Debray when he was at Havana University, which helps explain why he was there. I wanted to know how the relationship between Che and Regis had started. To be told Regis Debray and Ciro Bustos were wandering through the jungle hopping to interview the great Che Guevara I had accepted the explanation at first!

A question- How were they supposed to know where Che was going to be in October; when they were arrested in April?

I thought the files Elizabeth had stored in Stanford University California would be interesting to see. 'box/folder 15:7 Che Guevara 1967/69'. So I sent an email requesting them. I was told I could have the first ten pages and it was free of charge. As I put my thoughts to paper fourteen days have gone by, but an envelope from the university has not arrived.

I have sent Elizabeth a letter, the same letter as I have sent to my father. I have not received a reply to it yet!

What more do you want? Look at this film- 'Weg Der Revolution: Che Guevara. In the film 'Wege Der Revolution' www.icestorm.de Regie: Manuel Perez. You can see this man (Che Guevara!) in the scene where 'Benigno' Dariel Ramirez Alarcon is being greeted by Salvador Allende in Chili *1968*.

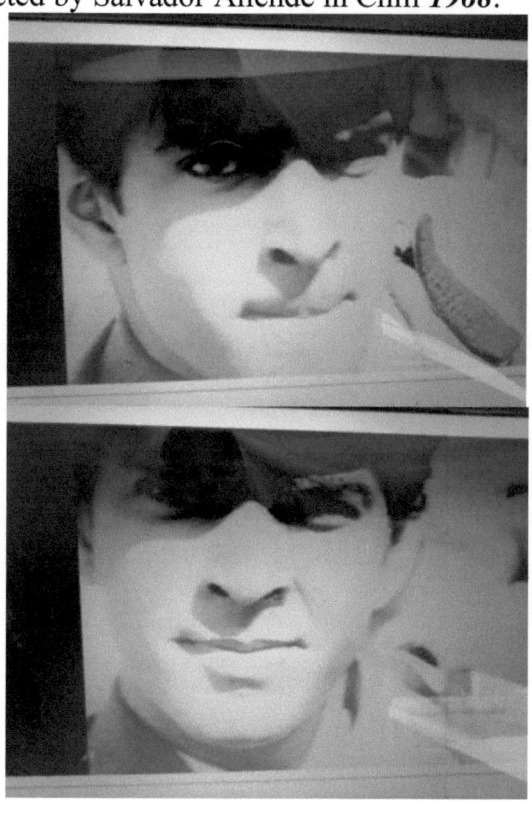

From the Youtube film!? YouTube has Che Guevara's name over the same bit of film!?

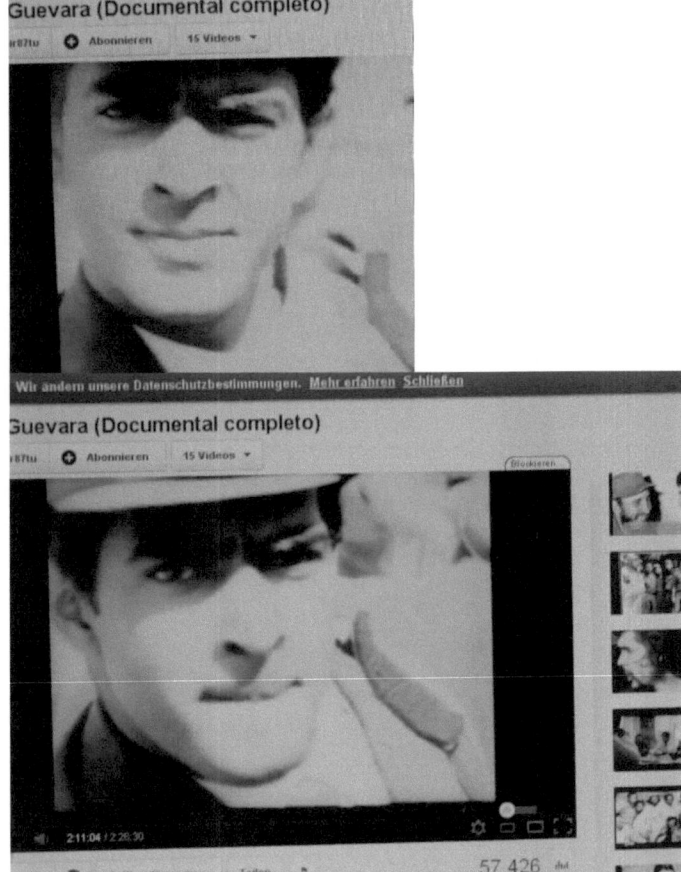

Chapter six.
Who knows?

Elizabath Burgos-Debray and Regis Debray.

A document from the Centre for Latin American Studies, University of California, Berkely. Says that Elizabeth and Regis were responsible for the planning for the Bolivian trip. And that she worked for the popular unity government of Salvador Allende in Chile.

Cristian Perez's study. Salvador Allende- Notes on his security Team. Also says Cuba /Castro trained men for Salvador Allende's private army.

Norberto Fuento wrote a book an Autobiography of Fidel Castro, the reader sees through the eyes of Fidel the revolution, it this time I have not read it. I hope it will give me an insight on the real relationship between Castro and Che.

I hope I have understood the relationship between Norberto and Castro. Norberto Fuento left Castro's side, they were intimate friends. I found his name in Cristain Perez papers. I sent Norberto Fuento a letter hopping he would shed light on Che and Castro's real relationship.

Who knows Che became Ciro?

There is one question that has found a place in my mind.

I want to read a copy of Ciro's book but it is in Spanish, now I found the internet has a translation portal I was planning to get a copy and put it through my scanner, page by page. I remembered the copy Ciro showed me had over five hundred pages! EL Che Quiere Verte.

The internet told me that Ann Wright was asked to translate this book; she even made a trip to Bolivia to feel better the words in the book. I sent her a letter asking when it would be ready! As of yet I have not had a reply.

To be surprised about anything should not happen anymore:
Ann Wright translated the book, 'Motorcycle Dairies- the version written by Che Guevara. And she wants to translate Ciro's book!

Ann Wright and Elizabeth Burgos-Debray worked on a book together. 'Rigoberta Menchie: An Indian Woman in Guatemala.

Elizabeth Burgos-Debray has translated 'Benigo'- Dariel Alaron Ramirez book, 'Memories of a Cuban Soldier.

Just to confuse me more, Lucia Alvarez de Toledo, who has written 'Story of Che Guevara.'

Lucia Alvarez de Toledo lived near the Guevara's, she is about ten years older than Che, and she has made interesting remarks about the family. She translated Alberto Grundo's book. His version of the motorcycle trip made me laugh; he makes funny little comments about why they made that trip. One reason was to... How shall I say, add to the population of the world. Had they known what I would understand about that that remark! (She is the mother of Che's half brother.)

I saw Aleida Guevara March made a speech in Sweden in February two thousand and six for Voz Populi, in Gothenburg.
Gutenberg is about two hours from Malmo.

Aleida's remark made in 'Freepublic.com/focuss/f-news' about Castro stuck in my mind. She says, Castro dreams Che is still alive! I have not forgotten Fidel Castro is Aleida's godfather.

If only Aleida knew I want to give her a hug.

I thought I would look up Uncle Alberto Guevara in.
'Collectivoepprosario.blogspot.com/2010_02_01_A Who is/was head of films in Cuba, but found Roberto Guevara Lynch. A program explaining Argentina thought he was a terrorist! A few mug shots further was a young man, they said was a half brother of Che Guevara. I noted the name Fernando L Chavaz Alvarez.

I landed in a program that told me about brothers and sisters of Che. Che's farther had another family giving Che half brothers. There is another half-brother had the name of Ramon Guevara Erra.

In this program I was looking to see if I could find the name Ann-Marie. This name was given as the wife of Ciro Bustos. I was wondering if Ann-Marie could be one of Che's sisters. A sister would be a covenant substitute wife, another program had told me that Elizabeth Burgos-Debray had visited Regis Debray in prison.

Archive Chile.

Archive Chile. Pagina 12. Histora Popitco social-2001. Mommesto Populaur. Who betrayed Che Guevara? Written by Miguel Bonasso. He is an Argentinean journalist, Also named as a terrorist in the same program.
'Collectivoepprosario.blogspot.com/2010_02_01_A'

I read the paper through once with the feeling I had found something, but not what. As with the nodules I had found about Frank Sturgis. I took it apart. By that I mean I took any name I did not know to see what I could find out. To know Miguel Enriquez was the son of Salvador Allende's general secretary. He was a CIA agent?!

Pagina 12 is explaining Regis Debray and Ciro Bustos point of view once they had been captured. Names like Vazquez reminded me, of the man I saw in Ciro's flat.

The fact the text in Pagina 12 is the one used in the documentary 'Sacrificio' creeps over me slowly. That's good their subtitles are helpful and their body language but to have the text makes it more interesting. That the people are discussing their point of view in a way that does not match with each other, comes as no surprise to me, if it had I would not be still looking.

The next name I decided to see what the internet has to tell me was Luciano Monteagudo. He reminds me of a face I have seen, it is in the program telling me two of Che's brothers were considered terrorists! Under the name Fernando L Chavaz Alvarez is the explanation, the aforementioned travelled around Europe raising funds for....terrorist activities.

Luciano Monteagudo is also portrayed as a writer, his field is writing for films. I find it connected to 'Sacrificio'.

Fernando and Luciano have similar faces, a little mole on their laugh line match as do a dimple in their chins.

If a drug dealer, who grew up in England had forty-seven aliases making him difficult to keep tracks on! Then, why not an uncle?

What made me sit up was in the paragraph under Luciano name. It says, 'Ciro Bustos currently living in southern Sweden, with a modest state pension. By Luciano Monteagudo.'

I did not know what to make of that! Maybe the internet translation has muddled things up! But not they are the same person.

I did not get far looking up Luciano when I found another name. Jean-Luc Godard. But he looks like Luciano Monteagudo! Jean-Luc Godard is a film producer and wife's name is Ann-Marie. (Did Ciro borrow his half-brother's wife? That would explain why Bustos family photos are missing in his flat in Malmo.)

While looking for Jean-Luc's address I found out the name of his accountant in France! Playing tax in France was good for his accountant but not good for him, he lives in Switzerland! So dose Ann-Marie.

I enjoyed the music he used in his blog. It reminded of the music they used in 'Sacrificio' only it is not used so strongly! Cinemaspargus.blogspot.com/2010/05/jean-luc godard.

Jean-Luc Godard is renown, as a film producer.

How do you address a letter to an uncle when you are not sure which name he would like? I sent him the same letter- a letter to my father. I want him as an uncle, I want a father and if I am honest I want something more but the right words fail me, this has been a long and hard road.

Christoph Röckerath.

While I am waiting to see if I get a reply to that letter the television offers me a program I have seen before, as there is nothing that interest me on any of the other channels I am happy to wander around Cuba with Christoph Röckerath, he is an USA correspondent for the television sender ZDF.

'An Island from another time, 'Insel aus einer anderen Zeit' this film tells how changes are being made in Cuba; folk are take business into their own hands to provide a living. Hay! Nice music, where have I heard that before?

*It is the same music Jean-Luc Godard uses in his blog! And Sacrificio!*

Jean-Luc Godard/ Luciano Monteagudo/ Fernando L Chavaz Alvarez are one person but now he has produced the film with Christoph Röckerath!

An Island from another time, and is connected to Sacrificio!?

I took out the photos in my file, 'Could you be my Uncle.' No mole but a clef in their chins, now there is a file, Could you be my cousin!)

Can piece of music betray them? I would never have thought a piece of music would lead me this way.

What if the third man I saw in Ciro's flat was Christoph?

This is not the time for my brain to go on strike! Ann-Marie had daughter with Jean-Luc Godard in the early seventies, the internet will not tell me if she had a son, but I can have Christoph's address!

On the news that evening I saw Christoph name, he is a USA correspondent as the internet says.

I sent him a letter not being able to answer my own questions.

My emotions have got the better of me, Jean-Luc Godard has been sent a letter on Friday, Christoph letter was taken by the nice lady from post on Saturday. Luciano Monteagudo/ Fernando L Chavaz Alvarez would have had letters sent to them too if I could have found their addressees! Lucio Claudio Garzon Maceda would have been sent a letter; this name belongs to Fernando L Chavaz Alvarez as will!

The name Lucio Claudio Garzon Maceda was used when he collected information about the USA.

It is Sunday; I had to write down why I have sent such letters before my mind gets lost in my emotions.

    Who must know?
    They must know!

I wonder if they will answer my letters.

No they will not answer my letters. Why should they? They are people that do not want to tarnish a hero.

All this time I have tried to contact those that don't want to lose a hero. They do not know I was looking for my roots not to knock heroes over. I find out more than emotion drives me to wanting the truth.

I have known Humberto Fontova is someone that does not see Che as a saint. His internet side called 'Murder' made me think he would be interested in what I have found out.

While I am waiting to see what he will say I look up a name an actor he describes as someone that was double for Che.

Cantinflas was a Mexican move star.

    Chapter seven.
    The movie busyness.

Che's double, Cantinflas a Mexican move star.

This is the first time I have heard of a double for Che, or even thought about there being one. That said; when the demise of Kennedy was being planned. It was common praxis to have doubles for the people they used. I wander how he was used? If Cantinflas was not used as a double the fact he was actor, comedian and a film producer from 1936 to 1984 and he was politically motivated. He would have been in contact with films fans in Che's family. (What a naive remark!)

## Ana Maria, Che's sister.

While I am waiting for all those people not to answer I have found I have a new file, 'Could you be my aunt?' I saw a photo of Che taken in nineteen sixty one, with him is a lady in a wonderful animal skin coat. Underneath was written Che with his sister, Ana Maria.

I had had in my mind that Ciro was said to have a wife with the same name. I came to the conclusion she was Che's half brothers wife. Now I am confused. I had started with the idea that Che/Bustos had used his sister as his wife, as Ana Maria was the name that was given in Parger 12.

Back to the internet, looking through family trees brought me the answer; both ideas were right! I was only to be confused again when I saw Ana Maria had a second name Anna Karina and she was married to Jean-Luc Godard and a singer and model and an film actress, funny so was/is Ana Maria Marville! I could be wrong it is much more difficult with women as fashion and makeup, style changes over the years. I have found a strong connection for Ana Maria as sister and wife to Jean-Luc Godard. Ana Maria Marville, Ana Maria Guevara (Che's sister) and Anna Karina are the one and same woman.

Look at the man behind Guevara la hermana del Che..

 Jean-Luc Godard. "'cupblog.org

### Fernando L. Chavez Alvarez:

Cuñado de Ernesto "Che" Guevara. Integrante de una familia tradicionalmente apátrida y terrorista. Es miembro de las bandas terroristas "EjÈrcito Revolucionario del Pueblo" (ERP), y de la "Juta de Coordinación Revolucionaria" (JCR). En Europa desplegó tareas afines a las que desarrolló su cuñado Roberto Guevara Lynch. Se hizo prófugo de la justicia Argentina.

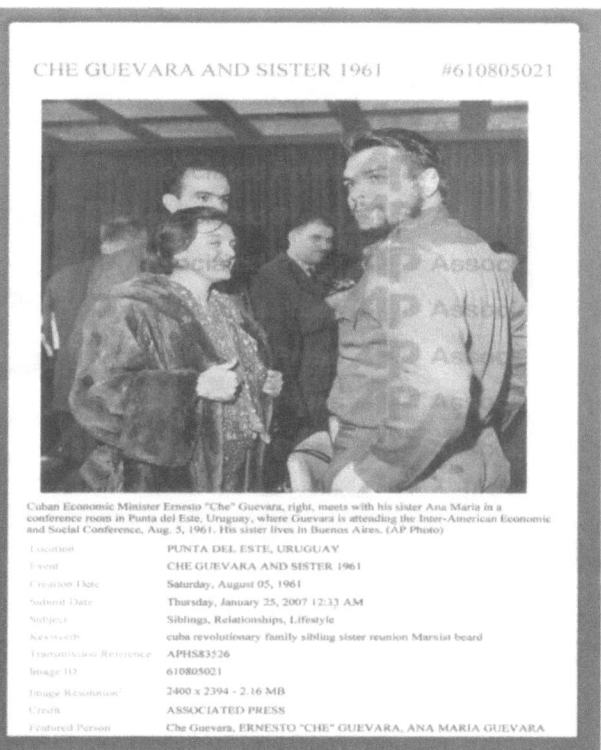

Elizabeth Burgos-Debray's news paper cuttings are informative. I should not have been surprised; they are mostly in French, not in Spanish.

The first thing they state is- Che was not believed to be in Bolivia. On article says he had been sighted but then had disappeared. The news papers enjoyed speculating where he could be.

Elizabeth Burgos-Debray's news paper cuttings stated that:

-La Higuera, the people in the village knew nothing about the 'Death party' execution.

-They knew apparently nothing about Che or any execution!

-The people from the village Alte Seco, not far away stated that they had never heard of Che Guevara. His body they had not seen.

-(Che's brother Roberto it was reported was not allowed to see the body, he had been told it had been burnt.) (I have a news paper cutting from The Spiegel talking about brother Robert. Elizabeth's news papers do not mention him.)

-Che's father was shown a body; he could not identify it as Che's. As he could not identify the body, or anybody the Argentinean government would not give position to bring the remains in Argentina.

-Che's father was reported to say he does not believe his son has been killed, he has not been shown any evidence of prove. He has not been shown his body, or anybody.

-Another article says that Che's body was buried just after it had been shot, due to strong political presser two days later it was dug up again! But, because of the condition of the body no one could identify it.

This version does not cover any of the others I have seen.

None of the versions cover each other! They would need a large amount of bodies to all cover all the stories going around.

The biography is by Josef Lawrezki. KGB
It amused me, to be lent a book written in Russian in nineteen seventy-two, translated into German in nineteen seventy-four, which has to said was completed within three years of Che's death! 'Laben and Kampf eines Revoltionars. Ernesto Che Guevara.' The biography is by Josef Lawrezki.

It was not just the fact this book was produced for the Deutsche Demokratische Republik I found interesting nor the fact Russian printing machines do not have a Q, it place is taken by a K.

It was the fact that the writer of this book also noticed that statements don't match! In fact the author's remarks match up with Elizabeth's news paper cuttings. To say others have noticed there is discrepancy in where the said body could be.

(I looked Josef Lawrezki up Wikipedia; it told me he was a KGB agent! Interesting to know, his other books cover Salvador Allende and Bolivia.)

To have two sauces stating, there was at the time mist trust over what was said about what happened to the 'Body' is comforting for me.

World News- Garderen Weekly-
I am trying to explain to a friend what I am working on.

Thanks to Silke's interest she found a piece of film that made us both sit up!

'Last moments with Che Guevara.

World News- Garderen Weekly- Steven Soderbergh. (Mejorentrevista a Ernesto Che Guevara. (invedotia))

Silke stumbles over the seine where (Benigo) Dariel Alaron Ramirez and Harry (Pombo) Tamayo Villegas and others are being greeted by Salvador Allende.

They have just left Bolivia.

Among the others you can see **Bustos/Che**.

This film is dated nineteen sixty eight.

There are more cuttings to this film. They show indirectly Che leaving Bolivar and Chile. And the scenes have been cut so you think he could be with the others returning to Cuba!

This film has similar scenes, as in 'Path Way to Revolution.' Where I saw Bustos/Che shown as an expert in guerrillas warfare, working for the CIA.

I and Silke spent time poring over more photos, trying to talk ourselves out of believing what we could see. I decided to ask the question; was Ciro Bustos in Prison?

Ciro pension and prison Camiri.

I read chapter twenty-four in 'The South America Years'

Ciro and Debray had been living in a pension in Camiri.

Debray was financed by his family whereas Ciro financed himself by selling his paintings and portraits. The thought came to me as thoughts do in the WC. If neither Silke nor I can live from our work it is two-thousand and twelve, how can you expect to feed yourself in nineteen sixty-seven in Bolivia!?

The 'The South America Years.' By (Mo) Mosies Garica put on line in two-thousand, gives me a vivid account of the court proceedings in Camiri. Everyone got so excited the judge broke his bevel trying to keep order. The remark Mo made that stuck in my mind was that made by Regis Debray. In the middle of all the theatre he says to the judge. 'I thank for the long sentence you will give me.' It came across to me as arrogant; the whole attention is focused on him. Bustos and three others are in the back ground.

The convicting evidence came from Che's dairy-informing that they were part of his plans. They are acquiesced of 'Rebellion, Murder, Theft, Wounds and Lesions.

The whole show must have been inspiring to see as Mo says.

In the up rough Debray and Bustos are sentenced to thirty years in prison each, even though Bustos had been expecting twenty. They moved from their pension on one side of the street into the prison on the other.

Mosies Garcia's account was fun to read, he is the only one to state Ciro Bustos was in a pension, the discussion was about getting Debray out of prison, I could not find anything to say Bustos was in prison. To stop myself from getting confused I remained myself that the year is nineteen sixty-seven and the month is November.

Chapter eight.<br>
Their Lawyers !

My husband had read a letter from Ciro Bustos to his lawyer, I read it too, and it is not a letter looking for advice but one of wishing to continue the mission he had started. I had put it to one side. I took up the concept of lawyer.

Bustos's lawyer's name is- Captain Raul Novillo.

Debray's lawyer's name is- Jaime Mandizabal.

I put their names into the internet and get the shock of my life!

Uncle Roberto's photo with this name appear in-

La Historia Clompleto.

http.//bp1.blogger.com/6bkpgg.

In fact I find he has another name, Rafael Miguez Roca contributed to him.

Uncle Roberto is Debray's lawyer!?

I did read in chapter twenty-four of the South America Years that Debray's father was not allowed to be his son's attorney.

I put in Ciro Bustos's lawyer's in, why am I surprised to see a photo of a man with many names, marked as a terrorist in program-

'Collectivoepprosario.blogspot.com/2010_02_01_A

Looking like Juan-Martin Guevara lynch!?

I also see a photo of a woman with the name of Mirta Tresa Gerelli looking like-Che's sister. She is named as a tourist in this program.

I took time looking at photos of Uncle Martin, Juan Martin Guevara, not wanting to confront myself with the fact-
***Two of Che Guevara's brothers are representing Debray and Bustos/Che at their trial.***

The script writer!
Strange to think Che's half-brother Fernando L Chavasz Alvarez under all the names he has used, has written history the way they want us to think it was. He is a film producer, script writer. Films I have got a lot of my information from were written by him!

What a script to write!
You plan the death party, direct the actors, smear on the makeup, set up the stuntmen- this explains why pictures and scenes in films don't quite match: they don't have to be filmed on the same day or the same place. You promote your work on a world stage.

There is so much distrust and smoke regarding the Che's Bolivian Dairies. I do not drought the dairies are real. You have to decide for which purpose they were written. And when were they written!? Were they written to be used in the court room? Or making the plot fit later? Do you want to close the film with the scene of them being sentenced to thirty years in prison, knowing. Your players are going to be freed.

Salvador Allende is kind enough to help bring (Benigo) and (Pombo) and Bustos/Che amongst

others to Chile. As shown in the film 'Last moments with Che Guevara.
World News- Garderen Weekly- Steven Soderbergh. (Mejorentrevista a Ernesto Che Guevara. (invedotia))

Steven Soderbergh had made a film called Che Revolucion. It was not German TV, Das Erst. (I missed seeing it.) And someone called Jonan Söderberg did the editing for Sacrifico!? New file- new relations!?

If I was to give an Oskar they would have it. They would have it for the biggest cover up me could think of. Only someone that wants to find her father would think to look under stones, other parties, like the CIA, are happy to cover their tracks. This explains why so much information did not match. Things do not have to match exactly, but somehow fit together. It never has till now!

I do not know if I want to kiss them or hit them. What a good film, best screen play!

Why are there so many of Che's family involved?

I feel as if I am walking around in fog. The question that is in my mind is, why are there so many if not all of Che's family involved, and involved in what?

I have found a photo on the internet where Debray can be seen with Uncle Martin, at first I missed the point; Martin is wearing a Bolivian uniform. www.larevuedesressources.org/spip.php?page=5. There is another photo showing Debray and Elizabeth Burgos with Uncle Martin, in the crowd

around them you can see Ana Maria! Why should I be surprised?
(I find other alias for one uncle or another and new names for my film star aunt and each time I am surprised.)
*(Cilia de la Serna was in prison in Argentina*

*Juan Martin, Cilia' youngest son was also in prison in Argentina. At the same time as Che's Mother.*

*I can connect Roberto to Osvaldo Chato Peredo, it is said of him. He took over Che's place as leader in Bolivia. They are young men then and under the photo in its blog it says they are training for the coup in Chile.*

*I can connect Juan Martin to Osvaldo Chato Peredo as older men.*

*I put in Osvaldo Chato Peredo into the computer to find the pictures to match those last two statements.*

*Ana Maria is on a wanted list from Brazil, her nick name is La Petti and her husband is a film director and half brother to Che.*

*Ernesto Guevara Lynch, Che's father where dose he come in? His second wife Ana Maria Guevara Erra is in one of Elizabeth's files. (All very cosy.)*

        Elizabeth Burgos-Debray's files.
        Hoover Institution Stanford University
            Hoover Institution
            434 Galvez Mall
            Stanford University
            Stanford. CA 94305-6010.

As a disclaimer I have not at the time of writing been able to visit this Institution. But on the internet the files are listed.

Elizabeth Burgos-Debray's file list is interesting in itself. There is a file with the name of Ernesto Guevara's second wife Ana Maria Guevara Lynch Erra, what makes her interesting?

Another- Ricardo Rojo, he is supposed to be Che's close friend, I had thought at one point that he could have been my father, which is why I picked out his name.

Humberto Vasquez has a file; he was supposed to have fallen from a chopper over the jungle, if certain reports are to be believed! I see there is one for Benigno and the defence lawyer's transcript arguments have their place.

Strange to think the lawyer is Uncle Martin.

I feel comfortable seeing there is a file with the authorizing her visits to see her husband in Camiri prison, 1968-1969.

But not so comfortable when I read the name of Pierre Kalfon, he has written about Che, I got the impression from the film Sacrificio that his books did not hold water. I looked him up on the internet:

He is an actor, author as well as a film producer that is interesting. On which side is he on? On which side; is not the question I should be asking! What is important in his role in this pantomime?

There are other names on Elizabeth's lists that at this time do not mean much to me and others like Charles de Gaulle that do. That Regis Debray family members have files do not surprise me. Elizabeth has her own files and there are files that relate to work she took on in and after the trial. Her last file dates 2007, not all her work is related to the time I am interested in.

I wonder what is in a file named 'Proposals, 1967-1970?'

The next says it is name is 'Escape Plan, 1970' my finger would have stayed there if the next one was not titled, 'Prisoner exchange, 1967-1968'

What surprises me is there is no mention of Ciro Bustos. No file has his name in it!

Why have files on those people and not one on one of the main characters? Debray may have had the leading role in the court room, Bustos played a part, but there is not a file about him!

       Archive Chile Pagina 12.

There is another name that keeps coming up, it is not on the list of files Elizabeth Burgos-Debray, but it connects to the Archive Chile Pagina 12.

Betencort. I put in numbers suggested in Pagina 12 after working my way though the names I found in it pages the internet gave me this name. If I put in the name of Godard I can also get the name Betencort. To have found both aunt and the uncles' alias connect to the name Betencort.

Lillian Betencort the internet tells me is one of the world's richest women.

The name Betencort connects to the Nazis.

The name Betencort is also in the Elizabeth Burgos-Debray's files.

Money, film making and politics need financial backing.

 If I had the resources I could go to the archives in Stanford to search for myself through Elizabeth Burgos-Debray's files. They have suggested I appoint a researcher to look for me, but there are so many names and faces 'now in my head!' the researcher would have to know all I know and have written French and spanish which I do not have; to draw out all the secrets those papers have. Sometimes you can have facts right under your nose but don't see what they mean to you. It may take weeks, months to understand what you have seen and now you are too far away to go back and look again-! Then I could ask someone to help as I would have exact questions to ask.

      Trying to find advice.

 After finding out that Che/Bustos had the best lawyers he could have, his brothers I contacted Jan, his is a journalist working in Holland. He did take me seriously which is a new sensation for me, but he found the jump from Che to Bustos to defalcate to make; he asked me what evidence I had. If you could have seen me than I looked like a fish, mouth opening and closing till I could say, 'I do have an example of hand writing I can offer as proof.'

 Ciro had written on one of my blue cards he had to Cuba in nineteen sixty-one the Bay of Pig invasion. It was not a large sample of his handwriting. The first time I met him he gave my three invitations/ flyers to announce his pictures were on show. In one of those is an introduction written by him, this matches with the writing on the blue cards.

(The blue cards had questions asking if he could go to Cuba, did he have family and friends there etc.)

I have keep the blue cards and the invitations safely so as not to disturb the DNA that they could provide, as only myself and the nice lady who tried to teach me Spanish had touched them, Ciro's DNA could be taken from them.

The DNA was important to me, but it could not, would not prove the man in Malmo was Che. Che's brothers and sisters nor his children would offer theirs for me to compeer. His hand writing has given me the proof I need! So I thought.

(I come to other conclusions in another chapter.)

It easy to get samples of Che's hand writing down from the internet. They covered my table as I matched them letter with letter to the samples I have. I peered at them through my magnifying glass, first one way then the next, I formed the letter they way they had been written, compared them to my own, I have always said my handwriting is like a doctor's scribble, really to hide I am dyslectic! I tried to find a sample of hand writing from someone that had learnt to write at the same time as Che. I did not want to send it to someone just so they could laugh at me. Silke has pocked her magnifying class at it, drawn down other samples of Che's hand writing. We both have got over excited about it. No, no we can't accept what we think we see. We are going to have to find someone that can confirm what we have before our own eyes.

I can now show as evidence a sample of hand writing. I can now say where Ciro was according to the dates shown on the invitations Ciro gave me, they span from nineteen seventy-nine to nineteen ninety-nine. They have been produced professionally not like the handmade versions I use, they can be verified by the printers and the cultural group that must have sponsored him.
'Grupo Cultral Del Sur.'

Now I have evidence that has not been filtered out of the internet! (Or I think I have) Somehow I feel further away from where I want to go, wherever that is! I had started this in hoped of finding a lost father, but the more I know the further away I feel I am. Somehow fascinated by the way 'they' have hoodwinked the world! I wonder what my next question is.

'They' should be easy to understand, as I have read the book Ultimate Sacrifice; it explains how people few can compile a plan so interlocked, with detail to every move that an individual was to make, when it came to killing a president. 'They' set more than one person to take the blame. The people who I have found connected to Che/Bustos are players in a game that I have not yet understood.

Not everyone would go to so much trouble just to save an artist! Ciro says, 'An artist wants to give something back.'

## Chapter nine
## Errol Flynn

Now that the excitement of handwriting has died down
The name of Errol Flynn pops up in my mind. It come out of the mists of my mind as an old friend told me there had been a film made by Errol Flynn about Cuba. I was not able to see it when it was presented on television some years ago. But now I am into producers and film stars the idea came to me to look for it on the internet.

The new surprise took some time to awaken me; I never would have accepted to see my aunt in the staring roll. She is about seventeen or nineteen, an ugly duckling staring next to Errol Flynn.

Beverly Aadland was the name she used, her English had an American twinge, and the film was made in nineteen fifty nine. I have a photo of her as Che's sister, where she is not such an ugly duckling wearing a coat I would have killed for.

It is so much more difficult deciding whether you are right or not, as fashion and styli do not help you, in the film she has very blond hair. In the photo of her with her brother Che, her hair is dark. Behind her is standing the film producer uncle!

As of yet I have not managed to see the whole film, it tile is Cuban Rebel Girls. Errol Flynn plays himself as a journalist. Che's sister plays the part of an American helping with the revolution. She is seen involved in smuggling weapons and ammunition and marching with the men through the mountains of Cuba. Though I have not seen the end, I ask myself what has this to do with- now I am stuck!

Errol Flynn makes a film about how Cuba financed its revolution, kissed my aunt under a romantic sky, I even saw her as a spy run through the streets of Havana.

I can find a photo of Errol Flynn talking to Castro, not yet come across a photo of Che with the film magnet. Errol Flynn was to die not long after he made this film.

The critics say it is the worst film he made, I can only say it is nineteen fifty American! But why did he make such a film? Why make a film with Che's sister? It dose mirror with what you have read about Frank Sturgis and the intrigue of Kennedy's death. A little pirate island with coves and caves where guns and ammunition could be hidden.

Just for interest I looked up Christopher Lee and Ian Fleming, it is said that they were cousins, whither that is right of wrong they were both involved in intrigue, secrete services and films!

I have put all my notes into files, there are six files side by side on my shelf. (There are more now) I did not know there was so much! I have made lists of all the books and films I have used and listed most of the internet programs.

Jorge Ricardo Masetti

The film made by Errol Flynn had a new face I could not place. There is a small clef in his chin, was he a member of the Guevara family?

Cuban Rebel Girls is as reported not the best film Errol Flynn made, I had hoped to see something that would state that show business had a bigger part in Cuba's revolution. It could have had subtitles saying just what I wanted to hear.

What it did show was a face; he is in the scene where one of the rebel girl's funeral is taking place. I am not sure why he is standing in the middle of the service, I know his face but cannot say why. It was not until Silke and I were comparing Che's hand writing again did the penny drop.

Silke rang to say look at the film she had found on the internet, it is called, La Palabra Empanada.

This film is produced by Martin Masetti. It is about Jorge Ricardo Masetti, Martin Masetti's father. Ciro Bustos is to be seen giving an interview! Jorge Ricardo Masetti happened to be a revolutionary by Che's side! He wrote a book called, 'El furor y el Delirio: itinerio de un hijo de la Revolucion Cuba.' Which Elisabeth Burgos-Debray has listed in her files and she has made first and second drafts for and she has kept its reviews. I should not be surprised; the circle is not as large as I at first thought.

In Errol Flynn's film you can see Che's sister and Jorge Ricardo Masetti! His book translated by

Elisabeth Burgos-Debray as is one by Che as himself and has contact to Ciro Bustos. It is the film producers that are interesting....
Jorge Ricardo Masetti and Martin Masetti they are also in the film busyness!

Why mention the hand writing again? We were looking for more examples of Che's hand writing. I remembered that Monika Ertl sitting at a table with Regis Debray in Havana, they were planning to capture her godfather Klaus Barbie.

A hand written love poem is used in the next seen it vials Monika's face it is said to have been written by the man that took over Che's leadership after his death party. Guido Alvaro Peredo Leigue 'Inty'
*Osvaldo Chato Peredo* is Inty's brother. (I have seen photos on the internet he is standing next to a young Uncle Roberto Guevara and as an older man he is standing with Uncle Martin.)

I thought the first time I saw it was Che's hand writing now Silke thinks the same. We used it to compeer it to the samples we have. As I was getting the CD out of its box a postcard drops out of it. We are surprised again! Kick is the production team for documentary and spiel films. They made the film about Monika Ertl. One of the little photos on the front of the card shows Martin Masetti! But he is the son of Jorge Ricardo Masetti! He was in Errol Flynn's film! Along with Che's sister!?

And! Under the name of Luciano Monteagudo, Che's half brother, the one married to Che's sister;

he has written an article for Pagina 12; it is in Archiv3-Daten der Kooperation Dritte Weld Archive. It is based in Berlin. It happen to be closed as I am writing this down. It will not be open till September 2012. I have tried to get a copy from other places but I have not had any luck!
 'Monika y el Che Padre nazi, hija guerrillera. In Pagina 12. Nr 1588 seite 26, dated 1992.
   Themen: Kultur; Guerilla; Brd; Lateinamerik; Bolivien; Uber die Deutsche Monika Ertl, die als Tochte eiens Nazi-filmers zu Klaus Barbie 'Onkel' sagte.
   The title alone is interesting! Without saying who wrote it! (Che's half brother.) He is also a film producer.
I cannot help thinking the whole thing is one big film production!

         To see Ciro again.
   I have been to see Ciro again. This time not with the need to know if he is my father. This I may never be able to prove, though I am happy to let my feelings guide me.
   Two years have passed since I have seen him. I have got to the point where he should know what I have found out. I made him up a folder; it is to explain how I think things went from the death party to his filmed escape in 1968.
'Last moments with Che Guevara. World News- Garderen Weekly- Steven Soderbergh.

(Mejorentrevista a Ernesto Che Guevara. (invedotia))

This is where Silke saw him among the others being greeted by Salvador Allende.

I would not have looked at this film again had Ciro not said that the photo we had taken from it was of Bingno. (Not of himself.)

What he said of the red folder I had made up for him was Bingno was a silly man the next day when we went to see him. (The only mention of Bingno in my folder is in Elizabeth Burgos-Debray's lists underlined with a marker pen.

I had not expected Ciro to write me a letter saying- Evelyn you are right! To go over what I have in the folder will take him more than one night.

I know Ciro has understood I know he is not who he says he is. Why state that Che shot himself by accident; showing Silke where the built had passed through his-Che's body leaving Ciro Bustos without any scaring. I would have laughed if I could; this was not the moment to do so, as Silke was having a hard enough time as it was. Ciro had said he did not understand French on Sundays but on Monday he did. Silke was trying to turn French words into Spanish words, there were German and English words hanging around trying to be helpful too.

Long ago I had wadded through many photos looking for scars to prove Bustos and Che were one. I fell for the idea that had been planted to lead me away from the truth. And now the same game is being played again! If Ciro Bustos does not have scars then he cannot be Che. But Che does not have scars on his face after he shot himself either! He just has a band aide at the time, to cover the graze!

I only mention it as it was an indication he knew why I was there.

It was a great relief to have Silke with me on this trip just to have someone on your side. Silke did most of the talking for our side. This gave me the chance to watch Ciro closely. He has the same mannerism as the photo shows, the one where he is in the background with Bingno and Leonardo Tamayo- 'Urbano.' and Harry Villegas- 'Urbano. The three men to have survived the experience in Bolivia, as Ciro pointed out.

(Don't worry Silke, I have this film at home we can double check the point Ciro made when he said the photo was Bingno.

Wege Der Revolution. (The film cover tells me the film martial comes out of the –Staatlichen Kubanischen Filmarchiv ICAIC. That it is Original!)

## Army Advisers surprise uncles!

I did not have much to do the day after we got home so I got the film out of its box and put it in to the lap top. Dozing with the drone of the mowing matches I nearly missed seeing Uncle Martin and Uncle Roberto! This time they were subtitled as Army Advisers! I know they had taken the parts of lawyers at Debray and Bustos' trial. Not that Ciro had replied when I had made a remark about that; and he had somehow forgotten Sister Anna Maria had played his wife at the trial! He did not recognise her name when I pointed it out. That was on the Sunday, on the Monday Anna Maria was a name he said belonged to a grandchild.

Good thing I had read in Pangea 12 what his half brother had written, Anna Maria had played the part of loving wife when the court case was taking place.

Ciro did not react to the photo I had in the file of Anna Maria with Elizabeth Burgos-Debray and Uncle Martin and Regis Debray in the crowded street as they were going to court.

(Not for one moment do I think Che/Ciro is losing it! he is like a tortuous that does not want you to know he can run like a hare.)

I have spent some time puzzling over the idea that two of Che's brothers were in the Bolivian army as army captains and then as Bolivian lawyers at the trial of Ciro and Debray. They have rolls as Military Intelligence Officers and are connected to the Centre of Instruction of Special Troops.

It is not a puzzle that is just where they should be! After all Felix Rodriguez and the Novo brothers Guillermo and Ignaoio attended the death party as did Gustavo Villida, they all were CIA members. They can be seen as standing around as Bolivian soldiers at Che's death party.

(Gustavo sold hair said to belong to Che on the internet!) Che shared allies with Felix Rodriguez;

that was why I thought Che was in evolved in Kennedy's demise; I had not expected to see him waiting in the wings to take charge of the planed Coup.

   Jon Lee Anderson lived in the flat above Ciro Bustos.
Jon Lee Anderson lived in the flat above Ciro Bustos in Malmo! Silke and I heard Ciro tell us that. Why would the biographer do that? Is he one of those that know the truth?

   He lived in Cuba for three years as he wrote his book. His family had the same nanny as Che's seconded wife had for her children. This is a cosy family. The group is getting smaller all the time.

   Monica Ertl knew how to use a film camera as did her father; he had strong Nazi connections such as Klaus Barbie. Che's sister and half brother are connected to showbiz. Masetti and his son are film producers, actors! Masetti can be seen in Errol Flynn's film, he in the scene where the funeral is taking place, Anna Maria in that seen also.

   I have read that Ciro lived with Masetti when he first came to Cuba. Ciro painted clay pots somewhere near Santiago de Cuba.

             Other bad boys/brothers/guerrillas.
Other bad boys/brothers/guerrillas have their names and photos in the Argentinean archives of terrorists. You can find 'La Petti,' Anna Maria named as a bad

girl along with her brother Martin in a similar Brazilian terrorist archive in the internet.

(Colectivoepprosario.Blogspot.com/2010_02_01_a) This program also lists other names Uncle Martin has used, along with the name he used as a lawyer at the trail.

Why does Ciro have my photo in his glass case?

My next question is if I am completely wrong why does Ciro have my photo in his glass case along with Che's first wife, she is standing next to a large blond journalist.

He interested me as he looks like a film producer that sung Jean-Luc Godard's praises in the film Nouvelle Vague. If he is the same man then he also can be seen in the Argentina terrorist archives. The name he uses is Nestor Carlos Kirchner. The same name can be found in the archives.

(A small twist here, Nestor Carlos Kirchner is the name of the Argentinean President. In fact they can be seen on a tank together!)

More films to look at.

I am having a bit of a tidy up in my mind, when looking for the film where Silke found Che escaping to Chile and on to Cuba. I found a film- 'Enter leyendas-Eresto Che Guevara en Bolivia.' Here I found it has the same material as Path Way to Revolution. It also has the two brothers in uniform and that photo of Che/Ciro and an interesting bit of film where you can see Che in disguise, he walks into the camp where his men are said to be waiting; at first they do not recognise him!

(I have seen this bit of film before, long time ago. I had recognised him the moment he came into the camera's shot, I was a little surprised that his men took so long to see through the disguise.) That was before I had found out it was a scene filmed for me to see, a part of the script in a much bigger production.

'Guerrilleros del "Che" Regresaran ala Habana.)

'Fronter De Chile Che Guevara. (Documental Completo) and the internet films. 'Septumber De 1967 – film 1 of 4 to 4 of 4 has the same information to offer. Put all the films together re-cut the film in your mind to get a better understanding of everybody's parts in this play.

I have to say Silke and I were Bond girls! I got another sample of Ciro's hand writing, this sample also has Silke's on it. No one can say it is a fake as it now witnessed.

I took his toothbrush. Not with idea to use it for another DNA test, to say to him, 'This is serious!'

I had put the brush in my sock; it was not a good place to put it as it slipped. I had the horrifying vision of the orange tooth brush marching down the stairs to the front door behind me! It did not, but it left me dancing back into the bathroom.

I had wanted to ask for a DNA test, one to see what his reaction would be, and two as another way to form a contact. But most of Ciro's remarks lead us away from this question.

He had hugged me; he had invited us into his flat where we drank coffee.

When Silke and I first got there we had to sit in the park opposite his flat we were not sure he would return, but as Bond girls we found out his windows away from the road were open. In the warm sun sitting in the park it was not so uncomfortable.

I did see the car Ciro drives race up the road with the same zest as any racing driver! A little while later he appeared looking like the old man disguise he had used in Bolivar.

I got my handy out and rang his number, we had not been able to use plan A as the man in the shop next door had forgotten the door code. Plan B was to get a young boy that happened to be passing, to ask Ciro to come to the window from where he could see me standing on the pavement, he did look surprised! At that moment a woman and her dog came out of the door. I pulled Silke after me; we reached it before it could close. This is the third time I have surprised him, I wish I could invite myself without have to take the risk that Ciro will fall from his balcony, when Swedish boy tries to tell him an English girl wants a cup of coffee!

I look at the photo I took of the glass case where I can see my photo, I cannot help wondering why he-

Ciro Bustos has kept my photo.... and why there is a photo of che's first wife but there are not any other family photos to be seen around his flat.

## Chapter ten
## Pierre Kalfon

Pierre Kalfon is a name on Elizabeth Burgos-Debray's list, he also wrote a biography about Che. Wonder why, well he was there, not only was he there he was also a film producer, an actor, a script writer! In a little green note book of mine I have written- 'A book states Pierre Kalfon is a brother.' What I did not do is say which book a found that remark in!

I have not found that refinance again.
But I did find Jean-Pierre Kalfon was directed in a film called 'Weekend' by Jean-Luc Godard! Playing with him was Mireille Darc. This is one of the names Ana Maria used! -Che's sister- (hcl.harvard.edu)

This is a Frence/Italy. 1968, color, 105 min and with French and English subtitles.

I have always wondered why the film quality was so bad for when it came to filming the Che death party. Special effects!

Did I mention Pierre Kalfon was a rock star and a professor in Chile, he wrote a book about Salvador Allende, and Bolivia! As will as being a diplomat and spending twenty five years in Latin America.

There is another man that has written a biography about Che, his name is Josef Lawrezki. He was a

Russian spy! Putting his life into a small paragraph seems mean; he was in Argentina working against the Germans. He must have had his feet in the pools of this story or he could not have written his books, he too has written books about Che and Bolivia and Salvador Allende. He became respectable and was given a doctor in history by the Russians.

(His remarks match those news paper cuttings from Elizabeth Burgos-Debray's files. No one had heard about Che nor his death part in the surrounding villages.)

As his book came out in nineteen seventy four it could have more to tell my but it is in DDR German! It would take me weeks, months, years to squeeze the juice out.

        Will Havana's streets shout my name?

The City stands as I knew it,
The peoples' voices are held within in its streets.
Is it my name that is on their breath?
I am here, but they cannot see me.

Am I the hero they think I am?
Were they told the jungle beat me?
The revolution goes where it can
I am here, but they cannot hear me.

Who told them I am a revolutionary man?
Why do they hold my name under their breath?
The words have been written before I ever spoke them.

I am here, what am I trying to give?

I am not the only one to have played this game.
Am I the only one to take the blame?
I have died so my name can live!
But, without my name I cannot rise again.

Will they understand I never went away?
It was a game I had to play.
The world did not want another way.
I am here to dread this day.

Now the truth is on their lips!
Will they stamp for joy, to hear I live?
Will Havana's streets shout my name?
Che! Che Guevara is here again!

                A list of who knows?
    I do not know if there is anyone I have mist, or if all of those I have named really know. But the list comes from a gut feeling; I say that to excuse some of the strange explanations!

Fidel Castro=he trained Salvador Allende's private army and they were best of friends.
Salvador Allende*=he had helped Che and other guerrillas to escape! As shown on many films.
Miguei Bonasso =reporter for Pangea 12 and a film maker.
Nestor Carlos Kirchner= as he is pictured

with Che's first wife in the same glass case as the photo of Ciro and myself.

His name and photo are to be found in the same terrorist archives as Uncle and Aunts.

Humberto Vazquez Viana= I saw him in Ciro's flat, he is known to have been involved.

Pierre Kalfon= He was there, written a book....

   'Benigo'- Dariel Alaron Ramirez.

   'Pombo.'- Harry Vallegas Tamayo.

   'Urbano.'- Leonardo Tamayo.

             Che's surviving guerrillas.

Felix Rodriguez= he lives of the falsified photo. There are a small group he worked with.

Orlando Lettelier= he is said to have arranged for Ciro Bustos and Debray's release from prison.

Elizabeth Burgos-Debray= she has kept files about this time and she was there.

Regis Debray= he was with Ciro!

Aleida Guevara March and family!

Josef Lawrezki.* I think he suspected things were not as they should have been,

Steven Soderbergh=they have made films about Che or Bustos

Jonan Söderberg=they have made films about Che or Bustos.

             Could be relations!?

Ana Maria= Che's sister-Bustos' wife for the trial.

Alberto Grunado*=a best friend, lifelong companion.

Lillian Betencort= for the financing.

Jon Lee Anderson= lived in the flat above Ciro Bustos in Malmo and he lived in Cuba for three years as he
wrote his book. His family had the same nanny as Che's seconded wife had for her children.
Monica Ertl*= because if the love poem.
*And Ann Wright as she is/ was Monika Ertl.*
Masetti, farther and son= Ciro lived with Masetti senior when he first came to Cuba.
They both are film producers etc! And terrorist!
Che's father* and second wife= as her name is to found in Elizabeth Burgos-Debray's list.
Che's Mother*= she lived alone when she died, her pockets were full of cinema tickets!
All of Che's brothers= script writers, film stars, producers, lawyers.
And me!=looking for my father.
*= those that have left the stage.

## Chapter eleven
### A Brazilian guerrilla in Bolivia.

It is at this point I thought I had learnt all I could. But-
You will never guess what I by chance found out!?

I had thought I had finished my manuscript I have even sent it of to Ciro in English; I also have sent him a copy translated into Spanish by the internet computer program. To use this method of translating can make reading the manuscript difficult; to decide exactly what is being said is a matter of hard work!

I have met a Cuban; he lives in the little town that is situated near where I live. He too has horses and loves to drive, just because he was organizing a fun drive out, he pop round to see us. Over the coffee we found out he come from Holguin in Cuba. We know the same places, but not so many people as he had not lived there for twenty-five years.

Pedro happened to say his father was in the Cuban army. I had not taken in his name correctly, the name I had took me to Marchuncuto, Venezuela, 1967, where I found a Pedro Cobrera Torres and Manuel Gil Custellonos, and they had been killed because the Island of Terror- Cuba had for some forty years made a (Bay of Pigs) attack on Venezuela. This happened at the same time as Che was attending his death party! *A book by Brian Lawtell about Fidel Castro would tell me more.* Pedro told me the next time I saw him: that his mother's family name was Cabrera, his father name is Pedro Julio Pena Quevedo.

To be allowed to come and study in what was the German Democratic Republic you had to be in a comfortable potion in the Cuban government. With that in mind I put the name into the little box the internet provides. To see he was a military man was no surprise. But after playing with the name as Pedro suggested I did get a surprise.

I put in Pedro Pena:
 *PDF Che: Behind the CIA's killing of a Revolutionary.*

This informs me that a Pedro Pena informed on Che! It is written by Michael Ratner and Michael Steven Smith.

There were other Pedro Penas' one a ballet dancer one a footballer. But I was surprised to have found myself back in a familiar circle.

While I was working with the name Pedro Pena, asked the internet to show me is selection of pictures. I did not expect to see a picture with of two people and a hand written letter. The hand writing was familiar, very familiar. It was the hand writing of ***Che Guevara***. (or syndicate)

Now I am surprised. How can this be?

Daniel Cassol has written an article.
*http://danielcassol.worldpress.com/2012/08/29/um-brasileiro-na-guerrilha-boliviana-2/*
A Brazilian guerrilla in Bolivia.

The familiar handwriting has written a letter to Susanna it is reportedly to be from Luiz Renato Almeida Pires. He is supposedly a member of the guerrillas in Bolivia even though he was said to be a Brazilin citizen.

He married Susana, when he disappeared she was expecting a child. (Another half sibling?)
Daniel Cassol's report tells me that Luiz Renato Almeida Pires was considered as candidate for the position of commissar of the guerrillas, but it was decided that Nestor Paz Bolivia Amora should take up this position.

Chato Osvaldo Peredo it said to have considered this possible, but Renato did not wish to take up this position as he did not think his Spanish was good enough!

All of this is revolving around Teoponte. Teoponte is a town the guerrilla group lead by Chato Osvaldo Peredo took in the third quarter of nineteen seventy. They were to hold it for about one hundred days.

General Candia promised a war without causalities or prisoners. Out of the sixty-seven men that involved nine survivors were taken over by Juan Jose Torres when he took over from General Alfredo Ovando Candia.

In 'Brazilian in Guerrilla Bolivian' it is stated that Chato Osvaldo Peredo and Luiz Renato Almeida Pires among the survivors, however Luiz Renato Almeida Pires would have been executed. The writer also says that the circumstance of his execution was never clarified, nor was his body found!

(Where have I heard that sort of thing before? Even though Vazquez Viana body was thrown into the jungle he has a death certificate as dose Luiz Renato Almeida Pires. But I met him in Ciro Bustos's flat and found his address in Sweden. In Italy he can be seen on the internet selling a book about Che Guevara!)

Talking of Ciro Bustos I sent him an email this time in Portuguese, not Spanish. I got a replay, I usually do when I say I am to go and see him. He usually says he cannot see me, he is ill or there is another problem, he did not seem to notice I had used Portuguese instead of Spanish; it is my habit to send him my messages in both English and Spanish.

What does that mean!? He says he does not speak English. The email I sent to Ciro was to point out he has both versions in English and Spanish.

In a replay to an email I sent him on the first of October two-thousand and twelve he ends his email by saying

'I do not like losing my toothbrush after the DNA of a ghost. Winter came. Until next summer, greetings.

In the replay to the email I used a Portuguese translation he says. 'I do not share obsessions; I am co-author of one, not romance novel character. I do not like pressure or you steal my brushes.'

I do not understand why he has confirmed I took his toothbrush! Not once but twice!

At this time I am confused, there are now four names connected to the same hand writing.

Che Guevara, his I have been able to follow from his childhood to the Bolivian diaries. He has the habit to make a fuss of one letter in his script. But so does Ciro Bustos! And Luiz Renato Almeida Pires!? And Monika Ertl in her lament to Inty; as the film shows. Gesucht: Monika Ertl, by Christian Baudissin.

Regis Debray says. 'Monika wrote it out of her sadness at the death of Guido Alvaro Peredo Leigue 'Inty'.

Ciro gave me on my first visit an invitation for one of his pictures presentations. In this invitation there is a hand written introduction. With other examples he gave me, one of which was witnessed by another person other than myself: we did confront him with the handwriting likeness. That was before seeing it again used by Luiz Renato Almeida Pires.

Four people cannot have the same handwriting. One man can!

I am angry! He has another family! There is another sibling! Why am I hurt? I want to know, how do I find out?

I get the copies of the computer translations. I have sent emails to Daniel Cassol, knowing he is not going to believe me but I need to know. He says do I know Mabel? No I do not but I want to, I replay not knowing at that time she could be the half sister I am looking for.

I do not want to tell him anything, knowing he will not believe me. But I did tell him to look at the hand writing.

I find at the end of Daniel's account he was able to contact Susana, companion of Renato and mother of Mabel. She lives in London. On the morning of July the twenty-fourth two thousand and twelve Susan answered the phone in England. She did not want to give an interview.

Daniel help me! He knows their family name. I wrote him another email I will bombard him with emails! I am cross with him, I am cross with Ciro and I am cross with myself. How do I proceed from here? I take down all the names in Daniel's report and from a report about Teoponte by Gustavo Rodriguez Ostria.

Gustavo Rodriguez Ostria is an historian he has written a book about Tarmara Bunke 'Tania'. He is working in the same circles. He became deputy minister of Education of Bolivia. The military archives of the period in Bolivia are still closed, even though Gustavo Rodriguez Ostria managed to get documents related to the guerrillas during his research for his book. Daniel report tells me among them are typewritten sheets of what could be part of Luiz Renatoto's diary. Gustavo Rodriguez Ostria would be interesting to talk to!

Daniel did send me an email asking who I am; he said he did not know much about Susana or Mabel. I told him my name and I do not want to carry the responsibility of what I have found out alone. He has not replied to this email. I had told him that the Guevara family was involved: I decide to write down for him, how each individual was woven into this.

I had made a start cross referencing all names in his report and Gustavo Rodriguez Ostria's.

Inty, one and two.

Guido Alvaro Peredo Leigue 'Inty'. He has a photo in 'cerrocolvo. Blogspot.com' as this program comes from Santa Clara where the Che Guevara museum is, you would think they would know! In the same program you can see Lucio Ediberto Galvan Hidalgo. He looks like Guido Alvaro Peredo Leigue 'Inty' even though his chin is missing!

Drop into gehealogiadelcheguevara.blogspot.com and have a look at their photo of the for-mentioned man.
(Since when did men with wavy hair decided to have tight curly hair?) It is like saying men that are bald will grow a good head of hair while they are in prison!

I want to see if the uncles are on this stage. They can be seen as advisers and integrators before Che's death party. They appear again as lawyers at the trial of Regis Debray and Ciro Bustos. If they are there, around Teoponte it will be difficult evidence to argue against.

So that leaves me thinking but not knowing in which direction to go in. I had wanted to stop, get on with being a housewife and artist. But the fact that Che's and Ciro's share the same hand writing; Regis Debray tell shows Monica Ertl using the same hand writing to lament the death of Inty. To top it all Luiz Renato Almeida Pires has the same handwriting has made an impression on my mind I cannot get rid of. (similar hand writing)

I started by putting all the uncles different name into the search program on the internet. I have to say I went round in circles bumping into names I know. In this way I came across the name Elvira Susana Miranda, it is said of her. She was a member in the ELN. Among other places I found her in 'Desaparecidos en Argentina.' www.desaprecidos.org/arg/victimas.

I note the word- Victmas.

In this program says she is missing. Teoponte on the eleventh of May ninety seventy-eight. She is said to be twenty five at this time, a nurse. Susana and another nurse Domingo Mather were taken to Santa Fe to a small arms factory. They were not take there to work or play they seem to have been under arrest, kept captive for her membership in the ENL.

In an internet program 'City Rossario in the province of Santa Fe' it says Elvira Susana Miranda and Jorge Horcio Novillo (One of the lawyers!) were charged with terrorism. A list of her and Jorge Horicon Novella crimes are in PDF'informepara querellantes.
www.aph.argentina.org.ar/.../hijos20090818.

As is Jorge Horcio Novillo- no conapepa:3628. He has been listed in Listado de Detentidos-Desaparcidos en Argentina.

I find this interesting! He is a Che brother and a Ciro Bustos lawyer and now a fellow prisoner!

Luiz Renato Almeida Pires and the name Elvira Susana Miranda name I found in 'Mortes e Despareaidoa' this program told me they were against the rule of dictators. This program only sets out lists.

I am not surprised to find the name Rodolfo Walsh popping up many of the programs. When I put in Susana Elvira Miranda.Teoponte a program Colectivoepposario.blogspot.com/.../Bolivia.info… I found Rudolfo Walsh again; the reference is on the page about digging up the bodies of those that fell in

Teoponte. He too is an ex-prisoner of the collective Pol-Sarvivor. Rosario. Two brothers and a Susana!

Jean Pierre Kalfon's name is in this soup.
He has worked with Jean-luc Godard another name used by Rodolfo Walsh amongst others that I don't want to repeat here a half-brother to Che.

Jean Pierre was a film star, Rock singer a Professor. A journalist and a diplomat, he was expelled from Chili after Salvador Allende was overthrown. He is an author/journalist with books about Che and the events connecting Teoponte.

I found another alias for him- Andre Durand-Mareuil.
(In a film called 'Prenom Carmen' produced by Jean-Luc Gudard. Jean Pierre looks like Che, they carry similar expressions. Could Jean Pierre Kalfon have played the part of Che's double? That Jean-luc Godard can also to be seen in one scene of this film! I am only thinking.)

Regis Debray is in this soup too. He has also written about Teoponte. I have not read their books but I will bet they do not explain why Luiz Renato Almeida Pires has the same hand writing as Che Guevara.

Chapter twelve.
Looking for evidence
The DNA is not of any use at this time!

I had been grumbling to friends that I feel I am sitting on something that is not mine. They asked me to coffee one Sunday. They said they knew someone that could be interested in my story. But as usual there was a, but. That person wanted evidence.

The evidence we were thinking of was the DNA from the toothbrush. There was more than one problem; the first was to find a firm to take on this test.

To use a German firm gave me the problem of needing Ciro's permission. As he had confirmed I had taken his toothbrush not once but twice, I did not think he would.

The next was if I used another name the test would only confirm the name had taken a DNA test. Not that it was Ciro Bustos, nor would it prove he is Che.

To use the name of Che Guevara had all read given me problems! Not everyone can cope with the idea of someone wanting a DNA test with someone they think is dead.

Using that name did not make it a legal document. A legal document meant asking a doctor to collect a sample from Ciro.

I have his toothbrush!

An English firm could offer me a soft test for peace of mind. The doctor or a witnessed written permission would make it a legal document.

I am going round in circles, to make a test with another name on it, would not help me. I could use my neighbour the father and daughter are in the same age group. Still does not provide my evidence. How am I going to match it with Che Guevara?

I was planning to go to Paris, try to find Anna Maria Che's sister. Her address is in the phone book, so is the half brother.
The Bond Girl's mind is working again. Plan A would be just to ask them. "You could be my aunt/uncle. Can I have a sample for a DNA test?" I don't think they will send me an email... "You have taken my toothbrush! Please replace it!"

I am not feeling very happy at this point, till the moment I thought 'eyes.' Eyes?

Why eyes? The moment I saw Ciro for the first time the light showed me a man with light brown eyes with a green/blue paler outer ring. And a brown flak in the right eye= goodbye Che hallow Ciro. So I had thought. On return from that first trip I spent the whole weekend on the internet looking for that moment where you can look into Che's eyes to find the same paten. The references are in my diary for that year. Then I forgot it. The fact my eyes have the same colour and the blue ring that can be seen when you look from the front as it can be seen with Ciro, took me on the road to a DNA test.

I spent the weekend on YouTube looking for the eye paten of Che. Three films gave me a good view of the paten I was looking for. But my camera was not able to make a clear copy.
The film Sacrefico was not making it easy to find, could be my laptop program is not made to show frame for frame.

I was not to cleaver with the YouTube films but they show what I am looking for.

The weekend brought me to a point where I thought I would not find what I was looking for. Up until the moment where I had the eye paten on my laptop screen and the matching paten from a YouTube film facing each other I could have been wrong. But there it is and a list of where to find it!

Weight fell from my shoulders; the nervousness of the past few days fell away. The stress from being in a position of not being able to prove that Ciro is Che had just disappeared.

The eyes looking at me are one and the same man.

The moment did not last long, now I have to find someone that has the right programs on their laptops and a camera that is capable of taking a photo that will show clearly the eye paten.

Frank has a book about island, we share the same publisher. We meet last weekend; he was giving a lecture on post card depicting island and the older towns on the island. When he was talking about reproducing some of the smaller cards so they could be used in an exhibition the penny dropped. Some of the cards are of visiting card form.

Frank is coming on Friday!

Frank did not come on Friday as the winter through snow over everything and the wind filled in the roads even as the snow ploughs did their best to keep the roads free.

To overcome the disappointment I decided to take a bath. It was in the bath an idea came uninvited into my mind.

The article from the Berlin archives had arrived by post; it had taken over a year as the archives had been relocated, the article had been sitting in packing boxes till I could persuade someone to take it out.

As the half brother had written it under the name of Luciano Monteagudo and it was titled Monika y el Che it had caught my eye.

Until I had taken that bath I was not impressed with it: It was advertising the film Gesucht: Monika Ertl, by Christian Baudissin.

Monika was under suspicion for the death of Roberto Quintanilla in Hamburg 1971. They were advertising this film in 1973 in a Bolivian news paper.

Christian Baudissin he was the producer of this film and guerrilla. Masitti is connected to Fliker films, his photo is in the DVD box as is his son. On the same page of the news paper, I got from Berlin, Regis Debray has written a column singing the films praises.

The point that makes this interesting is the timing of the film, ready for distribution shortly after Monika's death.

The thought that entered my head was if Monika was not killed as they portray, then who did she become?

Ann Wright came to mind! She has written a book with Ciro Bustos and Jon lee Anderson. 'Che wants to see you.'

I went to bed thinking I could not get any sillier!

The next day was spent studying photos on the internet.
Women are not as easy as men they change their look so often.
At the end of the weekend I had photos of Monika and Ann Wright on the table before me. How was I going to prove they were one and the same person?

Every photo with a good view into the eye was scrutinised.
Han Ertl has blue eyes with a darker blue ring edging it. Monika has this, her eyes have a fleck in the left eye above the fleck is a mark that does not reflect light. A good example can be found in the film about her.

(Good thing Frank could not come. Hope he can make a copy of this also.)

Ann's eyes photos had the help of colour. I found the fleck and the non reflecting mark, but the blue ring cannot be seen from a front view. I feel close to panic! Only to calm down again when I found a photo where the light passes through the eye from one side to show the blue ring.

The next day the idea to match the photos with the one small image I have found of Susanna gave me a surprise.

Monika Ertl had become Elvira Susana Miranda. It is said of her. She was a member in the ELN. Among other places I found her in 'Desaparecidos en Argentina.'
www.desaprecidos.org/arg/victimas.

Susanna was in prison with Che's brother using the name Jorge Horcio Novillo- no conapepa:3628. In Santa Fe.
He has been listed in Listado de Detentidos-Desaparcidos en Argentina.

Monika/Susanna took in the identity of Ann Wright a USA army cornel till she retired twenty nine years later. As Ann Wright she had written books with Elizabeth Burgs-Debray. Translated books for Ciro, Benigno, and and- -.

As Susanna was said to have married Luiz Renato Almeida Pires as found in Daniel Cassol and Rodriguez's reports of events around Teoponte.

The letter for Susanna I found on the internet in the same if not similar hand writing as Che's. This information came from a report from Daniel Cassol.

When Frank came I was too excited to find the right moments in the DVD Sacrifico nor could I control the YouTube programs will enough to take a useable photo from.

Frank was most helpful he has put a program on my computer, with this it is possible to print directly from the film. It might be better to say you catch the moment you want, take it onto your computer so you can print it, cutting out the camera. Sounds easy! I wonder how long it will take me to learn to use.

Frank dose know someone that has the knowhow and equipment to control films/DVDs frame for frame. Good thing is they are not too far from home.

I rang them! I was getting in a muddle.

Kathleen answered the phone, she was friendly but I did not dare to tell her why or whose eyes I wanted to make a match with. All I said was ask Frank.

The next day I walked into an office with five people round the table- for the first time I did not feel like a freak. But I might have preferred to have to choose between them and the dentist.

Part Two-
There is more to this than I thought.

I would like to show you the photos I found in my research. To use them I would need to get the owners permission. As I don't think they will be so pleased if they knew why I want them. I will say way where you can find them.

I have changed my mind. The misuse of propaganda, the lies used to do another's bidding should not go unchallenged.

Chapter thirteen.
Susan- Monica-Ann.

There has to be a seconded part of this story. To answer the question what did Che Guevara do after the death party?

I had started to wonder about it when I found the hand writing of Luiz Renato Almieda Pires in the letter to Susana. That lead me to believe Susana was Monika Ertl and that Monica took on the name of Ann Wright.

Monika.
This photo is from 'Gesucht: Monika Ertl. Die frou die Che Guevara Rachte. By Christian Baudissin. Christian Baudissin- He is also a guerrilla journerlist and film producer of the time.

 Susana Elvira Miranda
desaparecidos.orgThe photo of Susana is from 'Desaparecidos en Argentina.
www.desaprecidos.org/arg/victimas. Mortes,e, Desparecidoa`

The name given for the photo is Elvira Susana Miranda.

That Susana was a 'Militante do ELN' connected to the National Liberation Army. Susanna happened to have been held captive in Santa Fee, Argentina at the same time as Ciro Bustos, as was one uncle using the name of Mendizabel. I cannot be sure which one is which they swapped identities often; both were lawyers, useful to around when you have militant beliefs. This Susanna when missing at some point, no body was found was the remark I read.

Ann Wright
There are many photos in the internet.
Photo of Retired Colonel Ann Wright from ... islandbreath.blogspot.com

I had read from Daniel Cassol article that Susana had a daughter when she was married to Luiz Renato Almieda Pires her name was Mabel.

Mabel is interesting to me as she for me will be another half sister. Do I have a world record, having some many half siblings?

When I have straitened my thoughts I will begin the process of pulling the evidence out of the Internet, firstly I need to prove Monika is Ann Wright. (The same paten in Monika's eyes can be seen in Ann's.)

I do not know how I can prove that Susan Dixon is Mable.
Susan Dixon is a woman of the age that allows her to be Ann Wright's daughter. They work together! You are thinking this not the way to think! Here I will add I am learning to look for small intimate connections. Who is connected to who?

There is a red folder beside me, on its cover it says-
***Evidence of Eye Paten. Che Guevara/Ciro Bustos.***

If I had known I could find the eye paten! I never would have worried about DNA. Though the amount of films I have looked through and piles of photos was frightening. I was torn between knowing I had seen into Ciro's eyes, seen his eye paten and wanting to find it in Che's film/photos. Torn between believing and not believing I could find it.

Knowing if I could find it with the equipment I have, clear enough to see with the naked eye then a specialist camera can only confirm my findings. That file sits next to me now! I have done the same with Ann Wright.

I knew to be able to see the paten I needed to know they where there, for others to see was going to be hard. I had not reckoned that the man I showed then to would not take the trouble to even look at them, take a magnifying glass in his hand nor try to match the pixels.

To try to discuss with someone that has not taken the trouble to read or look into the material you have given them is frustrating. You cannot place arguments in front of someone who does not believe you. But if it was that easy then someone else would have found out the things I have; there would be a line of people in front of me!

With the disappointment of the response about the eye patens, I made my mind up to proved the evidence (they) needed. There are other options other than eye patens. Face mapping recognition for one and voice tracing for another. I have examples of the hand writing, as in photo copies, one example written by hand.

I have sent emails of to institutes that can offer me their forensic expertise. As it is Easter I am going to have to wait to get a reply.

There is reason to think they are on and the same person! Not just photos.

Gary Hart used a pen name when he wrote a book called 'I Che Guevara.' Gary Hart Wikipedia tells me an American politician, author, lawyer, professor. He served as a Democratic Senator representing Colorado (1984 and in 1988) he was considered as a frontrunner for the Democratic presidential nomination.

The fact that the book 'I Che Guevara.' Is about Che Guevara returning from the dead to start a new revolution in Cuba did strict me as interesting. (You cannot write about what you do not know!) The other book under his pen name John Blackthorn title is 'Sins of the Fathers' this book is about the cold war and nuclear stand that griped Cuba. The book revue tells me Gary Hart's books reads like someone who's been perusing this terrain for years.

This is where circles cross! Ann Wright is an active Democratic! Gary Hart is a Democratic! As is Daniel Ellsberg. He I am told in Wikipedia is a war political analyzer; working in the sixties-seventies and he is a translator as well as an author. He has written the foreword to 'Dissent: Voices of Conscience, by Ann Wright and Susan Dixon.

I can bring all these people into the same ring.

(Is Susan Dixon Ann Wright's daughter? They live on the same island; work at the same collage and write the same books.) If that is a question I want to answer; then I have a new question to add. (Is Christoph Röckerath Ann Wright's son?)

In the back of my mind is the growing thought- I had presumed that Christoph Röckerath was Che's half brothers son. Could he be Che/Ciro's son?

It was funny to think that the young man I sat next to in Ciro's flat as a cousin. Two years later to have the idea, he could be a half brother! If this thought is right then the number of half-siblings is thirteen.

I have come a long way from the woman standing under a dark night sky without any stars to state I am a member of the human race. Now I know I am part of a chain that every human wants to know, from where they come.


The Congo Diaries.
I asked myself the question- The Congo Diaries?
I started with the name-

Monika Ertl became Susana Elvira Miranda, she used the name Nancy Fanny on a trip to Hamburg, now using the name Ann Wright. It should not be a surprise to find her name connected to the books-

> Monticule Diaries. Written by Che.
> Bolivian Diaries.
> The Congo Diaries. Written by Ciro.

Che wants to see you.

*I have to point out that the titles differ as they change publishers But--- they are all owned by one man. Feltrinelli.*

Ann Wright was translating them and Patrick Camiller is also named as a translator. I have not yet looked fully into his profile but the quick glance I made, suggests he comes from the same stable. As do the other names that came up. Reading lists of names are boring but I do not know how best to explain this.

>The Book connection-
>Ann Wright.
>Che/Ciro
>Daniel Ellsberg.

*A USA military analyst, that likes to write forewords.*

*There is a documentary titled*
*'The Most Dangerous man in the world.'*

Jon Lee Anderson-

*(Not forgetting he spent three years with Aleida March. One year in a flat above Ciro Bustos. As Che/Ciro told me.)*

Lucia Alvarez de Toledo-

*Her name is credited to Alberto Granado's book 'Travelling with Che Guevara, the making of a Revolutionary.' (Mother of Che's half brother, She was a sectary to Che's father.)*

Lucia Alvarez de Toledo's *name is connected to-*
Elisabeth Burgos-Debray.

>Regis Debray. Richard Gott.

Richard Gott.
*He also likes writing forewords.*
Gabriel Garcia Marquer- he is a holder of a Nobel Prize for literature. *Elisabeth Burgos-Debray has also received a prize from them. The work was about Rigoberta Menchü a woman from Peru. It turned out to have been faked. This was discovered by David Stoll.*
Gabriel Garcia Marquer founded and served as Executive Director for the Film Institute Havana. Strange that is where you can find Alfrado Guevara, Che's Brother. No film is made in Cuba without his permission. It is easier to just say Gabriel Garcia Marquer is fully involved. His name pops up in another interesting circles!

     Giangiacomo Feltinelli.

Publishing house Giangiacomo Feltinelli Editor.
Giangiacomo Feltinelli.
He published all the books by
    Che Guevara
    Fidel Castro
    Regis Debray
    Ho Chi Minh
*Fidel Castro name connects with all lists. Pictures of him and those on the lists can be easily seen on the internet.*


    Chapter fourteen.
   Guests at the death party.
Photos as Evidence .

In the above picture you can see- Uncle Martin. Uncle Roberto.
Elisabeth Burges-Debary-Regis Debray- and Anna Karina- acting as Ciro Bustos' wife.

Look at the magazine- to see which players were there at the time! This includes Ciro Bustos' wife with another name- connected to Jean Luc Godard.

Magazine, Punto Final, where articles about-
Salvador Allende, Anna Karina- Jean Luc Godard-
Che Guevara and many others can be seen.

## Jean Luc Godard explica su arte

CON motivo de la presentación en Santiago del film Iban por lana (Bande a Part, con Anna Karina, Samy Frey y Claude Brasseur), del director francés Jean Luc Godard, es interesante analizar su modalidad cinematográfica a la luz de las propias explicaciones dadas por el cineasta. Dentro de una forma realista, multitemáticamente, este director va creando sobre la marcha, improvisando en el correr de la filmación, hasta dar con un clima, un espacio cinematográfico (que obedece a un elástico plan primitivo), y que se irá llenando con las captaciones que haga la cámara, junto al lenguaje y a los sonidos, en una banda sonora donde se confunden siempre —yuxtaponiéndose— la música y los ruidos de la calle.

Aunque cada película de Jean Luc Godard obedece a un tema central, el discurso del film muestra varias escenas o episodios que no siempre están imprescindiblemente ligados al asunto básico, sino que forman parte de cortea de la realidad, con los cuales se topa el ojo del director en los momentos en cine), es frecuente observar fuertes críticas a la estructura social que se da en la capital francesa. Hay, en la casi totalidad de sus films, escenas críticas captadas a la manera de un testimonio visual periodístico, pero elevado a una categoría estética: (por algo el propio Godard dice: "si algún sueño tengo, es el de poder ser algún día director del noticiero francés"). Esta dureza cinematográfica con el modo de vivir

Anna Karina, actriz que figura en el reparto de "Iban por lana" y en otros films de Godard.

Establishing who was there at the time.

Uncle Robert and Martin- as lawyers in Camiri for Ciro Bustos and Debray.

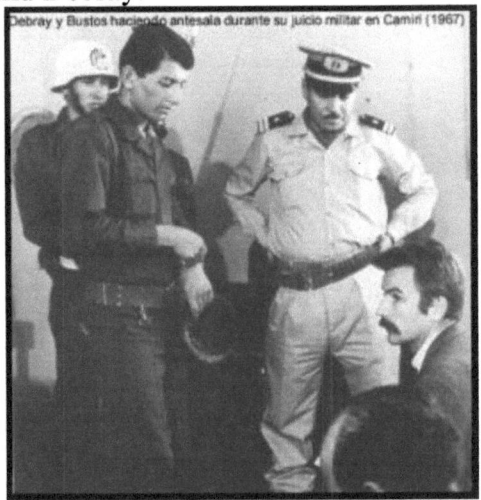

Website mit diesem Bild
... del Ejército Guerrillero del Pueblo (EGP),
que no fue capturado, ...
martinezestevez.wordpress.com

In the film 'Wege Der Revolution' www.icestorm.de
Regie: Manuel Perez, a Cuban.
In this film two men can be seen, Roberto Guevara- Martin Guevara- described as advisers and

integrators! Before the 'said' capture of Che Guevara.

Guests at the death party.
Supporting role guerrilla warier.
Giangiacomo Feltinelli.
*He it is said to have taken photos of Che's death pose, to send round the world.*
Richard Gott.
*A freelance journalist for the Guardian in Cuba, the Wikipedia page tells me he played a role in confirming the body was Che's.*
As Che's brothers were also attending this advent as military advisers. Not forgetting Che's half brother, who has written the script for Che/Ciro's film Sacrificio and is a prominent film producer Jean-luc Godard.

Other film producers like Jean-Pierre Kalfon, Jorge Masetti and Nestor Carlos Kirchner, who is a friend of Che's half brother and have known Che and Che's first wife in Mexico; Mexico is where Jorge G Castaneda came from, he is Guerrilla and author and a senior associate of the Institute for International Peace. *Ann Wright is a Peace activist. Elizabeth Burgos-Debray has his name in her files.* Richard Dingo who gave Jon Lee Anderson the Bolivian Diaries as Jon Lee Anderson states in his book. It is also said that Giangiacomo Feltinelli had them. (Feltinelli did print them.)

I have to ask the question, why Castro would want them. He is supposed to have left Che to rot in Bolivia.

Fifty million dollars

Christian Baudissin another film producer made the film 'Gesucht: Monika Ertl, Die Frau die Che Guevara Rachte'

She came to Hamburg to kill Roberto Quintanilla, the CIA/Bolivian Agent who is supposed to have given the order to shoot Che.

But when you read Jobst C. Knigge's 'Feltrinelli-Sine weg in den Terrorismus.' Humbolt Universitat (open Assess) Berlin 2010. Where it states----

*Giangiacomo Feltinelli- offered Roberto Quintanilla* **fifty million dollars** *for the life of Che Guevara.*

This makes you wonder!

The fact that Giangiacomo Feltinelli acted as escort and supplied the pistol Nancy Fanny/Monika

Ertl was supposed to have used to shoot Roberto Quintanilla in Hamburg.

My assumption is that Roberto Quintanilla's death was not to revenge Che's death- because he is not dead, but for the misuses of the funds Giangiacomo Feltinelli offered.

Feltrinelli: it is said provided the gun used to kill Roberto Quintanilla, Monika Ertl was given a choice of pistols. When I had read that statement, I asked myself why state that, why do you want me to look this way- Could Feltrinelli have been the killer? Monika Ertl would not have needed a wig, why drop her hand bag, pistol and then lose her wig.

My assumption is that it had all ready been decided to fake her death, date to be arranged. Feltrinelli was keen on keeping his cover; he did not need anyone accusing him of Roberto Quintanilla death. Fifty million is a strong motif.
(Feltinelli's violent death was a subject for conjecture.)

If I were to invite all these people to a party and those I have not at this point mentioned I would not have to introduce them to each other as they all ready know each other.

Giangiacomo Feltinelli was financing this action with his millions. The name Liliane Bettencourt has been mentioned before for her finical support for revolutionary ideas.

Elisabeth Burgos-Debray's Inventory Collection Summary records comments made by interviewees from former participants in guerrilla warfare in countries such as Venezuela, Guatemala, Colombia and Peru as well as Bolivia.

Other countries were looking for revolution. To the countries already mentioned add Chili.

(Sky News reported on the 24.5.2013 that nine Colombian soldiers were killed by ELN Marxist Guerrillas, Stemming from the ideas from Cuba.)

The statement Felix Rodriguez makes in the film Schnappschus mit Che comes to mind.

*The Bolivian people did not want nor did they require a revolution.*

I asked myself on hearing this statement why go there? Bolivia was the best place for a death party!?

Strangers celebrating in inaccessible places could create any information they needed to without being interrupted.

Elisabeth Burgos-Debray has kept news paper cutting from that time where they state that no one knew of Che's presence at the time of his death party.

*I wonder which stage I will find all thesis people on next.*

Feltrinelli- Sine Weg in den Terrorismus. By Jobst C. Knigge.

This document is proving to be most interesting. It is going to take me sometime to go through each name that has been mentioned. I had a few minutes to spare so I put in the name Lotta Continua. In my ignorance I had thought the name belonged to a person not a news paper.

This news paper was set up in Italy for the Fiat unions. Feltrinelli offered finical support. For this news paper to be legal in Italy it had to have a recognized reporter.

I had seen the name Pier Paolo Pasolini among the pages of 'Sine Weg in den Terrorismus' he was on my list. He is a film producer, a journalist. He was chosen to be the Lotta Continua's journalist.

Pier Paolo Pasolini, his face reminded of one of the two faces said to be that of Inti- Guodo Alvaro Peredo Leigue. (Che's replacement after his death party.) I am stunned by this thought.

I had wondered why there are photos showing two different Inties, Inti should be just one man. It had crossed my mind that one of the Inties was Roberto Guevara, Che's brother and Bustos lawyer. I had let the thought hang there, not knowing what to do with it.

Now Pier Paolo Pasolini face is in front of me, the likeness to the seconded Inti is very strong. As a god I turn the clock back to see the match strengthen. I decide that the tight curly hair seen on the seconded Inty's head has turned into strong wave hair can be explained away by those that have curly hair want straight hair, straight haired people want curls!

Now what! Feltrinelli and Pier Paolo Pasolini are in the game. Looking for Pier Paolo Pasolini has brought me back into the same circle, Teoponte.

Teoponte is where Luis Renato Almeida Pires/Che and the Inties are to be seen again. Bothe Daniel Cassol and Gustavo Rodriguez Ostra, the later was also a guerrilla warier, have written about this time.

The death of one Inti is explained to have happened at a safe house. Whereas Luis Renato Almeida Pires/Che body after it had been shot by the army was said to have been lost in the jungle.

The letter to Susan with Che's hand writing said to be that of Luis Renato Almeida Pires/Che brings me again into the circle leading to Ann Wright/Susana Elvira Miranda/Monika Ertl.

Guido Álvaro Peredo Leigue (Inti)

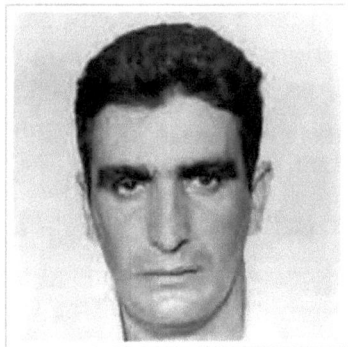

VILLACLARA
HÉROES ETERNOS DE LA PATRIA
Combatientes caídos en Bolivia

Guido Álvaro Peredo Leigue
cerrocalvo.blogspot.com

Guido Álvaro "Inti" Peredo
genealogiadelcheguevara.blogspot.com

Guido Alvaro Peredo Leigue 'Inty'. 'cerrocolvo. Blogspot.com' as this program comes from Santa Clara where the Che Guevara museum is, you would think they would know! In the same program you can see Lucio Ediberto Galvan Hidalgo. He looks like Guido Alvaro Peredo Leigue 'Inty' even though his chin is missing!

Drop into gehealogiadelcheguevara.blogspot.com

Pier Paolo Pasolini- paginecorsare.my blog.it.

Haydee Tamara Bunke/Susan Sontag

While reading Mr Knigge's Feltrinelli- Sein Weg in den Terrorismus. The idea was growing, if I thought the deaths of Che and one of the Inties and Monika were faked then could that be said of Tamara?

( Susan Sontag name also comes up at the end of 'Fidel & Gabo.' She was the lady that translated Che Guevara's work and she is connected to the ICAIC Insitituto Cubano del Art e Industria Cinematograficos and the UNEAC- Union of writers and artist of Cuba.)

Tamara Bunke and G Feltrinelli accusation can be seen in the Italian Wikipedia.

Feltrinelli's publishing has the book written by Ulises Estrada, about her time with Che. Ulises Estrada wanted to set up a home with Tamara Bunke and was with Che in Prague.

Susan Sontag's book 'Some Thought on the right way (for us) to love the Cuban Revolution.'

Haydée Tamara Bunke Bider - Wikipedia
https://it.wikipedia.org/.../Haydée_**Tamara_Bunke**_... ▼ Diese Seite übersetzen
Haydée **Tamara Bunke** Bider, più nota come Tania la Guerrigliera (Buenos Aires, 19 novembre .... inviata in Italia col nome di Marta Iriarte: impara l'italiano; (molto probabilmente è ospite presso l'editore Giangiacomo Feltrinelli a Milano).

There he attended high school and college, majoring in foreign languages.

- 1960 : Tania is the interpreter of Che Guevara , then Cuban minister, on a visit to the GDR
- 1961 : emigrated to Cuba and works to ' Havana as an interpreter at the ICAP, the Cuban Institute of Friendship with the Peoples, and at the Federation of Cuban Women
- 8 March 1963 : Tania is chosen by Che to join the revolutionary underground, and began attending the courses secrets of "illegal school" in Cienfuegos , Cuba
- 8 March 1964 : Tania is sent to Italy by the name of Martha Iriarte: learn Italian, (most likely a guest at the publisher Giangiacomo Feltrinelli in Milan.)
- Summer 1964 : it is the Cuban secret agent in West Germany and various European countries, Tania speaks several languages, German, English, Russian, French, Italian and Spanish
- Fall 1964 : it is sent in Latin America under the name of Laura Gutierrez Bauer, ethnologist of the profession, with Argentine citizenship; before going to Peru then he goes in Bolivia

 Haydee Tamara Bunke was born not far away from the Guevaras in Bonis Airas. Her family returned to East Germany where she studied. Coincidently at the same University as Mr. Knigge has placed his book. Humbolt in Berlin.

 Tamara had command of four languages, English, Russian, German and Spanish. Tamara loved photography, most photos of her show her with a camera.

 She was in Cuba for some time as a teacher, her teachers' identity card can be found on the internet.

 To say she was/is a spy extraordinaire is not to excaudate. The list of languages she could use made her attractive to many.

There is a film 'Che Guevara Der Tod und der Mythos. Documention, 1 2007 5-807-307. (I do not have a copy check) where it is stated while Tamara was traveling with Regis Debray and Ciro Bustos in Bolivia she was noted as being loud at a petrol station! And she left important documents in a car. In was inferred she was trying to draw attention to herself and her traveling companions. She trained in Cuban and East German-Russian centers, a spy of her caliber would not draw attention to her group *unless* they wished to draw attention to Che's planed death party!

Wikipedia states her body was pulled out of a river several days after she was said to have drowned. Her Paraná eaten remains are now in Cuba, Jan Lee Anderson offers this information.

After reading Mr. Knigge's Feltrinelli- Sein weg in den Terrorismus . I had a short list of women's names.

Two women's names proved interesting.
Yulene Olaizola and Susan Sontag.

Tamara Bunke 1964

Tamara.

http://www.juventudrebelde.cu/multimedia/fotografia/generales ...
martinezestevez.wordpress.com

Susan Sontag-sisyphe.org.

Looking at photos of Tamara and Yulene my first impression was Yulene Olaizola could be Susan Sontag's daughter!

Susan Sontag's photos and profile helped me to bring them together. Languages and the fact she is known as a translator. A keen photographer!

The fact Susan Sontag translated and edited Che's guerrilla warfare books cemented Tamara and Susan into one person.

Susan Sontag is in the same book circle as Ann Wright and Feltinelli's publishing house.

### Ulises Estrada Lescaille

Ulises Estrada Lescaille has written a book about Tamara.
He says they wanted to get married and have children.

Ulises Estrada Lescaille was with Che in Prague as well as in the Congo. His place in the skim of things is interesting. Guerrilla fighter, army commander, spy controller, drug trifling controller. He is known as an uprising organizer and closely connected to Che and Fidel Castro.

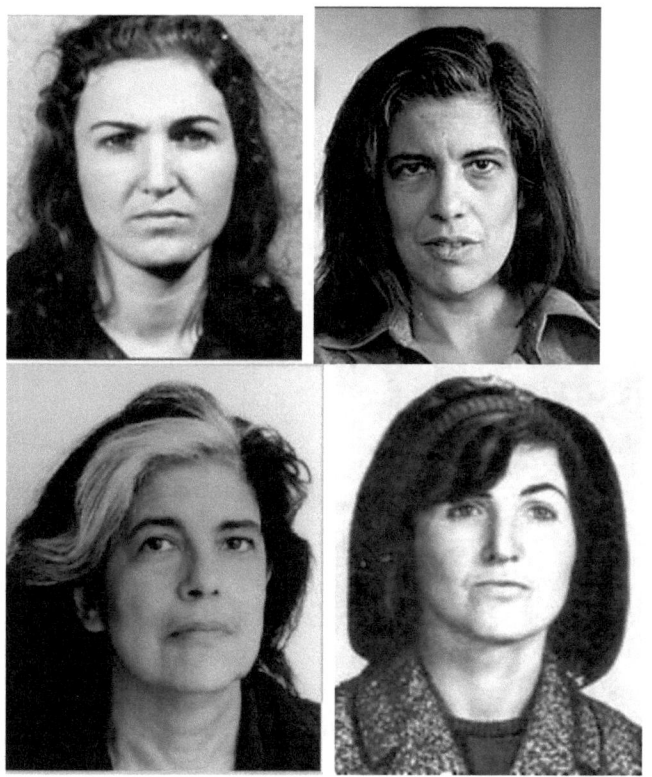

There are a few years between, but even so!

## Chapter fifteen
## The truth about the Revolution
## Cuba exported.

How can I now start to answer the question as to why go to all this trouble? Maybe this manuscript should be titled-

*The truth about the Revolution Cuba exported.*

A revolution exported by men and women using different names, faking their deaths to achieve a cover they could use in other countries and infiltrate left extreme groups, such as the Tupamaros, Black Panther, and PLO. Rot Brigade, Potere Operaio, others like RAF and Feltrinelli's GAP.
With the names of Giangiacomo Feltrinelli and Regis Debray, Rudi Dutschke, Andreas Baader, Raul Sendic.

Mix them in with prominent film producers, scriptwriters and actors to hide and disguise movements and plans.

There are so many names I could add here, many of those involved are still alive today.

*A lie would have no meaning if the truth is not perceived as dangerous.*

I read this while I was looking up Rafael Munoz Rivero. He writes about the Caribbean conspiracy, he has fifty five years of experience in public safety in the security area with state criminals.

Rafael Munoz Rivero words echo those of Juan F Benemelis who has written a document that offers an explanation. 'Las Guerras Secretas de Fidel Castro.'

Juan F Benemelis states that Fidel Castro spread a spy ring around the world.

Castro's ring interfered in all Latin America and African States. Undermined legally established governments.

Castro placed his spies into civil, tribal wars in other countries.

Took us all to close to a nuclear holocaust- many times!

Increase air piracy.

Castro continues to deploy disinformation to companies, espionage.

Sabotaging peaceful approaches to political problems.

Cuban armies ran Moscow's imperial designs. (Castro's guerrillas were never locked in the single purpose of Latin America. To name all the countries he has influenced would mean a long list spreading across the page. Influences, is not a word that should be used when violence is unlashed.)

I did sit up when I saw Northern Ireland name appear on the page written by Juan F Benemelis. I have watched over the years the Northern Ireland troubles, even sat at home while my first husband was serving in the English Army, there! I did not know his plans had an influence on my life even then.

I don't know then that Fidel Castro was controlling drug trafficking and its production or the need to course discontent around the world; using weapons and violence.

I know now why Bolivia was so important to Castro's plan. The land has a waterway known as the Green Road.

The Green Road tributaries have fingers that enter neighboring countries. It transport opportunities was what Castro wanted.

Jean Michel Cousteau made an expedition into the jungles of the Amazon in nineteen eighty one. He found a small Indian village with cocaine laboratories. The Indians questioned by Cousteau said on camera that cocaine was exchanged for weapons by the Cuban guerrilla group Guerrilleros 17group.

Not just countries like Bolivia were important to Castro's drug dealing. Angola had resources he need. Ships came to Hamburg to import and pick up raw materials need in processing heroin and cocaine.

I have left drugs to last as it shocked me to understand that Fidel Castro has his hands on all the drug production and its movement. He even sees it enters America.

*Juan F Benemelis' Las Guerras Secretas de Fidel Castro has opened my eyes as to why the world is as it is. He must know what he is talking about as he was an inner Cuban minister till he left in nineteen eighty eight. He is now living in Miami and he is a founder member of the Cuban museum, as is Felix Rodriguez the man that took the photo discussed in Snap Shot with Che, by Wilfried Huismann.*

Wilfried Huismann film points out that the photo is a montage. That was when I started to doubt that

Che's death was real. Juan F Benemelis's statements allow a Che Guevara death party and makes room for all the other changes of identity.

Castro's spies infiltrated, created a world I don't want to try to understand, but we live in, to say he was/is more dangerous as any leader/controller the modern world has ever seen is true and the more horrible as he has hidden in the shadows not wishing to be an enemy in the open. He is whispering his will into an all ready sick world.

Fidel Castro turned Cuba into a training camp, for warfare and specialist in spying techniques.

Juan F Benemelis's states that the Russians have in recent times have made costly investments in electronic surveillance in Lourdes, Havana. As Juan F Benemelis talks about events like Monika Lewinsky and other more resent happenings in the world today I have to except his statements.

*'Las Guerras Secretas de Fidel Castro.' Juan F Benemelis'*
*files lye next to Elizabeth Burgos-Debray's in the Hoover Instruction Archives.*

(Edward Snowden it was reported was planning to fly to or through Havana!)

What has this got to do with me? Che Guevara/Ciro Bustos was/is Castro's man.

When looking for information about Ricardo Alarcon De Quesada a Cuban minister and speaker in the EU; I found a paragraph that interested me. The writer is talking about the trial of Regis Debray and Ciro Bustos. He reminds me that they confirmed the presence of Che in Bolivia. But the remark in the Guardian newspaper that interested me the most is-

'The presence of Ernesto 'Che' Guevara in Bolivia has been confirmed by Argentine ***Castro-***communist Ciro Bustos.'
'hemeroteca-abc-es/nav/navigate.exe/…)

Ciro Bustos was a Castro man then, should not surprise anyone. Ciro has written a book with the help of Ann Wright and Jon Lee Anderson, Richard Gott and other members of Feltrinelli's book circle. 'Che wants to see you: Ciro Bustos. The untold story of Che Guevara.'

At this point I have not read his book; I am afraid I will not find the truth I am looking for in its pages.

## Chapter sixteen
## What now?

There is nothing to say I cannot present a short film. I can ask the question could this man, become this man? Why I think it is possible. And use the photo I took of the photo in Ciro's glass cabinet.

This photo was taken by me when I was in Ciro Bustos' flat. The photo of Ciro and I was taken when we first met. Over his head is the top half of Hilda Gadea and next to her is Carlos Nestor Kirchner the journalist and film producer who worked with Jean Juc Godard; he is with the Argentinean President with the same name.

(It has taken me a long time to come to terms with seeing my photo in Ciro's glass cabinet. You do not keep photos of people that do not mean anything to you. I would have long ago thrown away the photo if it did not mean something to me.)

My photo.

Carlos Nestor Kirchner is the name of the man standing next to Hilda Gadea; you can only see the top of her head above the photo of Ciro and me.

# Néstor Carlos Kirchner

Otro Cámpora, pero extemporáneo.

Carlos Nestor Kirchner is a film producer; I already knew that as he is in a film about film producers such as Jean Luc Godard, Truffaut. This film was on German television, 'Nouvella Vague-Aussenansichten.' I did see it on Art's internet side but I could not open it nor could get it to give me his name. He could have used another name as a film producer.

It is his name and face in the internet terrorist programs from Argentina.

To find Carlos Nestor Kirchner is the name of the president of Argentina, he was active politically at the same time as guerrilla Carlos Nestor Kirchner. I have even found a photo of both Carlos Nestor Kirchners riding on a tank with a Che Guevara flag.

abelfer.wordpress.com

2076896387. 86dc8d96f7 jpg Flickriver.com
It says under this photo, who they are, my opinion is president Kirchner is the third man from the left. Best of friends Kirchner is the first man from the right; I think the mug shot used in the terrorist programs has been taken from this.

Lahistoriaargentinacompleta.blogspot.com/2007
Diariopamperoarchivos.blogspot.com
Are programs where you can find many of the people I am talking about.

When I was with Ciro for the second time, it was he that told me Hilda was the sweet looking woman in his glass cabinet standing next to a tall young man and they were in Mexico City. It had to be in the fifties! Meaning the association with the big bear Carlos Nestor Kirchner was a long standing one. The president Carlos Nestor Kirchner was a small man with eyes that drew your attention.

The other men in the photo names are Eluardo Duhalde, Ramon Ortega, and Carlos Ruckauf. They can be found it programs where they are other interesting people such as Miguel Bonasso, another guerrilla, film producer and Rudolf Walsh, who I say used the name among others, Jean Jug Godard and is Che/Ciro's half brother.

There is another photo where I think both Carlos Nestor Kirchners are, this time with one of the Nestor's wives, Cristina she took on the Argentinean presidency after her husband's death.

Menenk png-Urgente24.com.

a) Carlos Nestor Kirchner was a close associate to Jean Luc Godard.
 He is photographed standing next to Hilda Gadea-Che Guevara's first wife!

This photo was taken when I visited Ciro Bustos.
b) Carlos Nestor Kirchner was the president of Argentina, His lady wife was president after him.

The question is did they use names as the American did to confuse everyone? Or just to confuse me?

While I was dipping in the internet programs about Carlos Nestor Kirchners I found this photo.

Soberania org – de como Fidel maneja a Chavez.
I also saw it in one of Juan F Benemdis programs. I had thought that Henry Engler could have been one of the men in my mother's album. Wikipedia did say he was born in nineteen forty-four. Henry Engler was nice enough to reply to an email, to say he would have been nine years old at the time of the photo.

The first man in the photo is Hector Perez Marcano, (el Macho) the footballer and the man in my mother's album?!

The second is a man called Almerico Siliva.

The next is Raul Menendez Tomassevich. (Toma)

Silvio Garcia and Moises Moleiro are the two men on the right.

It is Raul Menendez Tomassevich and Hector Perez Marcano that interest me. After making a mistake about Henry Engler I was more careful with my research before coming to any conclusion about them.

Raul Menendez Tomassevich was a general in Castro brother's military he can be seen as a close friend of Alfrado Guevara the head if films. He was a close friend of Fidel and was at school in Santiago de Cuba. Fidel Castro was also schooled in Santiago de Cuba.

He was one of the men that attacked the Moncada Barracks on July the twenty six, nineteen sixty three. It is celebrated today. (July 26 Movement.) (The July 26 movement was contributed to eighty two men- the same number as it was said the Granma carried to Cuba.)

Hector Perez Marcano was also a high ranking commander. He was known to have been with the Castros from the nineteen fifties onwards!

The two above men are more likely to be the men in the album. I put in brackets that the July 26 movement was contributed to eighty two men- the same number as it was said the Granma carried to Cuba according to Wikipedia.

According to Wikipedia the Granma was a boat built to carry twelve men. I ask how can such a boat carry so many men and the extra fuel it has been reported was need to make the journey from Tuxpan Mexico to the lower end of Cuba? Another tall story? I have not been able to find a list of the eighty two men involved in The July 26 Movement. I have not been able to find a list of the eighty two men said to have been on the Granma. (One of the Wikipedia's says there were twenty men, who can be said to have been on the Granma including Castro and Che. In the same Wikipedia it says only fifteen survived this trip.) I could not find out who had attended the training camp in Mexico. That there was a training camp is fact. I did find the name of the expert that instructed the men in Military combat and guerrilla warfare,

Alberto Bayo y Giroud.

Albert Bayo was born in eighteen ninety two in Cuba. Vikipedi 'the Spanish Wikipedia' tells me he was a teacher of English and French and had spent time in France; he had been active in the Spanish civil war. He became one of the most important commanders in the Cuban Revolution. It was he that chose the men from the Mexican training that were to go to start the Cuban Revolution. There are other ways to travel to Cuba and not waste the lives of trained men.

Alberto Bayo has written so many books about guerrilla and military combat they would fill a library.

I wonder is my birth mother's album the proof that Raul Menendez Tomassevich and Hector Perez Marcano were present at the camp. (I had always thought that Frank Pais was the younger man in the photo.)

Alberto Bayo, 1959 (Charlie Seiglie/Bohemia)
cuba1952-1959.blogspot.com
Alberto Bayo – Wikipedia
*de.wikipedia.org/wiki/Alberto_Bayo*
*Bayo* war Sohn des spanischen Offiziers Pedro *Bayo* Guia und der aus Puerto .... Mis versos de rebeldía (Mexiko 1958); Sangre en *Cuba* (Mexiko 1958); Mi aporte a la ... El *general* que adiestró a la guerrilla de Castro y el Che, Debate 2007.
Alberto Bayo - Wikipedia, the free encyclopedia
*en.wikipedia.org/wiki/Alberto_Bayo*
He was born in *Cuba* and studied in the United States and Spain. *Bayo's* most ... the same period.

Alberto *Bayo* died a *General* of the *Cuban* Armed Forces.

This man's profile is interesting! He was noted for his acts in the Spanish Civil War. He was the general that to trained the men for the Granma trip to Cuba. 1956. This man's image does not match that of General Bayo shown in Che Guevara's own account (OTRA VEZ).

 Bayo (Segundo de izquierda a derecha) independent.typepad.com

Or is he this man?
Alberto Bayo as seen in Back on the road.
(otra vez) Che Guevara.

Or is he this man?

General Enrique Jurado-
There is more to say about him-
'Gabriel Garcia Marquez the creator of Che Guevara.'

"Che" (centre) with Reinaldo Benítez Nápoles, Alberto Bayo and Universo Sánchez at the Miguel E. Schulz 136 prison.

"Che" (centre) with Reinaldo Benítez Nápoles, Alberto Bayo and Universo Sánchez at the Miguel E. Schulz 136 prison.

**Another pair of different men with the same names, closes to Che Guevara?**

General Enrique Jurado- General Bayo-

Chapter seventeen
-WATERGATE 1972-

You are wondering why I have written Watergate. I decided to look at Watergate because I remember that the burglars were said to have been Cuban.

The names I see are names I saw when looking into the death of Kennedy 1963.

Funny to think I thought- Che was on the killing team I would never have guest he was sitting in Dallas waiting to take his part in a Coup that Kennedy was plotting.

(I still cannot answer the question was he Kennedy's man or Castro's)

                Virgilio Gonazalez.
                Bernard Backer.
                James Mmcord.
                Frank Sturgis.
                Eugeno Martinez.

I read Eugeno Martinez's account of the brake in to the offices in the Watergate hotel compound. He brought my attention to Eduardo- Howard Hunt. (Another Kennedy death connection.)

Eugeno Martinez and the others were asked to enter the office of Dr Fielding. They had been asked to get Daniel Ellsberg's papers. Dr Fielding was supposed to be Daniel Ellsberg's psychiatrist.

The five Cubans were convinced Howard Hunt had an important position in the White House. Eugeno Martinez sates, they were given equipment that would not lead them back to the White house.

In Eugeno Martinez's account he states the he was told Eduardo- Howard Hunt had information that Fidel Castro and others were giving money to George McGovern.

George McGovern was the Democratic Party presidential nominee for the 1972 presidential elections. Their group was to break into the McGovern head quarters.

Eduardo- Howard Hunt informed them that Castro's money was going into the Democratic National head quarters.

**The Watergate brake in was to get evidence of this.**

Nixon had a million dollars to pay the men not to speak of their search for this evidence.

Daniel Ellsberg is a Democrat as is Ann Wright/Monika Ertl. Susan Sontag/Tamara Bunker is also in their political circles.

Castro was putting money into their political party. Frank Sturgis- he was connected to Marta Lorenz, Fidel Castro's lover, she was persuaded to make a murder attempt on him by Frank Sturgis and others. Frank Sturgis was in the same working cell as Lee Heavy Oswald.

Eduardo- Howard Hunt. Just read what Slate Magazine says.

The Slate Magazine asks questions like; did Hunt know what happened in the days before the death party? Did he know the real story?

To cut the answer short, he said, that our people at the National Security Agency kept tracks on Che's band. The Bolivians wanted to wash their hands of him. Hunts people kept the Bolivian Army informed.

Hunt was asked who killed Che, was it a Bay of Pigs member Felix Rodriguez? He said no it was the Bolivians.

Strange remark to make- We made it possible for Che to be killed. What did Hunt mean by deniability?

Slate asked if Hunt thought Che would become a hero? The answer was, no. But then he said; the Bolivian colonel with foresight cut Che's hands off. When was asked why Hunt replied, it was a good idea, he could not be identified by his fingerprints. A good idea if you don't want a body identified.

In the article I read it did not name the colonel! Hunt said he did not know whose idea it was; the Bolivian colonel or the CIA. Interestingly when Hunt discussed the death with Felix Rodriguez, he had said, they had fooled around with the body a day or two before disposing the body.

Here I have to say there is yet another version about what happened at Che's death party. I have seen many photos of Che on a medical table, he had his hands. Fancy, Hunt got the idea from Felix Rodriguez that the Bolivian colonel sloppy had a shallow grave dug to dump his body in.
This account does not match what he, Felix Rodriguez states in the film ´Schnappschuss mit Che.'

When I read Che's hands had been cut off so his body couldn't be identified by its fingerprints and that it was a pretty good idea—if you don't want somebody identified.
I could only nod.

Felix Rodriguez name is dominant-

Juan F Benemelis- was Castro's intern minister till 1988,
He has written Las Guerras Secretas de Fidel Castro.
Both men are in the same stable- Cuban Museum, Inc. And uses the same contact email address!

The Cuban Museum is filled with the Bay of Pigs invasion memorabilia and the artifacts Felix Rodriguez brought back from Che's death party.

The Slate asked Eduardo- Howard Hunt about Kennedy's death, Assassination. He is asked if he knew the conspiracy idea about David Atlee

Phillips—the Miami CIA station chief—was involved with the assassination of JFK. Hunt did not have anything to say.

The Slate thinks that Eduardo- Howard Hunt hired David Atlee Phillips to work with him in Mexico and to assist with Guatemalan propaganda.

Hunt said in the Slate that that David Atlee Phillips was one of the 'Briefers he ever saw' whatever that is.!

Eduardo- Howard Hunt was asked if he was in Dallas on the day of JFK Assassination. There is no record of a reply.

Frank Sturgis- was in and around Dallas at the time of Kennedy's assassination and so was Howard Hunt! And so was Che Guevara.

This not a history book it is an account of how I found how things came together. If you read between the lines Howard Hunt knew of Che Guevara from his time in Guatemala 1954 and he suggests Che had been in Cuba at this time.

Eduardo Howard Hunt you could call him a super spy master.

If you think I am telling a tall story- it was Fidel Castro that paid money to the Democrat party in the U.S.A To the very circle of people I see are involved in this cover-up.

## Otto Reich.

Sundays' afternoon can be boring, I took up an old habit, I put in Otto Reich's name in the search programs. His name I found when looking into

Watergate, having followed E Howard Hunt and his associates.

Otto Reich as it happens is an U.S.A diplomat, he was Ambassador to Venezuela, a Ragan man, a Bush man, and he was born in Cuba. Involved in the Contra affair in Nicaragua. His Wikipedia is interesting to read.

I put Ciro Bustos' name next to his, I had not taken Venezuela away.
(Under this hat are accounts of Che's Death party, people like Regis Debray's account amongst others.)
www.latogata.org/che/nuevos/che_ felixhtm gave me Felix Rodriguez Mendigutia: the man who killed Che. Was the first article to appear. Otto Reich is not mentioned in this article or any that followed and Ciro Bustos only gets a mention on passing.

This account explains the order of events leading up to the moment they said Che was shot.

The next account I read.
Felix Rodriguez Mendigutia El Hombre que asesino… Archive C
www.Archivechile.com
Varios Relatos sobre el asesinato del Che Guevara.
Baracuteycubano.blogspot.com/…/varios-relatos-sob…

They also explain the order of events leading up the moment they said Che was shot. The wording was the same but the names they used were different.

>As a normal person can only die once.
>Shot/killed by one built.

## Chapter eighteen
There should only be one account.
To answer the question, why so many different versions- they are to hide the real purpose of the sheared.

The second version of events is said to be believable as it comes from Jon Lee Anderson's stable. Jon Lee Anderson says he spoke with Ciro Bustos in Malmo, Sweden. (Ciro said as much when I was there with my friend Silk.)

The film 'Sacrificio' has its text written by Luciano Monteagudo, (he has a box address in Stockholm, Sweden) another name used by Jean Luc Godard, Che's half brother. The film 'Sacrificio' the company that made this film is in Jean Luc Godard hands. It is a Swedish company.

I thought there were many circles, but it is only one. Those acting as Guerrillas took me into the book circle. (Daniel Ellsberg and Ann Wright amongst others!) The book circle bleeds into the U.S.A Demarcate party, with the consequence of Watergate. (Watergate-money from Castro.) Watergate had the same gang of C.I.A men that were active in the assassination of Kennedy.

It is known C.I.A men shared the same code names, when working on the same projects- Che Guevara and Felix Rodriguez, Oliver North for instance!

The plan to kill Kennedy was a plan that was intended to get rid of a man who had put his nation between the U.S.A and U.S.S.R. Many of the actors were in Dallas on that day!

Just take another identity, start another field of unrest. Hide drug production in the mists of war to feed the need for weapons.

In the middle of this circle is one name Fidel Castro.
From this point the circle opens out to take us all in. It has touched all our lives, our husbands have been sent into war zones that have been manipulated. Lands have been rapped sending its folk to walk down unknown high streets. Our kids use drugs that have been in the hands of the drug godfather. If you control the world drugs you also control our medicines.

This was not what I was expecting to find when I started to look for my father. I wish this was a tall story.

## Chapter nineteen
## The Map

I made a map of events and the connection of people. I did this on clear paper, to look from above you see a spider's web! But peel away the different levels to see who, how and why.

The center of this web is Fidel Castro, Che Guevara, and Roul Castro.

Kennedy's assignation- Watergate- Che's death party how they entwine. With other members of the family threading through, the parts they played and how other people contributed to the spiders' web. To see which way money followed, to whom from whom gives a clear picture of why.

The next thing I did was to look at Ciro Bustos' toothbrush.

I have his DNA, I have a witness that can state I took it, and his emails remarking he is not pleased I took it.

It proves I have Ciro's DNA. Where else can you find his DNA? We are artist! We paint with hand and mind, which means his DNA will be in his work as mine is in my work.

(I can identify Ciro Bustos' DNA)

Che's letters and diaries have been through some many hands his DNA maybe lost- there must be a reliable source.

I would not trust a DNA sample give by those in the spiders' web. Though the uncles and aunt could provide that key should they wish!

It was while I was looking into where Ciro's work can be found I stumbled over something unexpected. Under the sample of hand writing that was familiar to me I read it was that of Tania. Tania Bunker. But then so did the sample saying it was a letter written by 'Victor' Casildo Condori to his wife Nancy de Condori and a third example this time contributed to 'Medico Moro' even I think this cannot be possible. Museo Ernesto Che Guevara Primer Muse Suramericano:ania la argentina comba…
http://museocheguevaraargentina.blogspot.de/2013/05/tania-la-argentina-combatiene-...

I have spent hours comparing Bustos/Che's handwriting and that of the lament to Inti' death, Regis Debray states it is written in Monika Ertl's own handwriting.

Five people with similar handwriting, not to mention Victor and Medico Moro. All in the same political circle, in the same place in time!

The explanation in Norberto Forgione's states the letters were recently found, some fifty years later. The letters were said to be for members of their families. It is interesting to note that the author of this report, Norberto. Suggest that Regis Debray and Ciro Bustos could have been intending to carry the letters to their recipients.

(It had to be Ciro Bustos. -*If I am right*- It makes sense to write such letters, it makes sense that Ciro/Che would write such letters- I wonder if they carried a message hidden in their wording?) (I have another solution to the handwriting muddle, I will explain in the chapter where I take the subject on!)

> Moisés: 157
>
> Ordena los hombres suficientes para hacerles la cosa a los zapateros si no entorpece otros trabajos por más importantes.
>
> En la primera oportunidad hay que hablar con Benítez. Se lo dices.
>
> Che
> Junio 11/58

cuba-cuban-signed-che-guevara-autograph-manuscript-document-ebay.com

> Ciro Bustos, pintor argentino que reside en Suecia desde hace unos ocho o nueve años, fue y es un gran amigo; a los dos años de estar yo en Buenos Aires nos conocimos y participábamos en una peña; la que frecuentábamos los sábados a la noche, allí el que no era pintor era periodista o dibujante. Los abatares de la vida nos separaron hace muchos años pero la amistad es de lazo más fuerte que une a los seres humanos de buena voluntad. La trayectoria de mi amigo Bustos está llena de emociones humanas las que hicieron de él un peregrino del arte. Esta muestra pictórica es el mensaje más íntimo y profundo que nos brinda en este mes de

Ciro Bustos

Chapter twenty
Letters found.

I am wondering around thinking I am a mad woman! I have sent an email right into the lion's den Norberto makes his living from the Che Guevara story; what's more he is a Gurvaraist! And he is a psychologist, activist. I did this without even thing to looking up who he is!

While I was waiting to see if Norberto will answer my email I look him up!

In INFO/news- is a film- the revolutionary, 'The official guerrila.' It is even worse that I thought! Norberto has directed a film about Che. 'De sus Queridas Presencias' It gets even worse- there is another man sitting next to Norberto.
Jorge Denti, a filmmaker. His film is titled, 'The footprint Doctor Ernesto Guevara.'

The third man makes my toes curl. Jean Martin Guevara.

Norberto is sitting next to my uncle. Small world! The English transcript of this program made comments that soothed me.

Uncle Martin talks about Che's birthday, he states it is the eighteenth of May not the fourteenth. (A bit suspect for a brother to have a four day difference for Che's birthday!) That Roul Castro and Che worked for a famous doctor researching allergies. Cats and dogs along with the rabbits around the hospital disappeared. Jorge Denti suggests that their disappearance was due to the researchers needing to excrement on live animals.

Uncle Martin confirms that Che met with Kennedy in secret. There are two names Uncle Martin mentions in his sentence about meeting with Kennedy.
Arturo Frondiz- Argentinien president 1958-1962.
Janio Quadros- Brasillin president 1961.
(Those names I have seen in Renato's hand written letters.)

Uncle Martin says that a Guevara cousin, Raul Lynch was Argentina's ambassador to Cuba when the revolution triumphed.

I find this statement interesting; Che must have found comfort knowing he had a cousin in Havana.

The next surprise was Norberto replayed to my email.

In his first statement he notes that sample-

(A) Is Che Guevara handwriting- it was from the sample for the art exposition invitation written by Ciro Bustos. Nineteen eighty seven.

(B) Sample (B) was from the diary hanging on the wall in 'Benigno' Dariel Alarcön's flat I took from the film 'Snapshot with Che'. Sample

(C) (C) Was from the letter to Susan.

(All similar and matching to Tania Bunkers letter!)

In Norberto's replay he suggests the writing is shown to an expert. For me that is a step forward!

I mutter in my next email that I am very careful about where I take my writing samples from. Had I not known that Inge Feltinelli- Giangiacomo Feltrinelli's wife at that time was Jewish I would have been suspicious of the sample the Jewish emestocheguevara-oleida.blogspot.com were annualizing. From their example I have taken a copy to show as Che's.

Please do not think I have against anything Jewish.

I am not at this point ready to talk with Norbert on Skype, but I suggested while we are waiting to install Skype could he answer some of my questions. I wanted to know If Uncle Martin is a friend of Norberto, what was his relationship with Jorge Denti.

Norberto told me he is friends with Uncle Martin. Jorge Denti lives in Mexico. That they are to be seen on the YouTube film-
http://www.youtube.com/watch?v=tvarybZjxOo

I did not want to spoil his fun by saying I had already seen it and was using its information.

I slipped in the name of Raffaele Bernetti as Norberto had said he was in Bolivia at the time the Body of Che was being sort for by the Argentine Forensic Anthropology team and the Cuban geophysicists.

Raffaela Bernetti and Stefano Missio made the Film 'Che Guevara the body and the legend.' A B&B Film s.r.l Italy 2007. I do not have an s.b.n number for it, as the copy I have was sent to me by Raffaela Bernetti, thankfully in English some years ago. I had offered him an explanation as to why I thought their findings were correct but they did not take me seriously. (They are not convinced that the body could be that of Che Guevara.)

Norberto said he knew Raffaela Bernetti had made a film about Che; I asked him to look at it.

I also asked him to show Uncle Martin the sample of hand writing. I want to know what Uncle Martin's reaction is. (At this point I have not said I am related.) (I wish I could be a fly in the wall when he dose confront Uncle Martin!)

While I am waiting to see what the reaction is to all of this is I decide to look Jorge Denti up! The first question that came to mind was- why is he interested in Che's younger life? Alberto Grundy was a friend of his. Where was I to look, in the world of film or Che's relationships in Mexico?

I took a pencil and made another map!
'On the Trail of Dr Ernesto Guevara.' is the film Jorge Denti has made, he is in the middle, Uncle Martin is one side of him and Ciro Bustos; is on the other. Wikipedia's Ciro's book is quoted as a reference Jorge Denti used. 'Che wants to see you.'

There is a line going down the middle of my map leading to Pier Paolo Pasolini- Jean Luc Godard, Che's film star sister.

In a Blog about Jorge Denti called Cinema dated 11/6/2013. It tells me he spent years in Italy from 1966. In Italy he formed the *Collective Third World Cinema*. He filmed in its name, in Palestine and Vietnam and Bolivia. He returned to his native Argentina in 1973 where he stayed until he took refuge in Mexico in 1976, following the abduction and murder of Raymundo Gleyzer, his friend and companion in the film group the *Collective Third World Cinema.*

When I looked up Raymundo Gleyzer, I found he looked like a young Jorge Denti. When I read that Raymundo Gleyzer and Jorge Muller along with Carmon Bueno had been tortured and then gone missing in 1976, I also saw Rodolfo Walsh's name on this list of those that had gone missing-

(*Rodolfo Walsh is a name Jean Luc Godard has used. Che Guevara's half-brother.*)

I was so surprised to see Che's half-brothers name I did not take down the reference, I did not panic to find it again as there are many websites stating the aforementioned had gone missing, their bodies had not been found. (Where have I heard that before?)

Jorge Muller and Carmon Bueno were in the film busyness, actress and camera man; their names are mentioned in the same references.

I am going to ask Norberto if he has access to face recognition programs.

Photos Raymundo Gleyzer.
 Raymundo Gleyzer peoplecheck.de
  (A)Website mit diesem Bild
Se extiende el plazo para la mandar proyectos en el Concurso ...abcguionistas.com
Desaparecidos:Raymund Gleyzer Desaparecidios.org

Jorge Denti: "Ernesto Guevara era el ejemplo de cómo tiene que ser ...laprimeraperu.pe

Festival Internacional de Cine en Guadalajara - La huella del Dr ...ficg.mx twicsy@searchles.com

It was with surprise when I could connect Norberto Forgione and Jorge Denti. Should you look up the above photos you will think the same! I mention this only to demonstrate to have different identities is more common than you think.
As it is none of my busyness I have not open the photos again.

*Collective Third World Cinema.*

Now I know who was in charge of the whole Film Industry in Latin America I understand better how they managed to get away with such a plan. To say the whole thing was planned as a film script is not to use the wrong metaphor.

Alfredo Guevara. Che's uncle was the big boss of the '*Collective Third World Cinema in Latin America.*' The film company had control over all productions!

Uncle Alfredo did not just control Cuba's film industry; he controlled all of Latin America as will. How am I going to explain to people like Norberto that we have been blinded by the light of the Guevara family and the Castros?

Members of Guevara family.
Alfredo Guevara Lynch- a brother of Che's father, Lynch side.

Alfredo Guevara. Che's uncle was the big boss of the '*Collective Third World Cinema in Latin America.*' The film company had control over all productions!

Uncle Alfredo did not just control Cuba's film industry; he controlled all of Latin America as will. Raul Lynch full name is Raul Aureliano Lynch y Fri.

He was an Argentina Admiral-ambassador in Cuba (1957-1983) Raul Lynch was Argentina's ambassador to Cuba when the revolution triumphed. If I had known there is more to this!
Gabriel Garcia Marquez the creator of Che Guevara!

Chapter twenty one
My Father's Book-
'Che Wants to see you. The untold story of Che Guevara.'

I had the original in my hands when I first visited Ciro in 2010. I even offered to translate for him as it had not been published in English. Joke really to say that; I would have translated it with a computer program! I did not know at the time of offering Ann Wright was in the process of translating it. The book circle!

It came out in March of 2013. I did not want to read it, but the Christmas of 2013 I diced to get a copy. For me it was not going to be a book to enjoy, I had decided to take it apart. It now has coloured markers in its pages and a collage block has notes and question arising from it. There were many names I recognized. I worked my way through the names I did not know and remixed names with those I did.

My notes.

Chapter 3= My journey to the Island-April 1961, tells of the trip to Cuba, of how the captain of the ship would not dock his ship in Havana as the Bay of Pigs invasion was in process.

   Ciro tells of the people trapped by the suspension of flights after the Bay of Pigs invasion; he flew with to Cuba's international airport.

   Jon Lee Anderson's book 'Che Guevara a Revolutionary Life.'
States on page 506 of the copy I have, the last paragraph states Ciro Bustos and his wife were in the crowd listening to Fidel Castro's historic speech. This is the moment when Ciro decides to join the revolution! Nest paragraph tells us that 1500 men strong Cuban exile Liberation Army came ashore at the Bay of Pigs, Playa Giron.

   It was the on reading Jon Lee Anderson's first reference to Ciro Bustos involvement and Jorge Casantaneda's lack of interest of Ciro in his book. I think it was he that told me that Ciro painted wonderful portraits of people without faces. Ciro had to be interesting as he is an artist.

I am an artist! This where I came in.

This might not be an important point to some, but to me it is, as it was at the first time my attention was drawn to Ciro, I remarked it was like a new actor was being placed in a novel- to be used later he had to start somewhere!

Jon Lee Anderson says he spent three years working on his biography in Cuba with Che's second wife.

Ciro told me and my friend Silke that Jon Lee Anderson had lived in the flat above him in Malmo for one year.
(Ciro moved down a flat between 2010 and the next time I visited him in 2012)(Jon Lee Anderson would have been there between 1993 and 1996, six months each way before his book was published in 1997) Copyright for Jon Lee Anderson's book 'Che Guevara a Revolutionary Life. 'Is dated 1997.

       Manuel Pineiro Losada

Manuel Pineiro Losada alias ‚'Red Beard' Fidel Castro's spymaster treated Jon Lee Anderson as a friend. He, Red Beard came out of the shadows to help clear up some of the mysteries created around Che! (Help write them!?)

Ciro Bustos states in his book the Manuel Pineiro Losada alias ‚'Red Beard'Fidel Castro's spymaster and his team leader knew his identity. (Good to have friends!) (When you are writing!)

       Tania Bunka

Tania Bunke's name came onto my computer screen it was in an article tell me about her death. They had cut her hair and removed her breasts. Horrible! Did I not read that she had been found drowned in a river, not easy to recognize as piranhas had eaten her. If I did not know she took on a new identity I would be so confused. You can only die once.

Norberto Forgione has found copies of the letters to be given to relations that I believe to be in Ciro/Che's handwriting, the discrepancies now can be explained. Ciro/Che had instruction in preparing documents-passports to fit any situation. Ciro is an artist/craftsman.

Looking up Alfredo Hellman he remarks in his had thirty different names to travel around the world with. Alfredo Hellman was Mendozer regional secretary and member of the Central Committee.

### Lenardo Werthein

Lenardo Werthein name lead me to a program titled, 'Jounal Pampero Cordubensis. The editor is a Gabriel Pautasso.

Three things came out of this that surprised me. (Point A I have not found much to confirm this.)

- A) My grandmother was from a Russian Jewish family.
- B) That Mario Vargas Llosa says that the bones in Cuba's mausoleum are not Che Guevara's.

Mario Vargas Llosa newspaper account from 10/3/2007 is the ‚Bones of Che'

C) The account Ciro tells about building a guerrilla arm matches nearly word for word an account in, 'Journal Pampero Cordubensis. By Masetti.

I had asked the editor of the journal who had written the report about the Salta Guerrillas as I was not sure the computer translation had not muddled up the author.

If Masetti was the author why is the account so near, word for word to the account I have read in Ciro Bustos book? As nothing before seems to match between one author to another is strange.

A revolutionary should be a solitary soul, but history shows they had lots of children, as if the starting point for revolution is love-Che want to see you. Stuck in my mind as both men used it. Masetti to make a revolution there must be love. - in Pampero Journal.

To talk about men dying of starvation, having to cook roots herbs is one thing but to use the same references is another!

The account written by Jon Lee Anderson of the time before the death party is also to liken to Ciro Bustos and Masetti's account of Salt. If you think I am thinking rubbish can you answer one question? Why make the same mistake twice?

A child only puts it fingers into a flame once.

My grandmother was from a Russian Jewish family.

I do not know how to take this, life is strange enough without having to face another- is this possible!?

In 'Jounal Pampero Cordubensis. Antonio Rodriguez says my grandmother was a sister to Ariel Sharon's father.

As he's state of health was remarked upon at the time I read Antonio Rodriguez's report I had the opportunity to see his face. It was not until the media reported his death after he had been in a comer for eight years, did I get a chance to look into his eyes. The question on my mind was; did he have similar eye paten as Celia Guevara? The question was not easy to answer as the eyes I could look into, shown on the television seemed to be a soft gray/brown but did show a dark blue outer ring.

When I have finished my research into other maters I will come back to seeing if there is a family connection to Ariel Sharon.

There is a positive side to this, when I was standing outside my farm house thirteen years ago, before my search began, I looked up into a starless sky. I was alone, without others like me. I was like a stone in a desert where no other stones were.

Now there are many stones that have become brothers and sisters, aunts and uncles, a mother a father and grandparents. Everything a normal human has. (Even if I cannot take them into my arms they are a part of me.)

That Mario Vargas Llosa says that the bones in Cuba's mausoleum are not Che Guevara's.

This newspaper account is from 10/3/2007 is the ‚Bones of Che, I found its' reference in 'Jounal Pampero Cordubensis.
As this is the second reference I have come across suggesting the body is not who they say it is.

The first being the film I saw by Raffaele Brunetti and Stefano Missio. 'Che Guevara: The Body and the Legend.' where the for-mentioned have the same opinion; they show how they formed their opinion.

The next reference I came across was from Alvaro Vargas Llosa. He tells me that Fidel Castro had given orders to provide evidence for his propaganda. Mario Vargas Llosa!

The penny did not drop till I compared their names and looked both men up in 'Wikipedia' they are father and son. Silly me they look alike.

Mario Vargas Llosa. He is in my book circle.

Mario Vargas Llosa- is interesting; he was a candidate for the governing penmanship in Peru. Now he is living in Spain.

Alvaro Vargas Llosa. Is a political commentator, his books about Fidel Castro or Che Guevara, do not seem to be complementary.

In the research to find email address and contact address I found Susana Abad. The internet media tells me she is married to Alvaro Vargas Llosa. With nothing to lose I asked her in a twitter to ask her husband to contact his communications manager. I had sent him an email requesting Alvaro Vargas

Llosa email address, which he gave me, but as no email has been replied to since. I decided to try other methods of communication.

My email side I used to send my twitter gave me a surprise. The last time I used twitter was about a year before when I wanted to ask Jon Lee Anderson to look at something I had put onto a home page. As the home page was not able to tell who had been looking at it, only how many times it had been visited I gave up the idea if using Twitter to contact anyone; till I saw Alvaro Vargas Llosa's wife was using Twitter.

My Twitter account told me of others that were of interest.

Amy Davidson's name was shown; her address said she is the editor of the New Yorker.

What is strange is her name came up year ago when I tried to twitter Jon Lee Anderson! I had even gone so far as to write it down.

There was another twitter address twitter had added as interesting- FNPI_org. The translator program told me the twitter said "This organization is working for Journalistic excellence and contribution to the processes of democracy and development in Latin American countries and the Caribbean."

Next surprise! How should I describe Gabriel Garcia Marquez? He is supporting the above organization. The FNPI is offering awards for journalism sponsored by Gabriel Garcia Marquez. His spits name is Gabo, is writer that won the Nobel

Prize in Literature in 1982. Best friend of Fidel Castro, never said a word against Castro- so says his Wikipedia.

Under the heading of 'Fame' in Gabriel Garcia Marquez's Wikipedia, it states that Mario Vargas Llosa punched Gabriel Garcia Marquez in the face!?

I was left thought less when I read this. Gabriel Garcia Marquez name is known to me; fair to say his name is part of this. His name is also mentioned in Ciro Bustos book, 'Che wants to see you.'

Gabriel Garcia Marquez's name had seen often and it appears in the 'book connection' I found.

Elisabeth Burgos-Debray has a file with his name. What she does not have is a file with Ciro's name on it: (Strange as he was in captivity with her husband! She made files listing the books he read and listed his letters.)

Question why did I find his name when I tried to twitter Mario Vargas Llosa's son's wife?

Page three-hundred and forty-seven of Ciro's book.
On this page Ciro states Gabriel Garcia Marquez took over their interrogation from Dr Gonzalez. Ciro states that-
*Gabriel Garcia Marquez was also a CIA agent.*

Fidel Castro and Elisabeth Burgos-Debray.

Website mit diesem Bild
Elizabeth Burgos is shown here with Fidel Castro in 1970; the photo is part ...
media.hoover.org

Fidel Castro and Gabriel Garcia- *Need I say more?*

Libertaddigital com

Gabriel Garcia Marquez.
- A) Fidel Castro's best friend.
- B) In Elisabeth Burgos-Debray's files.
- *C)* C) A CIA Agent.
- *D)* The 1982 Nobel Prize for Literature.

*E)* Contact to Giangiacomo Feltrinelli's publishing emporium.

*F)* (D) Ciro Bustos calls him *Gabriel!* Gabriel Garcia Marquez.

*( He also says he was interrogated by-Would you talk about your* interrogator using his Christen name?)

Is it my imagination?

The plans made for Che's death party were made using the Salta Guerrillas experience. Change the leading man's name from Masetti to Guevara. (Masetti was not the only man experienced in film making.)

Ciro Bustos was living opposite the court house, in the Fourth Division headquarters. Where Ciro himself says he had a room.

Another confirms this in his report about the trial. 'The South Amercia years- chapter 18 www.mogarcia.raintreeeditors.com/...chapter18.ht.

Elizabeth Burgos Debray also has filed reports about Regis Debray time in Camiri.
Hoover Insititution Standford University.

Ciro Bustos can sit on the accused bench in the courtroom and appear on set in the jungle with a wig, ready to play his part in the death party. This explains the misunderstanding about exactly which day it was. Not all the actors could get there on one day.   The theater was as the crow flies not that far away. As Ciro says there were two air strips near

Camiri. One military one private; helicopters, Jeeps and busies were common.

The parts of the lawyers where taken by Che's two brothers, they also were on set for the capture of Che, this time they resented Army advisers and interrogators. As seen and explained in the film, 'Wege der Revolution Che Guevara.'

Che's sister plays his wife; though she is married to Che's half brother, who I recognized as Jean Luc Godard, a prominent film maker, he too has the use of many names.

Add Feltrinelli a multi rich publisher connected too many of Castro's scams and enjoys his contact to the media world.

$50.000.000.

50 million dollars is a lot of money even now! Feltrinelli brings this sum into play. In Jobst C. Knigge's work 'Feltrinelli-Sine weg in den Terrorismus.' (page 35) he reports that the money was offered to Roberto Quintanilla to provide funds for Che's safety.

Add as the sequel 'Monica Ertl shoots the Bolivian ambassador. 'In Hamburg, Roberto Quintanilla. The same man that had been the recipient of the money!

Klaus Barbie plays the part of Monica Ertl's godfather and counter guerrilla military trainer sends his son to bring the hapless man's body back to Bolivia. Another film is made about her supposed demise. A whole industry is made up from this pantomime, with people disappearing and reinventing themselves. Books written, tee shirts printed- till I come along wanting to know about my father!

Not wanting to be left out Tania Bunke has had a book written about her. One of the books I am referring to was co-written by Che's best friends Ricardo Rojo's daughter Marta.

(Ricardo Rojo happens to be Che's best friend and Ciro Bustos also! This is stated in 'Che Wants to see you. Ciro's book.)

(Ricardo Rojo in standing behind my mother in a photo where Che and his first wife appear. In Jon Lee Anderson's book 'Che Guevara a Revolutionary Life.')

Che Guevara and Ricardo Rojo.

They are all together in Camiri!

Ricardo Rojo used the same editor for his book about his friendship with Che, as did Rudolfo Walsh who I say was another name used by Che's half brother, the one that married Che's sister.

Pierre Kalfon used Jorge Alvarez an editor; he wrote about Che Guevara and the political events around, he is also in files kept by Elizabeth Burgos Debray in the Hoover Institution Stanford University.

Jorge alvarez/rock.com.ar. This program talks about his music. Pierre Kalfon was also a film star and a pop star, Jorge Alvarez produced music in Paris. I only mention them as to prove what goes around comes around.

I quote from Ciro's book "One big lie is made up by innumerable small truths. " I cannot help wondering about the lives of the other twenty-nine he had.

How to turn Ciro Bustos into Che Guevara.

And back again

## Chapter twenty two.
## Continuing surprises from my father's book.

In the open letter- Peru 21 it states that Mario Vargas Llosa was hospitable to-
*Celia de la Serna Llosa. Che's mother, my grandmother.*

The lady that asked him to assist Celia was-
*Hilda Gadea- Che's first wife.*

(Mario Vargas Llosa remarks, 'Celia de la Serna Llosa did not have any money to pay for a hotel. She was in his house before returning to Buenos Aires where she was put in jail and would soon after her release die.)

With this remark in my mind and bearing in mind this is the man that questioned the body in Santa Clara is that of Che Guevara. I started to see what I could find out about her.

(To know about your grandmother is important to you. When Ciro/Che first met me he accompanied me to the bus station. When we embraced there were tears in his eyes that I could not explain. Later I wondered if he saw my grandmother in my face!?)

I am not at this point sure that there is a Jewish connection but I am sure Celia de la Serna Llosa was a close friend of Mario Vargas Llosa's family. He and his first wife Julia Urqnidi a Scriptwriter as it so happens, they were married in 1955. Julia Urqnidi tells me in her interview that their relationship was a close one; they live together, she and Celia went to the theater together and when Hilda Gadea needed help she was there to support her.

(From my half-brother Omar I had heard that both Hilda and her daughter Hildita, our half-sister had depression and fought the problems alcohol brings. This was when I visited him in 2009.)

To speculate only helps me to value the information I have found. But I did find information that suggests the Mario Vargas Llosa had a larger interest in Cuba and Fidel Castro's plans.

*Celia de la Serna Llosa speaks of her boys' involvement in unrest!*
*There is evidence that Peruvian men were additional solders in Sera Master:*
*luzpensamientoylibertad.blogspot.com/.../libro-hilda Written by Ricardo Gadea Acosta.*

Celia de la Serna Llosa. My grandmother.

To tell you she learned English and German and was an avid reader, she went out of her way to meet important authors. She was a forward thinking woman for the nineteen twenties. Celia took on the responsibility of teaching her children.

I am told by Froilan Gonzalez- a world renown racing car driver, travelled the word freely; an Argentinean, and publisher.

Adys M Cupull- is an author for a political publisher.

In 'Unfinished Song.' For which they won literary awards for in Cuba in 1998. (I found out that they are part of the propaganda machine. Nice that they could have prizes for their efforts.)

Political publisher- 'Unfinished Song.'

Celia travelled from Salto, Uruguay with abundant material proclaiming Fidel Castro's brand of communist propaganda; where she was arrested. They tell me it was the twenty third of April; she was registered as dangerous.

Celia was brought before a court charged with corruption and communist tendencies.

I do not like to think she was interrogated nor held incommunicado at the local prison. She was transferred to a prison for women in Buenos Aires. She was acquitted at that trial. But the executive did not accept the decision. Why he wanted an official from Fidel Castro's government.
(The article doses not say why.)

It appears that Celia had to sit in prison for another two months till a judge intervened, her trial ended in the early hours of June the twenty-fourth.

It is interesting to read that, outside were her sons and a senior Argentinean Military figure, he had his private car waiting to take her to his ranch near the Brazilian border.

The statement that says that Celia remained there sometime before pretended to be the senior Argentinean Military figure's wife crossed the border to reach Montevideo.

All of this was happening in 1963. I want to say my grandmother was very much involved in what was happening at the time. She chose to return to Argentina even though Argentina was under military rule. Celia had become one of the most wanted women, she had to live undercover. Celia refused to go into exile in Cuba or Uruguay.

At this point I wanted to give up! But somehow I could not; the thought that my grandmother was involved in all of this was intriguing. I asked the question who was behind Celia?

General Jose de la Serna was the last Viceroy of Peru.
(I am beginning to understand the connection to Mario Vargas Llosa.)

Juan-Martin de la Serna was her father, Edelmira Llosa was her mother. They were to die before they could bring her up,

Carman de la Serna; Celia's older sister became her parent along with Cayetono Cordova Iturbara.

Cayetono Cordova Iturbara- renown was a poet and writer, he's liturgy contacts would lead to contact with outer writers as did his political believes.

Carman de la Serna- had strong Leftist believes, she was a socialist as well as being concerned with women civil rights, an anticlerical feminist.

Both Carman de la Serna and Cayetono Cordova Iturbara were members of the communist party and were politically active.

Now it is not so difficult to understand how Celia could become involved in thesis worlds events. While looking for more information about my grandmother I found a reference to an invitation to the theater in Paris. Julia Urquidi and Mario Vargas Llosa had received the invitation from Jorge

Edwards. The invitation was extended to except Hilda Gadea and Celia.

Jorge Edwards even informs me in his statement 'Cuba and We' which play they went to see "Galileo Galilei" and Rue de Tournon was where Mario Vargas Llosa had his flat.

After recovering that Jorge Edward Valde was not just a lost poet sulking in Paris, that he was Chili's ambassador serving in France. He had met Fidel Castor in nineteen fifty nine after the fall of Fulegencio Batista at the Woodrow Wilson Center Affaires Public and International. Where Jorge Edward Valde was studying a postgraduate course in preparation for his Chilean diplomatic career. Mario Vargas Llosa was a member of the Peruvia parliament. Charger de Affairs to Chili. Writer and a Poet with a Nobel Prize and had the Venezuelan Romulo Gallegos Prize.

Gabriel Garcia Marquez is also a writer and a Poet with a Nobel Prize and the Venezuelan Romulo Gallegos Prize. He was also Cuba's ambassador serving in France. Best friends with Fidel Castro.

I have waded my way through pries wining writers, poet and journalist to see what their connection is. The more I looked the more I could image that their connections could go beyond poetry.

Alego Carpentier's name is connected to public money being hand over to the guerrilla Che Guevara there are many rumors floating on the internet about this.

As Alego Carpentier was in charge of Cuban state publishing and enjoyed a friendship with Jouis Jorvet a French theatrical director and was Cuba's ambassador to France 1975 and won the Cervantes Prize in 1977. This gave me the idea that 'Poets and their prizes could be a very useful way of transferring money and information.
Julio Cortazar- translator/poet/ UNESCO translator. actor/writer.

He connects to Jean Luc Godard and can be seen in Pier Paolo Pasolini's films.
As will as simpering with Fidel Castor and Salvador Allende.
Just out of interest the Wikipedia tells me he spent his childhood just outside of Buenos Aires, he was a teacher in a high school in Buenos Aires Chivilcoy and later in Bolivia. Interesting to read that he was a French professor French in the National University of Cuyo Mondoza.
One of the Wikipedia's tells me he was Chili's ambassador in France. He died in Paris 1984.

## Chapter twenty three.
## Other writers/poets/journalists!

Peru-
Lucho Loayza= writer/poet/journalist.
(Is in many photos with Mario Vargas Llosa.)

Raul Porras Barrenehea = writer/poet. Literary prize winner. Peruvian Canceller in Salvador Allande's

government. Believed to have been murdered shortly after Allande's demise,
Argentina-
Jorge Luis Borges= writer/poet/journalist.
Received the Jerusalem literary prize 1971.
Was at school with Ernesto Guevara Lynch, Che's father-who was expelled from that school for hitting the very same Jorge Luis Borges!
  He worked with Mario Vargas Llosa in the National Broadcasting System of Argentina.
Cuba-
Guillermo Cabrera Infante= writer/poet/journalist and translator/screenplays/film critic.
Worked in Brussels/Belgium/London.
Known at one time as a Castro supporter.
Jose/Pepe Rodriguez Feo= writer/poet/journalist/translator. Spanish to English, liter critic.
Nicolas Guillen= writer/poet/journalist. Songwriter. He wrote the song-Che Guevara. He was politically active.
Chili-
Jorge Edward Volde= writer/poet/journalist.
Won literary prizes.
Chili's ambassador in France
Pablo Neruda= writer/poet. Diplomat.
Accepted an award from the Peruvian government.
Was a member of Salvador Allende's government.
In every Wikipedia I read I am told that Pablo Neruda is Che Guevara's favorite poet.
Venezuela-

Republica Bolivarian de Venezula
Romules Gallegos= writer/poet/lawyer. Politian. Was an elected president the republic. Nobel Prize winner.
Spain-
Carlos Barral = writer/poet/journalist/actor/editor (Socillist party Catalonia Spain.)
To be seen in films directed by Pier Paolo Pasolini.

Lucia Alvaraz Toledo book 'The story of Che' the editorial is by Seix Barral. (Just a remark!) This lady is related to the de la Serna and the Llosa family, a stronger contact than living in the same neighborhood. (She could be the mother to Che's half brother Fernando L. Chavaz Alvarez, who I say used other identities such as Jean Luc Godard.)
All this people can be connected with each other as writers/poet prize winners- politicians
Poets like Vidadyo Telleboim. He was the Chilean leader of the communist Party.
Nicolas Guillen received the Stalin Peace Prize.
Emir Rodriguez Monegal form Uruguay also received liturgy prizes.

I do not know if they drank tea together but a network of communication has developed on the map I have drawn on a piece of wall paper. It is like my grandmother is showing me the world is a bigger place than I thought.
Alberto Szpunberg=Albertito. This name is coursing me some thought. Firstly he is poet, an Argentinean, a founder member of 'Brigada Masetti.' Alberto Szpunberg- Mistica, Lirica y politica - Revista N –

Clarin www.revistaenie.clarin.com/La_Academia de_de_Pi

A close friend of Ciro Bustos as is stated in Ciro's own book.

Alberto Szpunberg as an artist whose work I have often mistaken as Ciro's work on the internet.

(Ciro came to my notice in a paragraph in Jon Lee Anderson book where he said Ciro Bustos painted wonderful portraits of people without faces. This remark made him interesting to me.)

There is a question in my mind- They share the same the same political stage- that they are both Argentinean dose not bother me, but their closeness in their art work dose.

Portrait painting is an art you can learn. The fact that they have so much in common, opens the possibility that the said drawings could have been made by another hand.

Ciro Algaranaz- he is interesting as it is not clear what he was up to! I put in Ciro Bustos and Ciro Algaranaz into the network. The answers I got were, he was-

The Mayor of Camiri –

Che's neighbor in Bolivian prison!

On page three hundred and sixty-one Ciro Bustos tells me Ciro Algaranaz occupied the same cell as he. Ciro Algaranaz was being held for his connection to the suspected cocaine business.

Ricardo Gadea Acosta- is an author, a journalist who wrote a lament at the death of Javier Herard. One of the poets-Guerrillas lost in the Salsa campaign.

As an author Ricardo Gadea Acosta has spoken over the revolution and is influence in the Southern Americans. Many of his remarks are in a philosophy program on Cuban net.

I had read in Ricardo Gadea Acosta 2013, May 15 "Javier in the memory." That he had been in Cuba to share their defense in April 61 at the Bay of Pigs.

http://nuestrabandera.lamule.pe/2013/05/18/javier-en-el-recuerdo

As a Peruvian he had received military training, under Fidel Castro's instructions. He is Peruvian!?
*Ricardo Gadea Acosta is Hilda Gadea Acosta's brother.*
*Hilda Gadea Acosta was Che's first wife.*

Hilda Gadea Acosta was Che's first wife, mother of Hildita my half-sister, I have found a photo of her, (Wish I could hug her.) with Alberto Grundy. In this photo she looks so sweet, I wish I could have met her; it is said that she is dead, there are photos of her grave.(Who knows so many have used this way to gain another identity- just wishing.) One good thing is Hildita had two children and not just one. "Diario de Bolivia" books.google,de/books informed me about the brother/sister relationship and as Ciro's book also refers to the second child; for me to say family ties are of great importance is not unfair! 'Surviving Mexico's Dirty War.' A Political Prisoner's Memoir. Is a book written by Aurora Camacho Schmidt. She in turn is Hilda Gadea Acosta niece, my half sister's aunt.

Aurora Camacho Schmidt's photo is in an article written by Mario Vargas Llosa. The article says that she asked him to ghost write a book for her. 'Black and White.' Leereluniverso-blogspot-.com.
. Aurora Camacho Schmidt is still alive and is a professor of Spanish in the U.S.A.

It is strange for me to think that so many people related to me have stayed in Mario Vargas Llosa's flat!

Chapter twenty four.
Fidel Castro's Big Guns and their Supporters.

Naming the big guns and their supporters I hope to change your mind about the movement that was said to be set in place to save Che Guevara's life. Why? He was in most people's eyes a nuisance!

You are making a case against Ciro Bustos and Riges Debray as betrayers of Che Guevara.

I want to show there are other reasons for creating mass hysteria. It is common that heroes and anti heroes are created look at Harry Potter now his era is over a new one is being created, it is to be produced in over forty different countries.

Che Guevara was a big hit in the sixties and seventies and still is now, just go up on the internet and see what is being said and by whom, more and more information is being released. The whole story is making money, big money!

It takes a big organization to produce this sensation, I name some of those I found that are involved in the epic of Harry Potter- sorry Che Guevara's death party.

1) ***Fidel Castro-***
Is the first man to mention as all links go through him.

2) ***Manuel Pineiro***, red beard- Barba Roja-
He is Fidel Castro's head of secret service. Spy Master!

3) ***Luis Hernandez Ojeda-***He is also a Castro man. He was the first secretary in the Cuban Milan embassy in Italy His last job was as Cuba's ambassador to Nicaragua. He had a reputation of manipulating the political system and the media.

4) ***Jan Stage-*** he was in Cuba for eight years, a secret agent; their secret agent. It is not surprising he translated Gabriel Garcia Marques work for Feltrinelli.

5) ***Giangiaccomo Feltrninelli-***
He was the owner of the publishing house that published Doctor Zhivago. He obtained the rights from Fidel Castro for the Bolivian Diary, by Che Guevara. He was an activist in his own right.

6) ***Colonel Roberto Quintanilla-***
His participation in all of this, twists in and out of the master plan. He was offered 50,000,000 $ for services he could provide.

He is the man shot in Hamburg by the team- Giangiaccomo Feltrninelli and Monika Ertl and Jan Stage.

Jan Stage was Giangiaccomo Feltrninelli's contact in La Paz the August before Che Guevara's death party. Colonel Roberto Quintanilla entertained Giangiaccomo Feltrninelli for two days and a night or two nights and a day, depending on whose version you are reading. Carlos Feltrninelli book `Senior Service. 'or Claire Sterling's The Terror Network. Remember she was asked to give evidence in the USA congress. A big Gun!?

Colonel Roberto Quintanilla is the man responsible for the Bolivian military's part in Che Guevara's death party.

Colonel Roberto Quintanilla was the said interrogator of-

*Giangiaccomo Feltrninelli.*
*Che Guevara.*
*Ciro Bustos.*
*Riges Debray.*

7) ***Antonio Arguedas Mendieta-***
The Bolivian Minister Antonio Arguedas Mendieta to give him his full name: his name can be connected with which every 'Inty' that took over as leader after Che. Antonio Peredo had been a friend of the Bolivian Minister Antonio Arguedas for some considerable time. *(Look at this and from where the information comes.)*

Guido Álvaro Peredo Leigue

cerrocalvo.blogspot.com

Guido Álvaro "Inti" Peredo
genealogiadelcheguevara.blogspot.com

Pier Paolo Pasolini- paginecorsare.my blog.it
The Bolivian Minister Antonio Arguedas Mendieta
The Bolivian Minister personal intelligence adviser
was Gabriel Garcia Marquez.
 8) **Gabriel Garcia Marquez**-
Gabriel Garcia Marquez as well as Antonio
Arguedas Mendieta personal intelligence adviser
was an adviser to Ciro Bustos, Giangiaccomo
Feltrninelli published his books. A Castro follower.
9) *Tania Bunke*-
Claire Sterling that tells us Tania Bunke informed
the police Giangiaccomo Feltrninelli was in La Paz
so Colonel Roberto Quintanilla could interview him!
Tania Bunke was talked about as a spy.
10) *Ulises Estrada*-

He is working in the Cuban Embassy as coordinator of communication and contact. He happens to be personally involved with Tania Bunke, or so he says.

11) ***Elizabeth Burgos-Debray-***
Her part was to support Riges Debray. Ciro Bustos in his book remarks the she was an interpreter at the Cuban Ministry. With whom Debray had a relationship. Ciro Bustos does not mention that she is to be seen with Fidel Castro in a photo you can find on the internet, she is in her early teens, looks like they are having breakfast together.

11a) ***Daniel Alarcon Ramirez 'Benigno'-***
his book 'Memorias de un soldado Cubano.' was edited by Elizabeth Burgos-Debray as was Jorge Masetti's- EL furor y el delirio. The books that were published by the Feltrinelli group.

(*Rigoberta Menchu was one of the other projects Elisabeth Burgos-Debray was involved in this was also proved to be media invention. A lie.*) (It is said this story was to course unrest Guatemala and see the political changes were to Castro's' advantage.)
(*You will be surprised to know which name Ciro Bustos editor and translator, used to use.*)
Elizabeth Burgos-Debray has files in Stanford University; a list can be found on the internet it has been most useful in my studies. She has newspaper form that time where it is stated: no one knew who Che Guevara was and other interesting facts. You could say she has listed the sub-supporters.

The news papers also show who were Ciro Bustos and Riges Debray's lawyers were. Their faces are

remarkably like the brothers of Che Guevara. You can see the same faces in-
Lahistoriaargentinacompleta.blogspot.com/2007
Diariopamperoarchivos.blogspot.com
This time as Argentina terrorist.

***Ana Maria***, whichever name she was using- took the part of Ciro Bustos' wife; she is Che Guevara's sister. She was a film actor. She married Jean Luc Godard more than once under different names.

***12) Pier Paolo Pasolini-*** he is not the only film producer involved. He was also writer whose work was published by Giangiaccomo Feltrninelli's publishing houses. And they were personal friends.

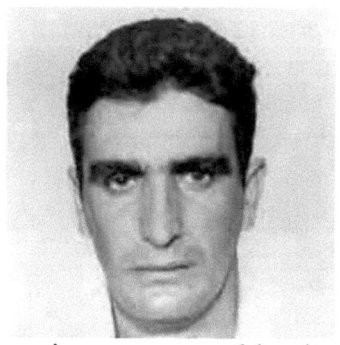

paginecorsare.my blog.it.
(Look at the photos above, he took the part of one of the Intys.) (Take the magazine: Punto Final. Dated Mayo de 1968 to confirm who was about at that time.)

I do not know which Inty, Monika Ertl was said to have been involved personally with, the one that resembles Roberto Guevara or Pier Paolo Pasolini. I cannot tell you which one was supposed to have been killed in the campaign Teoponte.

*Gustavo Rodrigues Ostria* writes in 'Bolivia Cycle in Guerrilla. Continuity and Differences 1963-1970 about three events. Salta. Bolivia. Teoponte. They were all designed to make a point.

A short list of members

You might like a short list of members of the media that were part of the machine Fidel Castro used.

*Eduardo Jozami.*

*Carlos Barral*- the leader of the publishing house *Seix Barral* (Long time friend of Che Guevara.)
*Alfrado Guevara*- the man leading the film and news distribution in the South Americas. And the head of the film industry based in Cuba.

Lawyers related to Ciro Bustos/Che Guevara!

 Tract pour la libération de Juan Martin Guevara, en 1976.

### Roberto Guevara Linch

Hermano del jefe de guerrilleros argentino-cubano Ernesto "Che" Guevara. Abogado de una clara definida vocación subversiva. Fue miembro de la banda terrorista "EjÈrcito Revolucionario del Pueblo" (ERP) En Europa militó en los denominados "Comités de Solidaridad" del "ERP", "JCA" y "CATS", con la misión de apologizar la guerrilla e instrumentar campañas de desprestigio al país Se hizo prófugo de justicia Argentina.

Website mit diesem Bild
... Argentine lawyer Roberto Guevara brother of Ernesto Che Guevara is shown ...
gettyimages.co.uk

La sala donde se llevará a efecto el proceso a Debray y los otros acusados, simplemente se le agregará un telón detrás de la mesa correspondiente al jurado, que llevará el escudo nacional y una leyenda en la que Bolivia reitera su derecho al mar

El doctor Novillo, defensor de oficio para los acusados de complicidad con las guerrillas, conversa con el Cnl. Remberto Iriarte, Fiscal de Guerra, quien se hace lustrar los zapatos, en el Casino Militar de Camiri.

Osvaldo Chato Peredo, sucesor del Inti

The same pair can be seen again with Inti's successor.

Website mit diesem Bild
Osvaldo Chato Peredo, sucesor del Inti. '
elortiba.org

Chapter twenty five
My conclusions at this point.
One of the key figures is Giangiaccomo Feltrninelli he can be connected to most figures

mentioned. From carrying information to printing their books-
How much money did Doctor Zhivago make?
How much money has the said Diaries of Che Guevara made?
50,000,000 $ was peanuts to the income received from the sale of Harry Potter- sorry the Che Guevara trilogy, and still is. Does it make any better when it is said that the proceeds went to revolutionists to fund their battles in South America?

Take an E-Fit photo program and get them to face map photos of Che Guevara and Ciro Bustos, As young men as old men, with hair without hair. I have photos you can use, as they come from those presented on the internet, you can pick your own. The fact that their head shape match fascinated me. Look at the baby photo of Che Guevara and match it with a bald Ciro Bustos, the bald head of Che Guevara is also available. Take a photo of a young Ciro Bustos and scribble on a beard and unruly hair. Do not be surprised to see both men become one man.
Why! 50,000,000 $ was Peanuts.

### Foot notes.

A foot note a- Why is Tania's black jeep relevant? Because it proves there were roads!
In fact there is a pipeline running between Cochabamba and Camiri. It can be seen on maps printed ten years before.

Foot note b- The hand written Bolivian Dairies were written by a syndicate, consisting of at least three men who were trained in Havana in the skills of forgery. Ciro Bustos, Riges Debray and Giangiaccomo Feltrninelli.
Giangiaccomo Feltrninelli saw that the Dairies were published within weeks of the death party.
Foot note c-
*Salta*- Could have the events in Salta been used to remove Jorge Masetti from center stage? He was in the film 'Cuban Rebels Girls' sponsored by Errol Flynn. Was he becoming too well known, actors have been hired throughout theses manipulated events? His said demise created much interest. This idea could be, was used again and again.
*Bolivia.* Was used to the stage the creation of a revolutionary romantic.
Teoponte. Teoponte was used to promote the need for heroes to continue financing the vast market the 'Big Guns' had created for revolutionary ideals in the South Americas.

Continuity and Differences 1963-1970 Salta. Bolivia. Teoponte.

   After cross referencing my father's book 'Che Wants to see you. The untold story of Che Guevara.' And wading through
Elizabeth Burgos-Debray lists of files. She has paced in Stanford University closed files which

cannot be opened before her death. In fact many involved have files stored there!

I have been able put faces to names already mentioned. And found others in the know.

I even have a copy of a magazine stating most of the actors were in or close to La Paz, or happily basking in the near, in Chill!
Ponto Final. Dated May the eighth nineteen sixty eight.

Nice photo of Allende on the front!
Nice photo of Anna Karina, Che's sister, the article is written by Lean Luc Godard, I say is Che's half-brother.
Regis Debray also has his photo in the magazine! The photo of Che is worth a look it is of a much younger man, not a man entering his forties.

I don't want to name all of them as their names are have already been written down!

How to organize a Death Party in Bolivia.
Step 1) Go where no one has heard of you.
(News paper cutting from Elisabeth Burgos-Debray's Inventory.) I have a copy stating that.
Step 2) Chose places within easy reach of each other.

Use similar maps to those in
The Bolivian Campaign-Che Guevara a Revolutionary Life by Jon Lee Anderson.
*Jon Lee Anderson, He was with Aleida March, Che's second wife for three years, when writing his book. Jon Lee Anderson was with Ciro Bustos- he lived above Ciro for one year.*

Südamerika. Verlag Volk und Welt. Berlin-1957.
This map and its book show how cultured Bolivia was in 1947/1957, with its terraced fields. A pipeline runs from Cochabamba through Camiri where the trial of Bustos/Debray was held to the Argentinean border.
Welt Atlas, printed in Germany 1972.
Within this aria the death stage was placed in radius in a 100 kilometers. Pipelines and roads, one engine airplanes were very much in daily use.
Getting everyone together on one day must have been a problem-explaining why there is a difference as to which date it was performed on.
Step3) Get members of your family to act on your behalf.

In film 'Weg der Revolution' Che's brothers can be seen as interrogators and advisers to those that were planning to capture Che.
In Elisabeth Burgos-Debray's Inventory there are photos of the same men this time dressed as Lawyers! Ciro Bustos and Regis Debray's. There are other Web Sites also giving this information.
Ciro Bustos was living in loggings opposite the court house. He was NOT under lock and key. This he states in his own book. He was free to put on his Che Guevara wig, pop over to the death set in La Higuera for his death seines.
Regis Debray is standing as front man- his mother was in the French government; Danielle Mitterrand

and Elisabeth Burgos-Debray were friends. Francios Mitterrand was only a French President.

Che's sister played Ciro Bustos' wife even though she was married to Che's half brother- Ferdnando L Chavaz Alvarez, who's mother live close to the Guevara's and she has also written a book about Che's life.

Ann Maria was a film star- she used many names. As did her half brother, among Ferdnando's alias is Jean Luc Godard- film director! He has other alias. I have a news paper proving they were on stage at the time, along with many interacting people you may know.

*Alfredo Guevara Lynch was the man in charge of* **Latin American films and distribution.**

**Jean Luc Godar or Fernando L Chavez Alvarez?**

 Jean-Luc Godard. "'cupblog.org

**Fernando L. Chavez Alvarez:**
Cuñado de Ernesto "Che" Guevara. Integrante de una familia tradicionalmente apátrida y terrorista. Es miembro de las bandas terroristas "EjÉrcito Revolucionario del Pueblo" (ERP), y de la "Juta de Coordinación Revolucionaria" (JCR). En Europa desplegó tareas afines a las que desarrolló su cuñado Roberto Guevara Lynch. Se hizo prófugo de la justicia Argentina.

Cuñado de Ernesto "Che" Guevara. Integrante de una familia tradicionalmente ...
lahistoriaargentinacompleta.blogspot.com

**Lucia Alvarez de Toledo**- La History Del Che Guevara. Author of 'The story of Che.' Forward by **Gabriel Garcia Marquez**.
She worked for-the National Broadcasting System of Argentina.
**She was Editor and translator of- Young Che by Ernesto Guevara Lynch, - said to be Che's father. Mother of- Che Guevara's half brother, Fernando L Chavaz Alvarez.**
(B) translator of-   Travelling with Che Guevara. By Alberto Granado.

(C) **Friend of -** Liaison officer *Ciro Bustos.*
(A) bol.com | the story of che guevara | Boeken
*www.bol.com/nl/s/engelse.../index.html*
(B) The Story of Che Guevara | *Lucìa Àlvarez De Toledo* ... Featuring a foreword by *Gabriel Garcia Marquez*

(B)
Cuñado de Ernesto "Che" Guevara. Integrante de una familia tradicionalmente ...
e.sb-10.com
Cuñado de Ernesto "Che" Guevara. Integrante de una familia tradicionalmente ...
e.sb-10.com

Stag4) Distribute the dairies. Giangiacomo Feltrinelli a Castro infatuated publisher printed and distributed world wide. Jobst C.Knigge's Feltrinelli-Sinn Weg in den Terrorismus points this out. Not only was Feltrinelli responsible for its publication he also made very large payments to persons involved in the cover up in Bolivia. 50,000.000 A lot money even now.

*(I have my theory about the dairies as Jon lee Anderson's match word for word with an account about a campaign in Salsa written by Masetti!)(Also a film producer.)(Masetti's account matches too closely with Ciro's version.)*

You know the power of advertising. Just look at Stair Wars or Harry Potter. You want to stop people from looking for your second head, show the world you have cut it off. The barite is not being looked for, a man without hair can continue to Castro-ise people's politics, their lives.

They used members of same team to do a nasty trick with Rigoberta Menchü, coursing mass disruption in Guatemala.

Dated in book 1944/1957. From Cochabamba to the Argentinean border.

Punto Final Magazine, sets the date.

I will mark people of interest for you and point out the date this magazine was printed. (They have used a very young Che as photo.)

  Klaus Barbie and son.

Part three.

Chapter twenty six

There is something I did not expect to find out!

Who would ever have thought a daughter of Che Guevara would find herself living in a small village next to an equally small village where the son of Klaus Barbie's son is living.

I can see the village where he lives from my window.

When I first met Dr Günter Schwesinger his garage doors were decorated with car number plates from Bolivar.

You cannot undo something you have done, why I told him what I had discovered I don't know. I thought I was asking a retired pathologist about the light in the said dead Che's eyes. I did not have the knowledge I have now.

Günter told me Che was a very charming man.

I like to shock those that have found this subject interesting, maybe I did not notice his surprise when he said, "Of all the people to walk into my house!" But, I did notice when he told me that Hans Ertl, Monika Ertl's father had said that Che had been a good husband to Monika.

Had Günter not said that I would never have thought to investigate her and the events around her. Never come to the conclusion she had taken on the identity of Ann Wright. With out the film- ´Gesucht: Monika Ertl. Die Frau die Che Guevara rächt.' I would never have found a sample of Che's hand writhing written after his death party. Never have found out that Klaus Barbie were Monika's Godfather! But while I was going through this phase I did not know that Klaus Barbie's son was among my acquaintances.

He did influence me enough to slow me down from making that first visit to Ciro in Malmo. I put it off for a year.

I had read that Klaus Barbie had a son, that he had died in an accident, hand gliding. This was before the time I have understood about changing identities, before the book about Kennedy's assassination explained to me the use of code names and aliases, how names connected people to projects.

I still would not have made the assumption that Günter had another life before he became a retired gentleman living in the village I can see from my window. I did feel he knew more but when you asked questions or tried to lead him to say more he would block you.

I am used to not being taken seriously, I did not expect to lose a coffee friendship in my village with the excuse that I put my friends at risk, that the C.I.A would be posing a risk to me and those I know if I continued with my investigations.

I have only taken facts from unrelated-related programs found openly on the internet- to come to the conclusions I have. This I have done for many years. I have done this because I want to prove that I am worthy of my father. If anyone had said Evelyn you are right; I would have arrived at where I want to be.

There is another village I can see from my window. Where a local writer lived, during the winter there are lectures and discussions about the history of this strange island. The weekend before the storm that kept me hiding from its strong winds, Günter was present at a lecture about its half city.

The lecturer did not like to see someone in his ordinance was asleep. Raising his voice did not bring back the dear man's attention. Others were asking when the lecture was going to stop. This was when Günter got up from his seat to thank the poor lecturer. I had not seen Günter for sometime; I did think anything of it as I was enjoying the afternoon's entertainment, but his face was fresh in my mind.

The storm blew for three days I had run out of things to do! There had been a program planed to be shown on Phoenix TV but it had been canceled, it was about Klaus Barbie. 'Klaus Barbie= My Enemy's Enemy.' I found on YouTube.

I had not gone more than a third through this film when I was struck by the similarities between Klaus Barbie and Günter Schlesinger. (He had Bolivian car number plates in his garage but he knew Monika Ertl.) Having made the connection between Norberto and his father I decided to trust my instinct.

Information about Klaus Georg Altmann, Klaus Barbie's son is to be found in the book- 'The Devil's Agent' by Peter McFarren and Fadrique Iglesias. But Information about Dr Günter Schlesinger is not to be found.

It is interesting to note the body of the ambassador, Bevor Quintanills. Monika Ertl was accused of shooting was brought back to Bolivia by Klaus Georg Altmann.

Klaus Georg Altmann was working for his father in his businesses and was part of his father's political actions worldwide.

It is also interesting to note that Regis Debray was involved in Klaus Barbie's deportation to France.

If you have been denied Spanish citizenship five times you have a need for another identity.

The pictures I took of Günter at the next meeting at the house of the local writer have not disproved my suspicion. I just wonder why I was so nerves about taking the photos. My hart was beating as it did in front of Ciro's front door, till I told myself not to be so silly. I had not come this far to be stopped by my own nerves.

There is another remark that Gunter made I remember; he stated that a red light was set in the window of Hans Ertl's house to warn Che Guevara not to return- a green light meant it was safe to return.

(This statement was made in front of witnesses other than me.)

In the film about Monika Ertl 'Gesucht' Hans Ertl describes the same warning system he used to safeguard himself.

## Chapter twenty seven.
### Hand written note books and diaries and other things.

There is something wrong somewhere! Felix Rodriguez states in, `Schnappschuss Mit Che.` by Wilfried Huismann, that he has the Rolex watch that belonged to Che; come to think he also states he has `the` note book from the afore mentioned.

In-`Che wants to see you.' by Ciro Bustos. Ciro states he had the Rolex watch belonging to Che.

Ciro Bustos says he had to leave Argentina; it was when he got onto a train to start this journey he was mugged and this was when the watch was taken, lost or stolen.

Question: how many watches did Che have? The same question can be asked about the diaries.

I have made the same mistake thinking there can only be one. Only one hand writing! I have even fallen into the trap by asking which of the dairies is the original one.

`Schnappschuss Mit Che.' by Wilfried Huismann, shows the diary set on the wall in Benigno's flat. The date of the finished film is 2007. (Benigno was said to be one of Che's companions, he also had his account of events written, I mean edited for him by Elisabeth Burgos-Debray and his name is on her list. Daniel Alarcon Ramirez. `Benigno'

The Bolivian government in a YouTube.com film. Hqdefault jpg; are waving a Che Guevara diary for us all to see. In the internet program `amigosdeboliniayperu.org.' This dates the diary's release as July the seventh, 2008.

We are told Bolivia unveils the original Che Guevara diary on the tenth of October 2012. Claire Sterling in her book, `The Terror Network.' tells us Feltrinielli went to Bolivia to help Che. She suggests that he may have visited Regis Debray in prison, who happened to be in the next cell to Ciro Bustos. Who in his turn says he studded forgery in Cuba.

Carlo Feltrinelli, Feltrinelli's son remarks in his book, ´Senior Service.' That his father was with

Regis Debray in Cuba. They studded forgery together. They all studded together?!

Both Claire Sterling and Carlo Feltrinelli remark that Feltrinelli spent two nights in prison while in Bolivia. But not why he was incarcerated! The experience must have made an impression as he wrote a pamphlet about it. (I have not been able to find a copy of it, yet.)

From the three copies of the diary I have had a look at when I was blinded by the idea that could only be one original. It was not the hand writing that told me to stop trying to decide, it was the fact the colour differed from dark red to cherry red for the covers of the 1967 diaries. The paper was, or was not creased- the ink smudged so it matched, nor not or the little bite shown on the covers. But the fact is that each one of the dairies was faked.

One was need to be used in the trial of Ciro Bustos and Regis Debray, as evidence.

Benigno had to have a copy for his wall; it can be seen in the film `Schnappschuss Mit Che.' by Wilfried Huismann.

Feltrinelli it is said microfilmed it so he could get it printed in 1968. Castro saw the streets of Havana filled with those that wished to get a copy. Big money was to be made all around the world.

The fact the hand writing style they used does not match that of Che's. The overall look picks out a likeness even I have fallen for. But look at the hand writing on the flag in

'Che… en. Wikicollecting.org' it sold for 100.000.000. A lot of money for a Cuban revolutionary romantic artifact!
(Fidel Castro has also placed his signature on this expensive flat.)

This signature of Che's matches the sample I have from Ciro Bustos much better. There is another example I trust as an example of Che's original, it comes from 'pfcauctions.com.'
Dated 1958. …a location in East of Cuba, the Sierra Maestro. Someone paid $1400, 000 for this note.

All the members were experienced forgers, from original passports with different identities added to them; to copying enough diaries to please everyone.

I have a theory. To save time thinking up new adventures they took the diaries of Jorge Masetti, he wrote about his problems in starting the revolution in Argentina, Salta. He is supposed to have lost his life but not before he wrote the material they needed. Of course I could be wrong, it is just a gut feeling I got after reading everyone's accounts of both events.

This team was active in other areas. If I have fallen for likenesses of hand writing, I found them in the same field on the same stage, linking the same people and objectives together.

The Motorcycle Diaries was such a success; the idea of making diaries to cover other years must have been tempting.

There is yet another diary attributed to Che! This time it is called, 'Diary of a Combatant,' it come out date is 16/6/2011. This one covers the years 1956 to

1959. They say to give a fresh insight into the father and son relationship between Castro and Che. No Comment.

Foot note- The hand written Bolivian Dairies were written by a syndicate, consisting of at least three men who were trained in Havana in the skills of forgery. Ciro Bustos, Riges Debray and Giangiaccomo Feltrninelli.

## Chapter twenty eight.
## Korda's photo!

If the expression caught on the photograph that Albert Korda took of Che Guevara is likened to the Mona Lisa smile, you cannot image what my expression was like when I realized what I was reading about, underlined my findings.

The copyright for this photo was taken out by Feltrninelli in 1967. In the spring or early summer of 1967, depending on whose account you read: Feltrninelli was in Havana where he got the wrights to publish the Bolivian Dairy.

I write again `in the spring or early summer of 1967.` Giangiaccomo Feltrninelli obtained the rights from Fidel Castro!

1) Why from Fidel Castro?

The photo was copyrighted to © Libreria Feltrninelli 1967. (In the lower left hand corner of the image.) It was used as the cover of the first edition published in Italy within weeks of Che's death party. Trisha Ziff- in aworldtowin.net tells me.

Here I have to ask more questions-

2) Why did Fidel Castro sell the rights of Che Guevara's Diary before Che's Death party? *Before his death*!?

Before Che's death.
It can be proven that Feltrninelli was looking for an image to cover the Diary of Che before his death party. Feltrninelli happened to ask the Cuban Communist Party for such a photo.

As to why Korda was neither paid, nor received the copyright is easy to explain as he was a member of the fore mentioned communist party.

3) Why did Feltrninelli go to Bolivia in August of 1967?
Did he really fly to La Paz to see what he could do to help one of his writers Riges Debray; who was in prison with Ciro Bustos?

It is said that Tania Bunke took the opportunity to inform the police that Feltrninelli was there. She herself was a writer belonging to Feltrninelli's publishing house under the name of Susan Sontag; she edited and translated for Che himself.
(It is Claire Sterling that tells us Tania Bunke was the informer.)

Feltrninelli has vanishes! It is the news papers of the time.
La Notte of Milan dates this the nineteenth of August. Many more Italian news papers report this There is such a fuss the Italian President Saragaty and his Foreign Minister Fanfani interven.

Feltrninelli was expelled from Bolivia on the twentieth of August.

Depending on which version you read; be it Clare Sterling's or Feltrninelli's son Carlo Feltrninelli's, Feltrninelli 'spent two days and a night or two nights and a day in prison.'

Did Feltrninelli's contact with Vazquez Viana family irritated Colonel Roberto Quintanilla. Or was it the 4,000 dollars he had on him?

(I met a member of Vazquez Viana family in Ciro Bustos' flat 2010.)

Colonel Roberto Quintanilla entertained Feltrninelli while he was staying in his prison.

Colonel Roberto Quintanilla was the man that it was said found and had Che killed!

Colonel Roberto Quintanilla was the man that Monika Ertl and Giangiaccomo Feltrninelli were suspected of killing in Hamburg in November of the year 1967.

50,000,000 $ is an exorbitant amount of money! It can be proved that Feltrninelli asked for this sum to be sent from his New York office. What I would like to suggest is, that it was not for the purpose to save Che Guevara's life. It was to smooth the way, to create the spectacle of the death party.

Feltrninelli was the publisher that went to great lengths to see Doctor Zhivargo was published.

The book the film made more money that anyone can think of. As would the Diaries for Che Guevara.

50,000.000 $ was peanuts to invest in such works.

If Colonel Roberto Quintanilla was shot by Feltrninelli and Monika Ertl, as Jobst C Knigge states. I suggest Colonel Roberto Quintanilla did not keep to the deal he made with Giangiaccomo Feltrninelli.

50,000,000 $ is a lot of money. Look into who is telling us-
Clair Sterling- read the chapter about my grandmother.

I point out she was called to give evidence in USA congress.

One of her books is titled 'The Terror Network.' Carlos Feltrninelli- explains in his Biography about his father

Giangiaccomo Feltrninelli. 'Senior Service.' Trisha Ziff- in aworldtowin.net, Korda's Che Moves Out into the World, dated January 2005. Trisha Ziff has directed a film about Che, 'Chevolution' Interestingly this lady was married to a Spanish Civil war refuge in Argentina, Mexico. All be it he was a baby when he left Spain. Jerry Adams the IRA leader was also a close friend of Trisha Ziff, she was in Northern Ireland with him when there was much political unrest. Just out of interest her name is connected to that of Robert Capa who it was said took the photo of a falling soldier in the Spanish Civil War; this photo was proven to have been faked, by his own admission. I say this to point out the power of Advising!

Che Guevara was a mass media produced hero.

A foot note or two- The other version is that in the spring of 1968 the diary was smuggled out La Paz by the disillusioned Bolivian Minister Antonio Arguedas who came to be a Castro follower: the operation is said to have been called 'Aunt Victoria.'

There are other funny stories about how long it took for Feltrinelli to translate the Diary, two nights. Whereas for a ten man team of Dutch journalist took one day! This tidbit comes from Carlos Feltrninelli book 'Senior Service.'

The Bolivian Minister Antonio Arguedas Mendieta to give him his full name: personal intelligence adviser was Gabriel Garcia, heard that name before? And the Bolivian Minister Antonio Arguedas's name can be connected with which every 'Inty' that took over as leader after Che. Antonio Peredo had been a friend of the Bolivian Minister Antonio Arguedas for some considerable time.

There are three more names that are of interest at this point: Manuel Pineiro, he has an interesting nick name, red beard- Barba Roja but what is more interesting is he is Castro's man in charge of state security for Cube between 1964 and 1968.

He had to leave that post as the Russians were upset by his actions. Not surprising as he is well known as Castro's Spy Master. Remember Spy Master!

Then there is a man named Luis Hernandez. He was more difficult to track down till I found a name to add, under Luis Hernandez Ojeda there was more to find. He was the first secretary in the Cuban Milan embassy in Italy His last job was as Cuba's ambassador to Nicaragua. He had a reputation of manipulating the political system and the media. One of the articles I read about him described him as a Career Spy. In fact it is not easy to say for which side he acted. I only found out about his activities when I put Claire Sterling's name beside his. (Read who I think she is in the next chapter.)

Today in History: Career Spy Posted as Ambassador to Nicaragua

Tags: America Area of the International Department of the Cuban Communist Party (PCC/ID/AA), America Department (DA), Daniel Ortega, Luis Hernandez Ojeda, Nicaragua

*Luis Hernandez Ojeda « Cuba Confidential*
https://cubaconfidential.wordpress.com/.../luis-herna...

*Editor's Note: The America Area of the International Department of the Cuban Communist Party (PCC/ID/AA) is the intelligence wing of the party's Central Committee. It is now predominantly focused on political intelligence operations. Previously known as the America Department (DA), the spy service was heavily involved in supporting revolutionaries and terrorists throughout the Cold War.*

I just want to point out that the two mentioned men are not small fish! They were advisers to Fidel

Castro and Feltrinelli. *It was under their instructions Feltrinelli travelled to La Paz that August 1967.*

There is another man of interest I want mention now-

Jan Stage. Unlike Luis Hernandez Ojeda there is a Wikipedia written about him and Manuel Pineiro, red beard- Barba Roja has in his Wikipedia the statement that his beard was in reality white!
Jan Stage was an accomplice at the shooting of Roberto Quintanilla in Hamburg?

Jan Stage it is said is Danish, a journalist, a writer in his own right. A translator, which would explain why he did a Danish translation of the Bolivian Diaries. When Jobst C Knigge remarked in 'Feltrinelli's way into Terrorism.'

That Jan Stage was suspected of being an accomplice at the shooting of Roberto Quintanilla in Hamburg. I should have fallen from my seat! I did when I read in Carlo Feltrinelli's book that the same Jan Stage was in Bolivia with his father.

Jan Stage had interesting tasks to fulfill. One was to hire a plane, a small cargo plane. Jan Stage had the fun job of accompanying Feltrinelli's girlfriend of the time, Sibilla. He destroyed Feltrinelli's contact books and his notes when Sibilla was arrested shortly after Feltrinelli was. I was going to say Jan Stage escorted her to the airport but it was Roberto Quintanilla.

Why be surprised when it is suggested that the same Jan Stage was the driver of the car waiting to take away Monika Ertl and Feltrinelli from the Bolivian embassy in Hamburg, after the shooting of Roberto Quintanilla.

Jobst C Knigge and a journalist Jorgen Schreiber have remarked on this.

The same Jan Stage's Wikipedia tells me he was in Cuba for eight years, a secret agent, and their secret agent. It is not surprising he translated Gabriel Garcia Marques work for Feltrinelli.

There is a lot to suggest he was a Spy Master. To have three heavy weight Spy Masters lurking in the background, hovering over unfolding events dose seem to me as if they wish to influence, control their plan.

So I say again that the Diaries cannot be original, that the death party was organized in the time Feltrinelli was with Roberto Quintanilla. There are 50,000,000 reasons why Roberto Quintanilla was executed in Hamburg.

Chapter twenty nine.
My grandmother.

You would have thought that my grandmother would be a simple mater, mother to my father- my grandmother. The only thing that is simple is to write down the names and identities I have found. Or though I thought when I made this list! (There is another name to come!)

Cilia de la Serna Llosa.    Grandmother- terrorist. Journalist

Anna Magnani.-Film star- terrorist.

Clair Sterling. -Terrorist expert. Journalist.
Journalist!
Grand mother- Cilia de la Serna Llosa.

A Grandmother with the name Cilia de la Serna Llosa I had got use to. I had always felt she must have been involved. I was excited to read she had taken refuse in Paris with Mario Vargas Llosa and Julia Urquidi, in nineteen sixty three. (It is also stated that Hilda Gadea was there at the same time.)

Knowing that had made sense of the entwining literary circles I was floundering in.

She had to leave Argentina as she had been spreading Castro propaganda. I have even found a photo where she is allegedly being arrested by the police. It is an EBay fined dated 2012.

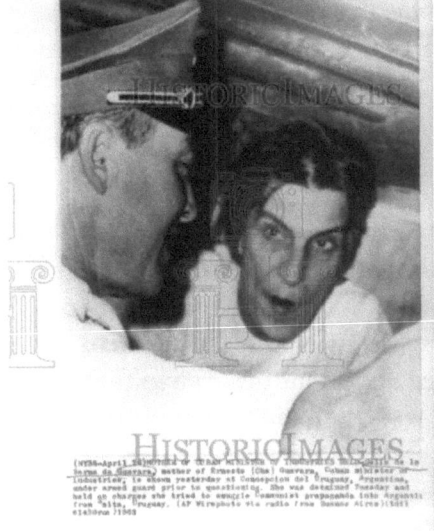

Someone that has been sent to prison carrying Castro propaganda must have done more than have a pamphlet in her handbag. I said as much to my partner the evening before I started on the check list I had made after reading, 'Terrousmo Subvesivo er la Argentine' This is a useful document if you want to understand how life was in Bolivia at the time of Che's death party. It has become a habit, any name I do not recognize I look up on the internet.

(NY36-April 18)NOTHER OF CUBAN MINISTER OF INDUSTRIES HELD-Celia de la Serna de Guevara, mother of Ernesto (Che) Guevara, Cuban minister of Industries, is shown yesterday at Concepcion del Uruguay, Argentina, under armed guard prior to questioning. She was detained Tuesday and held on charges she tried to smuggle Communist propaganda into Argentia from Salta, Uruguay. (AP Wirephoto via radio from Buenos Aires)(tdi1 61430rcm )1963

Google Bilder

Website mit diesem Bild
Katy Jurado, photographed by Sammy Davis, Jr.
undervintage.blogspot.com

Under the photo its says-(Ny36-April126)Mother of Cuban Minister of Industries 'Held-Cella de la Serna de Guevara, mother of (Che) Guevara, Cuban minister of industries, is shown yesterday at Concepcion del Uruguay, Argentina, under armed guard prior to questioning, She was detained Tuesday and held on charges, she tried to smuggle Communist Propaganda into Argentina from Uruguay. (AP Wirephoto via radio from Buenos Aires) (tdil 61420ron) 1963.

Uncle Martin- Juan Martin Guevara was in prison at the same time. He served a sentence for running Guns.

Roberto Che's brother is also named in as one of the terrorist bad boys.
Lahistoriaargentinacompleta.blogspot.com/2007
Diariopamperoarchivos.blogspot.com

Anna Magnani-Katy Jurardo-Celia de la Serna-Claire Sterling.

Clair Sterling

Clair Sterling is looking at me through the screen of my lap top. Her face, my face and that of Cilia de la Serna Llosa are merging into one!

The shock was pinning me to my seat. Her face my face-

To see that Cilia had lived a good thirty years more than I had thought was comforting. Comfort was not something I got when I saw Clair Sterling was renown as a terrorist expert.

*So renown she had given evidence in the American congress.*

Wikipedia cannot always be trusted to be accurate, but when it told me she had written many books on the subject of terrorism I must believe it. I got a copy of, 'The Terror Network. (Reading it through I suffered two days of feeling responsible, what she writes about made my hair stand on end)

There have been times where I grumbled that I did not get a chance to be involved. Now I am glad that I need to point out that all is not as they said it was.

Stop right there!
Anna Magnani!

The photo of Che Guevara dressed as a pirate looking down at my grandmother standing next to a man that I later found out was Clair Sterling's editor. But under this photo it says my grandmother's name is Anna Magnani!

Wikipedia tells me she was a renowned film star- I felt sick.
Anna Magnani had made films with Pier Pablo Pasolini- I felt sicker. Before I get any sicker I will add how I put it together.

With this I want to show you possibilities that have not been thought of before. I want to prove that the whole Che Guevara story was invented: invented to Romanize the idea of revolution to hide the dirty facts of the evil of war.

If you back a cake you decorate it, you make a war you give the course a Hero. If you don't have one in your pocket you invent one. In this case Che Guevara.

Medea 1966 regia giancarlo menotti anna magnani 1973 regia f enriquez valeria moriconi 1996 regia mario missiroli valeria moriconi altri

Medea 1966 regia giancarlo menotti anna.
archiviofoto.unita.it

   Have a look at this photo from the above website. You will be puzzled to see a pirate looking like Che. He is standing next to Anna Magnani, who I am going to tell you she is his mother. Among her many roles she played Cilia de la Serna.
(The man standing in the photo with Anna Magnani and Che, I feel is William Abrahams. He was her/Clair Sterling's editor.
In another photo he could be mistaken as Thomas Sterling, Clair Sterling's husband)

## Anna Magnani and Clair Sterling shared editors and husbands-

(Why have their identities been mixed?)

Thomas Sterling-husband -Clair Sterling

About Thomas Sterling · 39104. Thomas L. Sterling (* 1921; secretary, ... goodreads.com

*William Abrahams*

Website mit diesem Bild
USA. Museum of Modern Art re-opening. -
USA. New York,
magnumphotos.com

William Abrahams was Clair Sterling's editor:
-did he also play the part of her husband?
Max Ascoli-

Max Ascoli                    Thomas Sterling

USA. New York, NY. 1964. Editor, Max ASCOLI, at the reopening of the Museum of Modern Art.

Website mit diesem Bild
USA. Museum of Modern Art re-opening. -
USA. New York,
magnumphotos.com

Max Ascoli as editor of the magazine 'The Reporter' can be seen hugging Anna Magnai.
MEDEA 1966 REGIA GIANCARLO MENOTTI ANNA MAGNANI 1973 REGIA F ENRIQUEZ ...

*Not to be able to show this photo is sad as she can be seen wearing the same firs coat as Ana Maria, Che's sister.*

Medea 1966 regia giancarlo menotti anna magnani 1973 regia f enriquez valeria moriconi 1996 regia mario missiroli valeria moriconi altri

Anna Magnani

Anna Magnani.corradorizza.it
Look at that fur coat!
This is the same fur coat as Che's sister, Ana Maria; she is wearing in the news clip, it is not uncommon to wear cloths your mother wears. By the way in the background you can see the top of Che's half brother using the name of Jean Luc Godard. Ana Maria managed to marry him many times under different names she used in her film career. Bothe Ana Maria and her half-brother used many other names.
Ap::Images::Enlarged View::610805021-CHE GUEVARA AND SISTER 1961

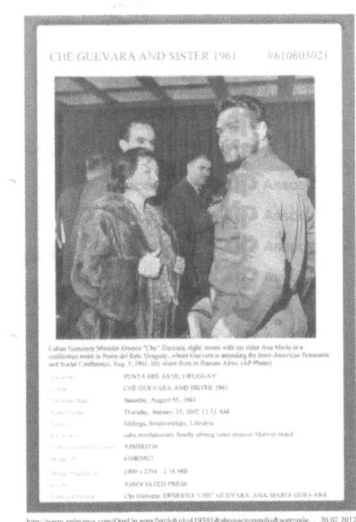

http://www.apimages.com/OneUp.aspx?st=K&id=419391&showact=results&sort=rele...20,02.2012

Anna Karina and Jean-Luc Godard, 1960's theredlist.com

This time dont look at her coat but at her face.

With these photos I want to show you other possibilities.

Anna is with her son- Luca. When I ask the internet to show me photos of him I have to ask what is his real name? Is it Franco Citti or is it Ettore Garfalo? Anyway I think his father is Pier Paolo Pasolini.

I do not write down what I think, but if you look at their faces you will understand why I am interested.

<u>Website mit diesem Bild</u> Anna Magnani and her son Luca. (Flag Image) allvoices.com

but he looks like the actor next to Silvana Corsini in Mamma Roma!

Mamma Roma - Silvana Corsini
nuovocinemalebowski.it

Anna Magnani    Pier Paolo Pasolini        ?

Silvana Corsini.
<u>Website mit diesem Bild</u>... pour pauvres ?), tout cela au milieu des vestiges écroulés de la gloire ...impetueux.com

Silvana Corsini.
... pour pauvres ?), tout cela au milieu des vestiges écroulés de la gloire ...impetueux.com

 I feel there is a connection between the young man, look at Silvana! You can find Silvana sitting in many photos with the Guevara family!

 If you look into this photo can you see Silvana!
You are wondering what is the conection? One of the conections is Mama Roma.
The next is you can see her sitting in the middle of the Guevara family.

Fue operada por primera vez, en que se le extrajo el tumor, sin tener que ... es.wikipedia.org

Che. Cilia. *Silvana*. Roberto. Martin.
Ernesto. Ana Maria.

***Mama Roma*** is a film by Pier Paolo Pasolini. Pier Paolo Pasolini played the part of one of the Inti's in Teoponte 1971.

With the 'Inty photos' I want to show how versatile an actor Pier Paolo Pasolini is. Teoponte was another campaign that took place in 1971. (I do have an explanation for this fact.)

Una de las dos caras de Inty.in Teoponte 1971. Guido Álvaro Peredo Leigue cerrocalvo.blogspot.com

Inty a) b) Pier Paolo Pasolini- Guido Alvaro "IntI" Peredo
a)genealogiadelcheguevara.blogspot.com.
b)paginecorsare.my blog.it.

Marginality and eroticism coupled with violence were key aspects of ...walterlippmann.com
Tells you how appreciated Pier Paolo Pasolini work was in Cuba.

## Carlos Barral

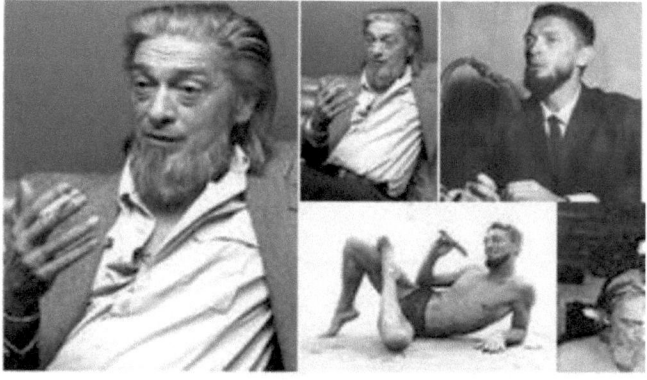

Carlos Barral he has acted for Pier Paolo Pasolini. To prove he has been involved in the making of Che there is a photo in Jon lee Anderson's book 'Che Guevara a Revolutionary life.'

You will notice Carlos Barral head above the others. The photo is courtesy of Carlos Barral. When looking for Carlos Barral I found him under the name of Carlos Boat! He took the Leadership of Publishing house Seix Barral.

Carlos Barral's image is from Jon Lee Anderson's book 'Che Guevara a Revolutionary life.' You can see a young Che sitting on the buss's bumper.

To proved Carlos Barral- Mario Varga Llosa and Gabriel Garcia Marquez connection.

El escritor cita a la localidad que visitó varias veces, en su obra 'Crónica ... diaridetarragona.com

García Márquez con Vargas Llosa, Gil de Biedma, Carlos Barral y otros autores en Calafell. Foto: DT

### A shorten Biography

Law degree from the University of Barcelona in 1950, was *Alma mater,* alongside Jaime Gil de Viedma, the literary generation of the fifties. Is poet more complex generation.

Upon assuming the leadership of publisher Seix Barral, family business founded textbooks by their parents in 1911, he printed a direction that led him to be the literary reference throughout the Hispanic world editing classic progressive culture of the fifties, sixties and seventies. Created a prize of publication internationally, the Formentor, the Biblioteca Breve and Barral novel award, and he was one of the architects of the Latin American boom and unveiled authors like Juan Marse. Mario Vargas Llosa. Alfredo Bryce Echenique and July Cortazar.

Seix Barral also a senator from Tarragona in 1982 and MEP by PSC-PSOE. In 1988 he won the Prix Comillas Tusquets Editors in the category of Memories by *When the swift hours.* He died in Barcelona in 1989.

Wrote thirty years of *Newspapers* and corresponded, among others, Max Aub , María Zambrano , Camilo José Cela , Miguel Delibes , Gonzalo Torrente Ballester , Barn Lane , Caballero Bonald , Alfredo Bryce Echenique , Giulio Einaudi , Alberto Oliart , Jaime Gil de Viedma , Jaime Salinas Bonmatí and political prisoners in Burgos. Your file is placed in the Library of Catalonia .

*Seix Barral* - Wikipedia, la enciclopedia libre
*es.wikipedia.org/wiki/Seix_Barral*Diese Seite übersetzen
*Seix Barral* es una compañía editorial con sede en Barcelona (España) que otorga anualmente el Premio Biblioteca Breve para novelas inéditas, el Premio ...· Grupo Planeta : Editorial *Seix Barral* : Grupo Planeta ...

*www.planeta.es/es/ES/.../Editorial-**Seix-Barral**.htm*<u>Diese Seite übersetzen</u>
La literatura del descubrimiento. *Seix Barral* fue fundada en 1911, como empresa de artes gráficas, y pronto se integró en la tradición editorial de Barcelona ...

- <u>Grupo Planeta : Editorial *Seix Barral* : Grupo Planeta ...</u>*www.planeta.es/en/GB/.../Editorial-**Seix-Barral**.htm* Literature of discovery. *Seix Barral* was founded in 1911 as a graphic arts company, and it soon became integrated into Barcelona's publishing tradition and ...

Why mention him or mention I have read 'Terrousmo Subvesino er la Argentina.' You can find this when entering the name Trivino Consuelo. He has taken notice of Clair Sterling and her book 'Terrorist Net Work.' And Ciro Bustos' book, 'Che wants to see you.'

As I can prove Ciro Bustos and Che Guevara are one and the same man why should I be surprised to see Clair Sterling looks like my grandmother, Cilia de la Serna Llosa!

Is there another part that Anna Magnani played?
"Clair Sterling it is said she had two children Luck Cortona and Abibail Vazquez. Clair lived outside of Cortona, near Arezzo in Italy."

Clair Sterling and Gabriel Garcia Marquez have a connection, she it is said went to his school of journalism. Are you feeling you are going round in circles?!

**<u>289 - My WN</u>**
*my.wn.com/search/washington_(name)?p=28800...* - Diese Seite übersetzen
*Claire* Sterling (née *Neikind*)(October 21, 1919 - June 17, 1995) was an ..... (FNPI), the journalism school for Latin-America created by *Gabriel García Márquez.*

Gabrial Garcia Marquez, Pier Paolo Pasolini, Giangiacomo feltrinellii, Carlos Barrel-Sexis Barral- -- I could go on-

Mairo Vargas Llosa , Carlos Barral   Ciro Bustos' wife again!

Website mit diesem Bild Con Vargas Llosa y Carlos Barral

**eldesvandelailusion.blogspot.com**
**Con Vargas Llosa y Carlos Barral**
eldesvandelailusion.blogspot.com
Carlos Barral's conection to Jean Luc Godard and Che's sister.
Con Joaquín Soler Serrano
Viernes 22 de junio de 2012, por Caja de resonancia
Carlos Barral y Agesta (Barcelona, España, 1928- Barcelona, España, 1989) fue, además de poeta, editor e impulsor de importantes proyectos literarios o, como suele decirse, culturales en el período de la post-guerra española. Editoriales como Seix-Barral o Barral Editores fueron nutridos y administrados por él durante años, siendo Barral mismo quien en muchos sentidos "descubrió" o "confeccionó" editorialmente fenómenos mercadológicos y literarios como puede ser el así llamado "boom latinoamericano".
Las ediciones viejas de *Barral Editores* o de *Seix-Barral*, bien sea en sus colecciones *HISPANICA NOVA* (Barral) o *Formentor* (Seix-Barral), son consideradas por muchos como verdaderas perlas de dedicado trabajo editorial, gráfico y de diseño.

In this you can see the Barral name.

But she looks like-
Jean-Luc Godard por Jean-Luc Godard
Barral Editores, 1971.Nos interesa en todo caso destacar varios puntos en la entrevista de Carlos Barral: por un lado
Tusquets editors- (One of their edtors- Nahir Gutierrez, commuercation management for Seix Barral.)

I have not bothered to translate the above; it is just to point out that they know each other.   Their names or connections I found in Elisabeth Burgos-Debray's Inventory: I have doggedly gone through the names in her inventory; without it I would never have found my grandmother, whoever she was.
 Saverio Tutino  another member!
He was born in Milan July 7th 1923. Joined the faculty of law, has to interrupt his studies because of the war. Participates in actions of resistance in the

Aosta Valley and Canavese. After the war he worked as a correspondent in the Communist press and corresponding in different countries of the world, particularly in Latin America. He participated in 1975 at the birth of the newspaper 'La Repubblica', where he worked until 1985.

In 1984 the idea of founding in Pieve Santo Stefano a place to accept the autobiographical writings of Italian and immediately think of a *competition to create diaries*. It 'was cultural director of the Parish Award and the Foundation Diary Archive, has published several books including 'Gaullist and workers' struggle.' 'The Cuban October.' and the volume of short stories 'The barefoot girl' for the Einaudi. 'The Che in Bolivia' and 'The Eye of the Barracuda.

'For Feltrinelli.' The Years of Cuba, 'Travels in Somalia .' From Chile 'for editions Mazzotta. 'Cicloneros' for the joints and 'Guevara at the time of Guevara.' for Editori Riuniti (1996). In 1998 he founded in Anghiari, together with Duccio Demetrio, the Free University of and began to publish the bi-annual magazine in Pieve Primapersona, he was director. He died in Rome November 28, 2011 at the age of 88 years. Saverio Tuntino has his name on Elisabeth Burgos-Debray's lists and he was an assonate of Feltrinelli.

## Chapter thirty.
## Katy Jurado.
## Maria Cristina Estela Marcela Jurado.

When I made the first list I did not have this name to add -

Katy Jurado. Maria Cristina Estela Marcela Jurado. A film stair!

Ok, they say she was born in 1924, so people lie about their age! Before I got lost in the labyrinth of birth dates I concentrated on what they had in common.

I had asked myself what had made Claire Sterling?
Claire Sterling the terrorist expert? She took the part of Cilia de la Serna Llosa would have been enough for me. Poking my nose into the internet did not offer me another explanation until I saw a photo of Anna Magnani with long hair, she looks younger in this photo than the others you can see under the name of Anna Magnani.

Katy Jurado in a promotion picture for the film San Antone. from Wikipedia The little crucifix. This also tells me she died 2002.

Anna Magnani Jargang 1908, war eine italienische Schauspielerin des italienischen nackrigskino. Sie erhieit als erste Italien den Oscar fur die beste Houptrolle in dem film ‚Mamma Roma' von 1962 spield sie die Prostituiete ‚Mamma Roma', die Tragish Ate an.

Roma', que Tragish Ate.

Anna Magnani in Mamma Roma
quotesgram.com

Katy Jurado es.wikipedia
In this film Anna Magnani reveals a remarkable performer with the painful **...**
famouspeopleinfo.com

*Look for the little cross they are wearing!*

In this film Anna Magnani reveals a remarkable performer with the painful sensitivity, in part by Pina, a Roman who was killed while trying to reach the truck on which her man is about to be deported by the Nazis.

The little crucifix that hangs around her neck the same way as it does in the same photo with the name Katy Jurado! This photo is used in Katy Jurado Wikipedia. And again in: Max Herre-Abserviert Lyrics on Rap Genius: rapgenius.com
Could this be a mistake!? Do they make mistakes?

*Anna Magnani: Triumph neorealist.*
Famouspeopleinfo.com/anna-magnani-triumph-neor- have used the same mistake, only this time the photo with the little crucifix as next to a more mature Anna Magnani.

Cilia de la Serna Llosa's grave can be seen on the internet in Bono Arias. 1965 (Attended to by Uncle Martin)

Anna Magnani body has been interned in Roberto Rossellini's family mausoleum. Italy. 1973

Clair Sterling's Wikipedia informs me she died in hospital in Arezzo. Italy. 1975

Whereas Katy Jurado has left this planet according to Wikipedia: in 2002. Which is ok for me, she would have been into her nineties by then.

It was not until I started to write this down did I start to believe what I am writing. Until now I have been blown about like a single cloud on a windy day.

The Wikipedia that uses the photo with the little crucifix and Katy Jurado's name has the most interesting indicators as how to make a- Make a what? Make an actress, a terrorist expert! A terrorist?

In the Wikipedia I have taken down in Katy Jurado's 'Early Life (1924-1943) it states that she studied Journalism in 1927. Here I have to ask, did they train three year olds as journalist in those days?

It was when I saw that Katy Jurado's cousin was Mexico's president; his presidents started in 1928.

**Anna Magnani: Triumph neorealist - Famous People Informati...**
famouspeopleinfo.com/**anna-magnani-triumph-neor**... ▼ Diese Seite übersetzen
27.03.2012 - In this film **Anna Magnani** reveals a remarkable performer with the painful sensitivity, in part by Pina, a Roman who was killed while trying to ...

## ¿También tocaron Celia de la Serna?

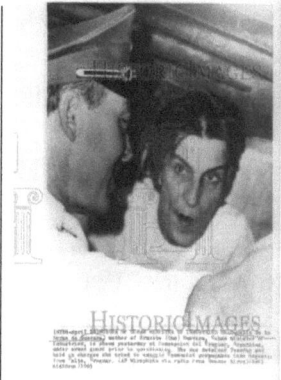

I could not resist looking him up, Emilio portes Gil Talking of look names up, I also put in Katy's farther Luis Jurado Ochoa and Luis Raul Ochoa her cousin. On doing this the photographic side of the internet showed me old friends. But when I entered Emilo Portes Gil with his wife's' name which happens to be Carmen Garcia Gonzalez en Teran, did the full meaning of seeing old friends hit me! Emilio Portes Gil wrote a book. 'Institutional Revolutionary Party.' This is a family that lost a lot of land that was later to become the state of Texas.

Emilio Portes Gil was president of Mexico.

Fidel Castro was a guest of Emilo Portes Gil in 1928. That he was two years old at the time does not stop him being a guest. (I don't remember exactly where I read that Castor was a guest of Emilo Portes Gil. As a two year old he would not have been there to talk about politicks. Therefore he must have been in the company of a guardian or a parent. I would be interested to see if there is a connection between this family; as there has been with others, active in South American.

Gabriel Garcia Marquez did not live in Colombia where he was born; he was in Mexico at the same time as others menchoied. (He grounded a journalist institute don't forget.)
There is a lovely photo of him with a black eye he received from Mario Vargas Llosa; who also grounded a journalist institute this time not in Columbia but in Peru.

In fact it is safe to say the whole band were there; form Pablo Nerudo to- … I could add names till I ran out of space.

## Chapter thirty one.
## My Grand Father.

In the book written by my grandfather about his life he says that Che's mother at the time of the Spanish Civil war was in Spain, as a war correspondent sent by the 'Critical' newspaper. Cilia was correspondent for Spanish civil war?! www.kaosenlared.net/.../80432-enestro-''che''-guevara...

This is my interpolation of events. A young man would be remembered for years to come especially if he was acting as if he owned the town. Not far from the truth if your mother's cousin was, or had been president.

This is the point where the Che Guevara story can begin. The players/actors are there. Not forgetting Raul Castro was seen with Che often in Mexico. Who would know that the parents of the flash youngster did or did not come from Argentina? Would anyone ask for the documents proving he was a doctor?

(I know the question of where theses papers could be found have been asked before.)(When I asked the university if Ciro Bustos had studded there, they could not answer that question for me.)

The story has to start in Mexico City because my birth mother was there in the training camp that had been set up to start the ball rolling for the campaigns they had planned.

If she had not been there I would not be writing about it now.

Every campaign needs a hero why not Che? All you need to do was invent his history before Mexico, excaudate it afterwards, invent a dramatic death, so you can continue to influence the world.

Why use the name of Guevara? Until I know better I will say it is because the Guevara's had control of the news media's and film distribution over Latin America. That and the fact the Guevara family were established in the political society.

As Katy Juado's Wikipedia says she was movie columnist, a radio reporter and a bullfight critic! Being a bullfight critic could explain why under one of the names I found for Roberto Guevara there was one that told me he was a matador. I think the name was Miguel Fenandez –Diez. The name has popped up now and again.

The best bit written in Katy Juado's Wikipedia is- She is like Anna Magnani. (!!!!) There is another funny bit for me it is when they say she received love letters from Louis L'Amour. He I was told was an American member of the family of my first husband! Hope I can find the book with his signature in it to prove this.

In her Personal Life Katy Juado's Wikipedia states that she abandoned her acting career for a few years, due to the sadness she felt over the loss of her son; Victor.

I like to think Katy used this time to grow into her next role Anna Magnani. There aren't any photos of spelled the end of more than one era. Even a left-wing dictator, it seemed, could be seduced by the glamour of celluloid. Politics and the cinema have become ever closer as the years pass by."

I was taking a look at the diaries said to have been written by Che. I asked the internet to show me anything to with Che's hand writing. In bookthrift.blogspot.com there is a revue of a book written, compiled by Ernesto Guevara-Lynch, my grandfather. 'The making of Che Guevara.' The forward is written by Lucia Alvarez de Toledo. Who happens to be the mother of Che's half brother-Jean Luc Godard, amongst other names he used. She just happens to be my grandfather's editor and translator. Small world, she also has written about Che Guevara.

This was not the only interesting point I found in the book review. This tells me that the Guevara forefather Francisco Lynch, on my grandfather's side; left Buenos Aires for Uruguay, as he did not wish to live under the then current dictatorship. Francisco Lynch in California made a huge fortune. Note California!

Juan Anonio Guevara was a direct descendent of the founders of the city Mendoza. His line of the family can be traced back to Chile.

It has been said that Celia de la Serna's family was extremely rich. The family owned vast ranches. The book revenuer notes she became interested in politics; she gave lectures on the logic of justice and the Cuban Revolution.

The most exciting paragraph in the book review is where the writer tells me- Che was only a boy when the Spanish Civil war had started. The family was close to some of the Republican exiles, in particular Enrique JURADO. Heard that name before? General Jurado visited the Guevara-Lynch family many times to tell stories of the civil war.

Katy Jurado's family wealth came from Texas; California is in the state of Texas. In fact they owned the land that became Texas. Much of their wealth was lost during the Mexican revolution, even so the Jurado father was known as a cattle baron with orange farms. Katy's cousin was a president of Mexico.

What I want to say here is that the whole family moved in very high society circles. There is an old saying, 'It is not what you know but who you know.'

(The Motorcycle Diaries was such a success that the idea of making diaries to cover other years must have been tempting.)

(There is yet another diary attributed to Che! This time it is called, 'Diary of a Combatant,' it come out date is 16/6/2011. This one covers the years 1956 to 1959. They say to give fresh insight into the father and son relationship between Castro and Che.)

Another interesting point that came out of the book review is that Hilda, Che's first wife was working for the United Nations.

That is a big organization you need connections to get a job there! Hilda Gadea joined Che in Mexico as she was pregnant.

I only saw this as the revue remarks that: Che Guevara's handwriting was likened to a doctor's, it was indecipherable. It is dated Friday the fifth of July 2013.

Emilio Portes Gil

Katy Jurado's family- Emilio Portes Gil
britannica.com
Cousin- Emilo Portes Gil Mexico's president 1928/1930, he had his offices in-
                Palacio de Bellas Artes.
Godfather- Pedro Armeadariz, he was a Mexican actor and lawyer. He had his offices in-
                Palacio de Bellas Artes.
Godfather- Jorge Negrate was a Mexican actor and lawyer, **who** helped found the Union of
        Film Production in Mexico, and the National Association of Actors. He had his offices
                in- Palacio de Bellas Artes.
First husband of Katy Jurado- Victor Velasquez- actor and lawyer. He had his offices in-
                Palacio de Bellas Artes.
Brother of Katy Jurado- Barnabe Jurado lawyer with his offices in-        Palacio de Bellas Artes.

*(The lawyer Barnabe Jurado used was the same lawyer as Bugsy Siegel, Jose Vasconcelos.*
*Jose Vasconcelos was lawyer to the top members of the mafia; Who had his offices in-*
*Palacio de Bellas Artes.*

Uncle- Belisario de Jesus Garcia de la Garza. In the Military and a renowned musician.
Abelardo L Rodriguez ,Mexican president owned the land that would tune into Las Vagus.
had his offices in- Palacio de Bellas Artes.

*(Aides Sullivan's family owned the Santa Rosa Ranch; She was Abelardo L Rodriguez wife.)*

Barnabe Jurado
Acercarce a Susana Cora, implicaba también, llegar al hombre del poder. esquivel-zubiri.blogspot.com

**Victor Velazquez** (Katy Jurado's first husband) was a prominent lawyer, in the scandalous divorce of Rosita Fornes and Manuel Medel; he was Manuel Medel's lawyer. Rosita Fornes' lawyer was **Barnabe Jurado**.
Rosita Fornes can be seen with Mario Moreno.
**(Who was known to have been Che Guevara's double.)**

Rosita y Mario Moreno, "Cantinflas"

Rosita y Mario Moreno, "Cantinflas" gumucio.blogspot.com

All of this and more becomes interesting when you say Katy/Anna Magnani played Che's Mother- and Claire Sterling as a CIA go-between.

(Chapters 6&7 in Gabriel Garcia Marquez the creator of Che Guevara.)

Chapter thirty two.
Family members and connections.

Ricardo Gadea Acosta was Che's first wife's brother. Ricardo was Castro's contact to Eesterban the drug baron. Esterban was involved in has country's politics even stood for president. He had close contacts to the king of the drug busyness, Fidel Castro.

Katy Jurado cousin was the president of Mexico. She was a political atavist; the film world she worked in was filled with powerful names. They in turn were interested in political matters.

Errol Flynn when so far as to make films to finance the rebel course. Cuban Rebel Girls, where

you can see Che's sister in a leading role and Jorge Masetti.
Feltrinelli produced book after book, diary after diary to finance and promote the course. Film after film had been produced to manipulate the way we think.

Cantinflas was a member of the Antimarxista Party. He was to play as a Che Guevara double in the early sixties. I think Pierre Kalfon doubled for Che later, P Kalfon was an actor.

If you think Cantinflas skin was to dark, a good makeup artist could take care of that. The film producers could use every trick available to them at the time. What they did not have were contact lenses as they do now, to disguise eyes, change the colure, create a death mask.

The author of 'Cantinflas in the land of Fairies.' Described Cantinflas as a tax collector, lazy, grouchy and rude to the public. At times a poet. His critics blasted him for having lost his sense of humor, sold out to the Bourgeoisie of the argentine guerrilla commander Ernesto Che Guevara.

Had I not read the Cantinflas was a close friend Katy Jurado, who took on roles of Cilia de la Serna, Ann Magnani, and Clare Sterling amongst others I have not found. Remembering that Che had at least identities contributed to him. To say I do not know the name of my father is true.

Robert Redford=<u>*CHE'S* MOTORCYCLE FOLLIES - Guaracabuya</u> *www.amigospaisguaracabuya.org/oag aq119.php*<u>Diese Seite übersetzen</u>

"I might add that Dr. *Guevara*, like all his fellow comic-book characters, ... This comparison with *Cantinflas*, the late famous Mexican comic movie star, evoked my ...

Cantinflas-*Cantinflas da un discurso Nacionalista y Antimarxista Parte ...*

*Cantinflas* and the Chaos of Mexican Modernity
*books.google.de/books?isbn=0842027718* -
Jeffrey M. Pilcher - 2001 - History

The author of "*Cantinflas* in the Land of Fairies" described him as "a tax ... out to the bourgeoisie, the Argentine guerrilla commander, Ernesto "*Che*" *Guevara*, ...

► 9:38 ► 9:38
*www.youtube.com/watch?v=FmKDW-HTfQo*
15.10.2009 - Hochgeladen von Restaurador Venezuela
... genial como Mario Moreno "*Cantinflas*" puede conocer más a fondo las ... Discurso de *Che guevara* ...

Cantinflas of a speech and antiMarxist Nationalist Party ...

Video zu "Cantinflas + Che Guevara" ► 9: 9:38 38 ►
www.youtube.com/watch?v=FmKDW-HTfQo

Conclusion.
We have been Hoodwinked.
Chapter one
The New Zealand Maritime Museum.
www.nzmaritime.org

Cuban television on the Saturday fifth of May 2007, Jon Lee Anderson's biography, Che Guevara A Revolutionary.
Back on the road (Otra Vez) Ernesto Che Guevara.
CeiberWeiber- Frauen Onlinemagazine- Artkel 'Herstory' jhd `Freauen um Che'.
Biograph Castaneada.
Image:Aleida Guevara March.jpg- Wikipedia
www Poetry international web
CeiberWeiber- Frauen Onlinemagazine- Artkel 'Herstory' jhd `Freauen um Che'
Die Letzten Tage einer Legende. 500851065.
The Life and Death of Che Guevara Companero.
    By Jorge G Castaneda.
film 'Sacrifico who betrayed Che Guevara?'
Wilfried Huismann 'Schnappschuss mit Che.'
Christopher Loving, 'Che die fotobiografie.
Pageina/12.com.

## Chapter two.

Ei Diaro del Che en Bolivia. 'Evocacion' by Aleida, Che Guevara- Der Tod und Der Mythos. Raffaele Bruntti.

## Chapter three.

Che Guevara CIA- State Dept- Dept of Defence Files.

## Chapter four.

Che Fotobiografie. Christopher Loving.
Che Guevara CIA -State Dept- Dept of Defence Files.
The CIA files are from Informer Enterprises.

Che Guevara, The way to revolution.' directed by Manuel Perez.
Weg Der Revolution. Paco Prats.
Revolutionary Life, Jon Lee Anderson
Film 'Gesucht Monika Ertl. The woman who revenged Che Guevara's death.
Jan Lee Anderson's book Funny Man.
TV= Eyes of grandmother and a young Che.
Cheguevaravideos.blogspot.com
Guevara, Part 3
    Part 4
    Part 5- As Castro reads Che's farewell letter.
    Part 6- At the very beginning of the film.
=At the moment where locks of hair are being cut from his head the eyes can be seen.
The photo by Alberto Korda.

                              Chapter five.

The photo by Alberto Korda.
Humberto Vazquez Viana -Wikipedia
Rondon Aristides Velasquez Che Guevara institute in Santa Clara,Cuba.
Christoph Röckerath 'Insel au seiner anderen Zeit' a film about Cuba tradition.
Recruiting Nazis=www.angelfire.com.
Jim Garrison's 1967 Play Boy interview (part 1)
www.maebrussell.com/.../Garrison. Oct 1967
Chehasta.navod.ru/bol_4.hfm.
The other side of the Barricades. 'Wege Der Revolution.'Regie: Manuel Perez.

**Death of Che.**
Wwwgwu.edu/~nsarchiv/nsaebb/nsaebb5/-
National Security Ardine briefing, book no5.
Dept of defense Intelligence Information Report.)
(RoJo 218)
www.amigospais-guaracbuga,org.oagmf026.pfp.
*wwwwikipeda.org: says Hasenfus*
*Secrets of the CIA: In bed with the Nazis* Felix
Ramos+Edurado Gonzoler+1967+CIA.
wwwleandokatz.com/…
ChronoEnglishChefourhtml.
legion the last day in the life of Che Guevara
wwwleandokatz.com/…
ChronoEnglishChefourhtml.
Don't Shoot I am Che. By Grul Arnallo
Sauoedo Palozor.
Travelling adventures with Alberto Grando
Ultimate Sacrifice.
http:ajweberman.com/nodulex25pdf
Nodulx10.
Larmar Warldron and Thom Hartmann's book
(Ultimate Sacrifice)
The State Dept-Dept of Defence (The way to
Revolution) bestell-nr 69095/
Film 'Snap shot with Che.'
Elizabeth Burgos-Debray Stanford University
California 'box/folder 15:7 Che Guevara 1967/69'.

Chapter six.

Centre for Latin American Studies,
University of California, Cristian Perez's study.
Salvador Allende- Notes on his security Team.

Norberto Fuento- Autobiography of Fidel Castro.
EL Che Quiere Verte.
Ann Wright translated the book, 'Motorcycle Dairies- the version written by Che Guevara.
'Benigo'- Dariel Alaron Ramirez book, 'Memories of a Cuban Soldier.
Lucia Alvarez de Toledo, 'Story of Che Guevara.' and translated Alberto Grundo's book.
'Freepublic.com/focuss/f-news'
about'Collectivoepprosario.
blogspot.com/2010_02_01_A
Archive Chile. Pagina 12. Histora Popitco social- 2001. Archive Chile.
Pagina 12. Histora Popitco social-2001. Mommesto Populaur.
Who betrayed Che Guevara? Written by Miguel Bonasso.
'Collectivoepprosario.blogspot.com/2010_02_01_A'
Cinemaspargus.blogspot.com/2010/05/jean-luc godard.
 ZDF. 'Insel aus einer anderen Zeit'

                                            Chapter seven.

Parger 12.
Elizabeth Burgos-Debray's news paper cuttings
Laben and Kampf eines Revoltionars. Ernesto Che Guevara.'
The biography is by Josef Lawrezki.
Josef Lawrezki up Wikipedia
Last moments with Che Guevara.
World News- Garderen Weekly- Steven Soderbergh.

(Mejorentrevista a Ernesto Che Guevara.
(invedotia))
Path Way to Revolution.
The South America Years.' By (Mo) Mosies Garica

                                Chapter eight.

La Historia Clompleto.
http.//bp1.blogger.com/6bkpgg.
South America Years
'Collectivoepprosario.blogspot.com/2010_02_01_A
World News- Garderen Weekly- Steven Soderbergh.
(Mejorentrevista a Ernesto Che Guevara.
(invedotia))
Steven Soderbergh -Che Revolucion
www.larevuedesressources.org/spip.php?page=5.
Elizabeth Burgos-Debray's files.
Hoover Institution Stanford University
   Hoover Institution 434 Galvez Mall
   Stanford University Stanford. CA 94305-6010.
Archive Chile Pagina 12.
Grupo Cultral Del Sur

                                Chapter nine.

Cuban Rebel Girls.
La Palabra Empanada.
El furor y el Delirio: itinerio de un hijo de la
Revolucion Cuba.
Pagina 12
Archiv3-Daten der Kooperation Dritte Weld
Archive.
Monika y el Che Padre nazi, hija guerrillera. In
Pagina 12. Nr 1588 seite 26, dated 1992.

Last moments with Che Guevara. World News-Garderen Weekly- Steven Soderbergh.
Mejorentrevista a Ernesto Che Guevara. (invedotia))
Wege Der Revolution. (The film cover tells me the film martial comes out of the –Staatlichen Kubanischen Filmarchiv ICAIC. That it is Original!)
Pangea 12
Colectivoepprosario.Blogspot.com/2010_02_01_a
Enter leyendas-Eresto Che Guevara en Bolivia.
Guerrilleros del "Che" Regresaran ala Habana.)
Fronter De Chile Che Guevara. (Documental Completo)
internet films.'Septumber De 1967 – film 1 of 4 to 4.
Weekend' by Jean-Luc Godard(hcl.harvard.edu.

                                Chapter ten.
Perri Kaflon.
                                Chapter eleven.
Marchuncuto, Venezuela, 1967.
*PDF Che: Behind the CIA's killing of a Revolutionary.*
*http://danielcassol.worldpress.com/2012/08/29/um-brasileiro-na-guerrilha-boliviana-2/*
A Brazilian guerrilla in Bolivia.
cerrocolvo. Blogspot.com''Desaparecidos en Argentina.' www.desaprecidos.org/arg/victimas.
PDF'informepara querellantes.
www.aph.argentina.org.ar/.../hijos20090818.
Jorge Horcio Novillo- no conapepa:3628.
Listado de Detentidos-Desaparcidos en Argentina.

Mortes e Despareaidoa'Elvira Miranda.Teoponte a program
Colectivoepposario.blogspot.com/…/Bolivia.info…
Prenom Carmen' produced by Jean-Luc Gudard.

                              Chapter twelve.

Fliker films.
Luciano Monteagudo and it was titled Monika y el Che Gesucht: Monika Ertl, by Christian Baudissin.
Desaparecidos en Argentina.
www.desaprecidos.org/arg/victimas.
Jorge Horcio Novillo- no conapepa:3628.
    In Santa Fe Sacrifico

                    Part two.  Chapter thirteen.

Gesucht: Monika Ertl. Die frou die Che Guevara Rachte. By Christian Baudissin.
Desaparecidos en Argentina.
www.desaprecidos.org/arg/victimas.
Mortes,e, Desparecidoa.
I Che Guevara.' Gary Hart Wikipedia Monticule Diaries. Written by Che.
    Bolivian Diaries.
    The Congo Diaries.
    Che wants to see you. Written by CiroBustos
                          Chapter fourteen.
Gesucht: Monika Ertl, Die Frau die Che Guevara Rachte
Jobst C. Knigge's 'Feltrinelli- Sine weg in den Terrorismus.
Humbolt Universitat (open Assess) Berlin 2010.
Sky News reported on the 24.5.2013 that nine

Colombian soldiers were killed by ELN Marxist Guerrillas, Stemming from the ideas from Cuba.
Schnappschus mit Che.
Guido Álvaro Peredo Leigue- cerrocalvo.blogspot.com
Guido Álvaro "Inti" Peredo- gehealogiadelcheguevara.blogspot.com
Pier Paolo Pasolini- paginecorsare.my blog.it.
Humbolt in Berlin.-Che Guevara Der Tod und der Mythos. Documention, 1 2007 5-807-307.
Wikipedia
http://www.juventudrebelde.cu/multimedia/fotografia/generales ...
martinezestevez.wordpress.com
Susan Sontag-sisyphe.org.
Che.1.Ipg   Taringa net.
borealidad.com.ar

Chapter fifteen.
Las Guerras Secretas de Fidel Castro.' Juan F Benemelis
*Snap Shot with Che, by Wilfried Huismann.*
Che wants to see you: Ciro Bustos. The untold story of Che Guevara.'
hemeroteca-abc-es/nav/navigate.exe/...

Chapter sixteen.
Nouvella Vague-Aussenansichten.' 2076896387.
86dc8d96f7 jpg Flickriver.com
Lahistoriaargentinacompleta.blogspot.com/2007
Diariopamperoarchivos.blogspot.com

Cudando Duhale/Bolivia/Ruckauf vetaron a jaua, el bolivar Bolivariano. Photo 5. Jpg. Xa.ying.com.
Menenk png-Urgente24.com.
Soberania org – de como Fidel maneja a Chavez.
Vikipedi 'the Spanish Wikipedia'

                                Chapter seventeen.

The Slate Magazine
´Schnappschuss mit Che.'
Juan F Benemelis-Las Guerras Secretas de Fidel Castro.
The Cuban Museumwww.latogata.org/che/nuevos/che_ felixhtm
      Felix Rodriguez Mendigutia: the man who killed Che.
Felix Rodriguez Mendigutia El Hombre que asesino… Archive C
www.Archivechile.com
Varios Relatos sobre el asesinato del Che Guevara. Baracuteycubano.blogspot.com/…/varios-relatos-sob…

                                Chapter eighteen.

The film 'Sacrificio'

                                Chapter nineteen.

Museo Ernesto Che Guevara Primer Muse Suramericano:ania la argentina comba…
http://museocheguevaraagentina.blogspot.de/2013/05/tania-la-argentina-combatiene-...

                                Chapter twenty .

INFO/news- is a film- the revolutionary,
The official guerrilla.

De sus Queridas Presencias'His film is 'The footprint Doctor Ernesto Guevara.'
Benigno' Dariel Alarcön's flat I took from the film 'Snapshot with Che'.
ernestocheguevara-oleida.blogspot.com
YouTube film- http://www.youtube.com/watch?v=tvarybZjxOo
Raffaela Bernetti and Stefano Missio made the Film Che Guevara the body and the legend.'
   -A B&B Film s.r.l Italy 2007.
On the Trail of Dr Ernesto Guevara.' Jorge Denti
*Collective Third World Cinema.*
Raymundo Gleyzer peoplecheck.de
abcguionistas.com
Raymundo Gleyzer: desaparecidos.org
Festival Internacional de Cine en Guadalajara - La huella del Dr ...ficg.mx twicsy@searchles.com
*Collective Third World Cinema in Latin America.*

## Chapter twenty one.

Che Wants to see you. The untold story of Che Guevara.
Jon Lee Anderson's book 'Che Guevara a Revolutionary Life.'
www.alfredohelman.it  Alfredo Hellman
Jounal Pampero Cordubensis. Lenardo Werthein
Mario Vargas Llosa newspaper account from 10/3/2007 is not the Bones of Che.
Journal Pampero Cordubensis. By Masetti.

Jounal Pampero Cordubensis. Antonio Rodriguez interesting- FNPI_org. organization
Journalistic excellence 'Fame' in Gabriel Garcia Marquez's Wikipedia .
Bild zu Fidel Castro and Elisabeth Burgos-Debray- Libertaddigital com
The South Amercia years- chapter 18
www.mogarcia.raintreeeditors.com/...chapter18.ht.
Hoover Insititution Standford University.
Wege der Revolution Che Guevara.
Jobst C. Knigge's 'Feltrinelli-Sine weg in den Terrorismus.'
Page 35 Jon Lee Anderson's book 'Che Guevara a Revolutionary Life.')
Jorge alvarez/rock.com.ar.

                        Chapter twenty two.

The open letter- Peru 21
*luzpensamientoylibertad.blogspot.com/.../libro-hilda*
     *Written by Ricardo Gadea Acosta.*
Adys M Cupull- is an author for a political publisher.
Unfinished Song.' Jorge Edwards statement 'Cuba and We'
Cortazar- translator/poet/ UNESCO translator. actor/writer.

                        Chapter twenty three.

www.revistaenie.clarin.com/La_Academia de_de_Pi
http://nuestrabandera.lamule.pe/2013/05/18/javier-en-el-recuerdo
Surviving Mexico's Dirty War.' A Political Prisoner's Memoir.

Diario de Bolivia. books.google,de/books .
Black and White.' Leereluniverso-blogspot-.com.
leereluniverso.blogspot.com

      Chapter twenty four.

Guido Álvaro Peredo Leigue-
cerrocalvo.blogspot.com
Guido Álvaro "Inti" Peredo-
genealogiadelcheguevara.blogspot.com
Memorias de un soldado Cubano. edited by
Elizabeth Burgos-Debray
Jorge Masetti's- EL furor y el delirio.
Published by the Feltrinelli group.
Lahistoriaargentinacompleta.blogspot.com/2007
Diariopamperoarchivos.blogspot.com
paginecorsare.my blog.it.
The magazine: Punto Final. Dated Mayo de 1968
*Gustavo Rodrigues Ostria* writes in 'Bolivia Cycle
in Guerrilla.
Continuity and Differences 1963-1970

      Chapter twenty five.

Che Wants to see you. The untold story of Che
Guevara.'
Ponto Final. Dated May the eighth, nineteen sixty
eight.
News paper cutting from Elisabeth Burgos-Debray's
Inventory.
Film 'Weg der Revolution'
Jobst C.Knigge's Feltrinelli-Sinn Weg
Punto Final Magazine.

    Part three. Chapter twenty six.

Film- ´Gesucht: Monika Ertl. Die Frau die Che Guevara rächt
Phoenix TV 'Klaus Barbie= My Enemy's Enemy.' YouTube.
The Devil's Agent' by Peter McFarren and Fadrique Iglesias.
Klaus Georg Altmann, Klaus Barbie.

### Chapter twenty seven.

Schnappschuss Mit Che.` by Wilfried Huismann.
Che wants to see you. by Ciro Bustos.
The Bolivian government in a YouTube.com film. Hqdefault jpg; are waving a Che Guevara diary for us all to see. `amigosdeboliniayperu.org.` Claire Sterling. The Terror Network.
Carlo Feltrinelli, ´Senior Service `Che… en. Wikicollecting.org'Dated 1958. ...
The Motorcycle Diaries 'Diary of a Combatant,' it come out date is 16/6/2011
The hand written Bolivian Dairies.

### Chapter twenty eight.

The photo was copyrighted to © Libreria Feltrninelli 1967.
La Notte of Milan Italian news papers.
Trisha Ziff has directed a film about Che, 'Chevolution'
The Terror Network. By Clare Sterling.
Giangiaccomo Feltrninelli. 'Senior Service.'
Trisha Ziff- in aworldtowin.net
https://cubaconfidential.wordpress.com/.../luis-herna...
*Luis Hernandez Ojeda « Cuba* Confidential

Jan Stage. Wikipedia Danish translation of the Bolivian Diaries.
Jobst C Knigge remarked in 'Feltrinelli's way into Terrorism.'
                              Chapter twenty nine.
Pier Paolo Pasolini-paginecorsare.my blog.it.
walterlippmann.com
Jon lee Anderson's book 'Che Guevara a Revolutionary life.'

*Seix Barral* - Wikipedia, la enciclopedia libre
          *es.wikipedia.org/wiki/Seix_Barral·*
Grupo Planeta : Editorial *Seix Barral* : Grupo Planeta ...*www.planeta.es/es/ES/.../Editorial-Seix-Barral.htm*
Grupo Planeta : Editorial *Seix Barral* : Grupo Planeta ...
*www.planeta.es/en/GB/.../Editorial-Seix-Barral.htm*
'Terrousmo Subvesino er la Argentina. Clair Sterling,'Terrorist Net Work. Ciro Bustos''Che wants to see you.'
289 - My WN
*my.wn.com/search/washington_(name)?p=28800...*
Con Vargas Llosa y Carlos Barral
eldesvandelailusion.blogspot.com
Con Joaquín Soler Serrano
Viernes 22 de junio de 2012, por Caja de resonancia
Jean-Luc Godard por Jean-Luc Godard
Barral Editores, 1971.
Thomas Sterling · 39104. Thomas L. Sterling (* 1921; secretary, ... goodreads.com

USA.Museum of Moden Art re-opening- USA. New York, Magnumphotos. com
newspaper 'La Repubblica' . 'The Che in Bolivia' and 'The Eye of the Barracuda.
bi-annual magazine in Pieve Primapersona

Chapter thirty.

WordPress.org famouspeopleinfo.com
Max Herre-Abserviert Lyrics on Rap Genius: rapgenius.com
Famouspeopleinfo.com/anna-magnani-triumph-neor
Wikipedia
Wikipedia -Katy Jurado's 'Early Life (1924-1943)
Institutional Revolutionary Party.
Anna Magnani.corradorizza.it Look at that fur coat!
Ap::Images::Enlarged View::610805021-CHE GUEVARA AND SISTER 1961 Seite 1von 2

Chapter thirty one

www.kaosenlared.net/.../80432-enestro-''che''-guevara... SANVIO CORP.
Carribbean.com - Issue 12.
Cuban Rebel Girls' Errol Flynn.
bookthrift.blogspot.com.
Ernesto Guevara-Lynch, The making of Che Guevara.
The Motorcycle Diaries.
Diary of a Combatant,' it come out date is 16/6/2011.covers the years 1956 to 1959.

Chapter thirty two.**Robert Redford=_CHE'S MOTORCYCLE FOLLIES - Guaracabuya_**
*www.amigospais-guaracabuya.org/oagaq119.php*

"I might add that Dr. *Guevara*, like all his fellow comic-book characters, ... This comparison with *Cantinflas*, the late famous Mexican comic movie star, evoked my ...
Cantinflas-*Cantinflas* da un discurso Nacionalista y Antimarxista Parte ...
☐ *Cantinflas* and the Chaos of Mexican Modernity *books.google.de/books?isbn=0842027718* - Jeffrey M. Pilcher - 2001 - History
The author of "*Cantinflas* in the Land of Fairies" described him as "a tax ... out to the bourgeoisie, the Argentine guerrilla commander, Ernesto "*Che*" *Guevara*, ...
► 9:38► 9:38
*www.youtube.com/watch?v=FmKDW-HTfQo*
15.10.2009 - Hochgeladen von Restaurador Venezuela... genial como Mario Moreno "*Cantinflas*" puede conocer más a fondo las ... Discurso de *Che guevara* ...
Cantinflas of a speech and antiMarxist Nationalist Party ...
Video zu "Cantinflas + Che Guevara" ► 9: 9:38 38►
www.youtube.com/watch?v=FmKDW-HTfQo
'Weg Der Revolution: Che Guevara. In the film 'Wege Der Revolution' www.icestorm.de Regie: Manuel Perez. You can see this man (Che Guevara!) in the scene where 'Benigno' Dariel Ramirez Alarcon is being greeted by Salvador Allende in Chili *1968*. YouTube has Che Guevara's name over the same bit of film!?